"*The Polyglot Lovers* is a bracing and sharp exploration of identity, gender, and literature, told in prose and images that constantly unsettle the reader. It is also an exquisite act of literary revenge and should confirm Lina Wolff's status as a major voice in world literature."

Josh Cook, Porter Square Books, Cambridge, MA

"An exquisite and insightful dive into the delights and horrors of our constant search for human connection, and what happens when women decide to set fire to the literary male gaze."

Emma Ramadan, Riffraff, Providence, RI

"I absolutely loved it. Wolff's characters come to life with poignancy and dark humour. *The Polyglot Lovers* cuts to the heart."

Tom Harris, Mr B's Emporium, Bath

"Lina Wolff's *The Polyglot Lovers* is a punch you in the face, grab you by the collar, and throw you across the room kind of novel. Brilliantly written, incisive and engaging, it is a stunning work. If you haven't yet (and why haven't you?) now would be a good time to add Wolff to your to-be-read pile."

Tom Flynn, Volumes Bookcafe, Chicago, IL

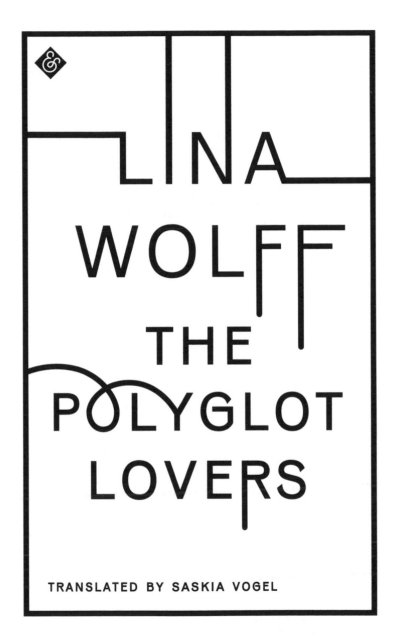

LINA
WOLFF
THE
POLYGLOT
LOVERS

TRANSLATED BY SASKIA VOGEL

First published in 2019 by
And Other Stories
Sheffield – London – New York
www.andotherstories.org

First published as *De polyglotta älskarna* in 2016 by Albert Bonniers Förlag, Stockholm.
English-language translation © 2019 Saskia Vogel

9 8 7 6 5 4 3 2 1

This book is a work of fiction. Any resemblance to actual persons, living or dead, events or places is entirely coincidental. Changes to character names for the English translation are at the author's request.

Acknowledgments:
The Stephen King epigraph is from *Hearts in Atlantis*; the quote on p. 110 is from *Gerald's Game*; the Michel Houellebecq epigraph is from *The Possibility of an Island*, translated by Gavin Bowd; the Djuna Barnes quote is from *Nightwood*; the paraphrasing of Borges ('Borges writes that mirrors and copulation are abominable, since they both cause the population to multiply') is from 'Tlön, Uqbar, Orbis Tertius' in Borges' *Fictions*.

ISBN: 9781911508441
eBook ISBN: 9781911508458

Editor: Anna Glendenning; Copy-editor: Ellie Robins; Proofreader: Sarah Terry; Typesetter: Tetragon, London; Typefaces: Linotype Swift Neue and Verlag; Cover and Inserts Design: Lotta Kühlhorn. Printed and bound by TJ International, Padstow, Cornwall, UK.

This book has been selected to receive financial assistance from English PEN's PEN Translates programme. English PEN exists to promote literature and our understanding of it, to uphold writers' freedoms around the world, to campaign against the persecution and imprisonment of writers for stating their views, and to promote the friendly co-operation of writers and the free exchange of ideas. www.englishpen.org.

We gratefully acknowledge that the cost of this translation was defrayed by a subsidy from the Swedish Arts Council.

And Other Stories is supported using public funding by Arts Council England.

I. ELLINOR

Hearts can break. Yes, hearts can break. Sometimes I think it would be better if we died when they did, but we don't.

STEPHEN KING

When trying to find the one, I'd never thought the internet would be my thing. There was something commercial about it, not to mention I'd never written a personal ad, or anything else for that matter, and had no idea how to sell myself in writing. My boyfriends had always been regular guys from my village. The first one, for instance, was called "Johnny" and there was nothing special about him at all, at least not on the surface, at least not until it became clear that he was in fact sick. We were in the same class at school and it started with him saying:

"Is there anything you've always dreamed a man would do for you?"

I guess he'd heard it in a movie and, in all seriousness, already actually thought he was a man. And I suppose he wasn't expecting the answer I gave him, but something more like: "Yes, I've always wished for a man who could make me lose my mind in bed." Or a concrete wish that would help him along. But I said:

"I've always wanted to be taught how to fight."

And when he didn't look as surprised as I'd thought he would, I added:

"Fight like a motherfucker."

Johnny nodded slowly, spat on the ground, and said:

"If that's what you want, doll."

That very night he took me to what he called his fight club. It was a bunch of people who'd seen and been inspired by the movie, but unlike the people in the film, they actually practiced various martial arts and met up three times a week to fight. Everyone went up against everyone else. You had to go into a basement beneath a school. It had tiles that faded from brown to orange; a strange matte tile that didn't behave as tile usually does, but seemed to absorb every sound. From there, you went deep inside a series of corridors. Everyone was dead silent, barefoot, and had bags full of gym clothes slung over their shoulders. Only the fans made a noise. Then you entered the room and there they were, the people from our village who wanted to fight. A temporary captain was appointed, and we all warmed up together. Everyone was flexible, even the guys, and no one was ashamed of showing that they could do forward or side splits. People farted loudly, stretched out like that, but not laughing was an unwritten rule. Then we fought. I was the only beginner and had one thing going for me: I was scared to death. Being scared to death gives you an edge, Johnny said. Being really fucking afraid had some hidden benefits – the body was smarter than you thought, and when you let it run on autopilot, it was capable of almost anything. But then you had to take control.

"Most people aren't angry because they get attacked, they're angry because they can't defend themselves," Johnny said.

Johnny could do more than fight. He could shoot, too. We used to visit a firing range on the way from our village to the next. We walked around wearing orange earmuffs, watching the people shooting handguns and then the ones shooting rifles. Johnny showed me how to take a wide stance, lift the rifle, and nail a clay pigeon. First in a simulator and then in real life. One day he said I was ready – he could take me hunting now. He talked a lot about that hunt before we went, how you had to go out after dark, use your night vision, and keep real quiet the whole time.

Only one shot was fired the time I joined the hunters, at a wild boar. The shot cracked the silence, and you could hear the boar still running, not like before, but clumsily, branches breaking around it, and in the end limping and confused, as if it knew it was going to die and was pulling itself through the brushwood in a panic. As we came closer, Johnny swung the beam of his flashlight upward. I saw the beech's bare branches, like long, dark bones reaching for the night sky. Johnny took my hand, clamped the flashlight between his legs, and started rubbing his buzz cut back and forth, and I wanted to ask him why but kept quiet. He was just about to whisper in my ear – I think it was going to be something big, about us – but one of the hunters interrupted, saying he'd found the pig. He shined a light on it. A clean shot to the shoulder, blood pumping out over the black bristles. It was a large sow, and we all had to help carry her on a pole to the pickup. The next day it was going to be cut up in Johnny's friend's yard. We headed over after breakfast, and by the time we arrived there was blood and bristles everywhere because no one actually knew anything about butchery. Everyone went at it as best they knew how, all the while saying it had to be fast. I never went poaching again.

One night I told Johnny that if he was ready, so was I. He smiled at me, and I was thinking this was the first time I'd ever really seen his teeth, and they were big and white like sugar cubes, perfectly set in his mouth, an odd contrast to his face, which was irregular and acne-scarred. We did it on the bed of his pickup, and the jacket he'd spread underneath me got covered in blood.

"Girls today don't normally bleed their first time," the school nurse told us during sex ed. "Because they go riding and biking, jump and bounce around, their hymens aren't normally intact."

I must've had an incredibly subdued childhood, because my hymen was absolutely still intact. The sight of all that blood didn't disgust Johnny at all, in fact it only took him seconds to come. I didn't know what to say when he was done. But I could already tell that Johnny was a person to watch out for. Of course, like most of the guys in my village, he had violent tendencies, was uneducated and horny and would be for the rest of his life. But there was more to him.

"I didn't know you were a virgin," he said.

"What about you?" I asked.

"Yeah. I was too."

He looked at his stained jacket and said:

"I guess you gotta start somewhere."

The next time was much better. Not to mention the third, fourth, and fifth times. Johnny said he thought the two of us, we fucked like porn stars.

When we were sixteen years old, I broke Johnny's nose with the back of my hand. It wasn't on purpose in the sense that I wanted it to happen, my arm just flew out by reflex, it had nothing to do with martial arts. Anyhow, it turned into a big thing, because we were in high school and everyone heard about it, the teachers and the nurse and Johnny's parents and mine. Johnny's mother said:

"I don't want you seeing that girl anymore."

We were in the schoolyard and his nose was bleeding.

His mother had rushed over as soon as she found out and was standing there giving me dirty looks.

"Mom, Ellinor isn't some little girl," Johnny said. "She's a lady. And what a lady she is."

He smiled at me, hair falling over his eyes.

"And what a lady she is," he repeated, smiling even wider with those sugar cubes of his.

I wanted to say, don't stand there grinning, remember how hot my blood got you, you're a sick fuck, Johnny, there's no hiding that kind of thing. That's what I wanted to say, but I suppose it was the bloody nose that made me feel differently, and so I went over and hugged him. The gesture was unusual for us. We did everything together. We helped each other with the repeating rifles and other weapons, we fought and we fucked, but we never hugged. And yet here we were, and I could feel his hot blood dripping down my neck.

"Now you've learned everything I wanted to teach you," he said.

But he added that if I ever used what he'd taught me against him again, he wouldn't think twice about killing me.

"Just you try," I replied.

"Don't piss me off," he said, and his eyes went black.

Soon we fell into a sort of sexual routine, even if you couldn't really call it a routine, the way we were back then.

"Let's go to my place," he'd declare, sliding his hand between my legs while driving.

Going to his place meant his dad's hunting cabin outside the village, where you could be left alone. It was a small cabin with gnarled bead and butt paneling and bright yellow curtains with white stripes that his mother must have hung. The cabin had two small bedrooms plus a living room with a stove. We went into one of the bedrooms and he said:

"Take your clothes off and get on the bed."

While I did that, he went to the kitchen and made coffee. He returned with his cup, dragged the chair over to the bed, and drank it as he looked at me lying there on my back, legs spread. It felt like he could see right into me, up and through my interior, if you can say that, as if there was a dark channel inside me, and if you followed that channel, you'd surface somewhere else entirely.

"Do you have to stare like that?" I asked.

"Think about the actors in porn. They've got no problem showing themselves off."

"Think about when I broke your nose," I replied.

"You're like bread between my teeth," he said and raised his cup, proposing a toast.

He went on sitting there, drinking his coffee. When he'd finished it, he put the cup on a shelf and started taking off his trousers.

"When are you going to let me do you in the butt?" he groaned once when we were getting it on.

I replied that if I was a truck driver and had access to a nice, comfortable garage, I'd never even consider parking my vehicle down in a ditch. Johnny laughed, but didn't ask about it again.

A few years later I put on some weight. I never really got fat, but it was enough for Johnny to stop finding me attractive. We met up less and less, and eventually he stopped calling. Once I plucked up the courage to call him.

"Should we go shooting one of these days?" I asked. "Or fighting?"

He told me he'd met someone. After that I saw him in the village with her. She was thin and fit with long dark hair tied in a ponytail that hung all the way down her back.

I wondered what it was like for them in bed, if he sat at its foot, drinking his coffee while taking her in and if so, what she thought about it.

I kept up the fighting over the years. Like other people play bridge, sing in a choir or dance a few nights a week, taking comfort in it as they get older – a pursuit, so to speak, that shores you up against old age, or at least lessens its effects – I kept going back to that basement and spent time with the people there. Fighting was good; you got better with age. Being young and good-looking didn't buy you any cred, nothing came for free, and every last thing had to be fought for. Later, when I found friends who came from other places, they said they couldn't understand why a person would choose to spend their time like that when they could be spending it with a good book, good company, or a glass of wine instead.

"Not much in life compares to fighting," I'd reply.

I knew how it must have sounded to them, but I still think it's true. I've never been as close to anyone as I have in that basement over the years. It has to do with concentration and how you read people's eyes. Sex doesn't work like that. There are people who close their eyes and jack off their whole lives, into their own hands or between someone's legs, and nothing ever goes on in their brains. But when you face an opponent, there's a moment when you can see right into them and understand exactly who they are. Not to mention, and this is what I told my friends, you're not really old as long as you can kick someone taller than you in the head.

Sometimes I thought about Johnny and how he was a sick fuck. But sick or not, I'd come to understand that wasn't what's important. What's important is not being alone.

I ended up having a number of boyfriends over the years, pretty normal ones too, at least compared with what was to come. I never moved in with them. I was more the kind of person who just lived, took each day as it came, and didn't get worked up for no reason. I wasn't really serious about any of the men in my life before the thing with Ruben and the manuscript happened. And that began with me creating a profile on a dating site with the following introduction:

I'm thirty-six years old and seeking a tender, but not too tender, man.

I left "interests" blank, I left "favorite authors" blank. Same with "favorite food" and "favorite places in the world." But in the space for your motto, I did write: *Meeting the aforementioned man.* Then it occurred to me that a motto is actually something else, a sentence or phrase that can act like a word of wisdom would in various situations. But I've never had that kind of motto, so I left the sentence there, even if it did say something about me, suggesting a laconic side some people might find off-putting. But on the other hand, I wasn't after a verbal person. I also included a picture of myself. It's a picture a friend of mine took where I'm lying on my stomach on his bed. The signs of my age aren't visible because the only light source in that picture is a few candles, and like my friend says, most people look pretty decent in the glow of a few of those.

A week went by before I logged on again. I'd gotten a ton of replies. Surprised, I worked my way through them, one by one. I've never been the kind of girl who gets shown any appreciation. Once Johnny said I was like an onion, you had to peel away the layers to get inside. Most girls would have been insulted if you said something like that to them, but I could tell Johnny meant it as a compliment. And now when I opened my email in the mornings I had dozens of responses. An older man promised me "economic freedom" in exchange for "satisfying him" sexually three times a week. A twenty-year-old wondered if I could school him. I sat there, coffee in hand, laughing out loud. I was touched, but not so much because these men were showing me appreciation (the photo, when all was said and done, was a con) but because I understood that the people writing to me actually believed in love, in the sense that I'd be able to give them what they were looking for.

Some time passed before I next visited the site. Things came up, but when I finally logged back on I saw that several of the men who'd replied had kept writing to me. Some of them had written almost every day for weeks. The twenty-year-old who thought I could teach him something seemed to have become a little obsessed with me, and wrote in a message that *I've always had girls who talk and talk, they never want to do anything but talk, but you seem wordless and genuine.* Wordless and genuine. I thought that was nicely put. I wrote to him:

I guess you're inviting them to have a conversation, plain and simple. Try inviting them to do something else. Kind regards, E

Some sounded threatening. Not that they were threatening me, but because they were telling me about other men who were threatening other women on the site.

This world is no exception to the real world, wrote one. *Girls get threatened here, like anywhere else, you have to watch out here, too.*

So I guess I'll block you now, you psycho, I wrote back, and that was the end of that.

Sometimes I thought: Why did you leave, Johnny? Why couldn't you just take care of me? Now I'm swimming out in this cold water and God knows if I'll survive.

But I survived, otherwise I wouldn't be sitting here writing this.

My next boyfriend was called Klaus Bjerre and came from Copenhagen. He liked that I called him my "boyfriend," it made him feel young, he said. In Danish you say *kæreste*: dearest. He lived in an apartment not far from one of the areas where you could score heroin. At that time, there were still whole areas where you could score in Copenhagen, and you could see people standing around and sleeping on street corners in the December fog. Klaus Bjerre said they were harmless, and they were. I mostly stayed at home, since Bjerre used to say that "anything can happen in Copenhagen," gesturing at the window. On the other side was a red brick facade. I've always liked Copenhagen, but I wondered why Bjerre was looking for a partner in Sweden. I thought there might be something about him that Danes saw at once, but that he hoped Swedes wouldn't figure out. Danes think Swedes are dumb. Being from Skåne is no exception; same shit, they think. We're good for selling food, building a bridge, and tending our forests so they can come over on the weekend and go for walks. Maybe we were even good enough to be wives or at least lovers. I guess that's what Bjerre was trying to find out.

"I only have one small flaw," he said the first time we met, "and that's that I drink quite a lot."

It didn't worry me then, because I didn't know anything about drinking and thought it wouldn't change anything at all, at least not to begin with. But then he touched me and later I still stank of his hands. The bed we slept in also smelled of him, and sometimes when he got up I buried my nose in his pillow, thinking I might vomit. It smelled of liquor and dirt, a physical dirt, like his body didn't know what to do with all that poison and so had started to produce its own musty antidote. In the beginning he made me feel sick, but I got used to it. I liked the apartment he lived in. It was in Frederiksberg and was warm and had a heater under the kitchen table that you could press your leg against while drinking your coffee.

Nothing special happened between us, nothing that doesn't happen between normal couples. The biggest thing that happened was Bjerre talking about our future. He sketched it out before him like some sort of castle, and as he did a look of happiness would appear in his eyes, and he'd even forget to drink while he was talking. He said I could come live with him, and he'd buy a bigger bed and other things I might want. We'd have friends that we could invite over, and he'd make sure there was money in the bank and a year's salary of savings in case anything happened.

"I'm going to make sure of it," he said. "This is my responsibility, you should be able to relax with me and know that I'm behind you, taking care of everything."

I replied that if he wanted to get his life in order, the first thing he had to do was stop drinking. He nodded and took a sip from his glass.

"True," he said. "You're not telling me what I want to hear, you're telling me what I *need* to hear. And that's why you're a true friend, Ellinor."

He looked at me with those bloodshot eyes of his when he said it. They had a shine to them, as though he were always on the verge of tears. He took my hand; his fingers were long and his nails chewed off. He leaned in for a kiss, but the smell coming from him was so nauseating I turned my head away. He took another sip and blinked away the shine.

"When I think about the life I want," he said, "the calm, warm, cozy life I want to have with you, Ellinor, I feel like I can do anything. I'm prepared to do anything. Tomorrow we'll take out all the bottles I've hidden, and we'll pour them down the drain. It'll be like a fresh start."

He gave me another smile, and his hand gripped mine.

"Should we get a car?" he asked. "Then we can drive all around Skåne on the weekends. Walk in the forest and buy cheap food in Malmö."

I said that we didn't need a car; one of the nice things about Copenhagen was that you could borrow bicycles everywhere, and if you wanted to go to Skåne there was a train. Bjerre looked worried, as though the car were a prerequisite for all the rest.

"What about a dog?" he asked.

I shook my head.

"We have it good as it is," I said. "All you have to do is stop drinking."

The next day we were supposed to throw away all the bottles. Pour the liquor out, throw away all the bottles and start that new, stable life. Klaus Bjerre got up early that morning, showered and put on aftershave, and drank coffee, but without touching any of the bottles in the kitchen.

When he looked at me, the whites of his eyes seemed less bloodshot.

"You'll see, everything will be fine," I said. "With enough determination, you can make anything work."

"Yes," said Klaus. "I'm going to the office now. Then I'll come home, and we'll eat dinner and drink water with it. Then we'll deal with the bottles."

I lingered in the doorway as he made his way out. He turned around when he got to the banister, waved at me, and smiled.

I went back into the apartment, sat in the kitchen, and had breakfast. Maybe half an hour after Klaus had left, there came a knock at the door. It was a hard, firm knock. I hadn't heard any footsteps on the stairs, so I thought the person knocking must have been standing outside the door for a while. Mustering the courage, then lifting their hand and delivering three determined knocks. I stopped chewing and set my cup on the table. It must be a salesman or a Jehovah's Witness, I thought. But I knew that a salesman or a Jehovah's Witness would never knock like that. With their very first knock, they'd make sure the person in the apartment perceived them as a friend, as someone who could improve your life. When I didn't respond, there was another knock. Hard and insistent, as though the person knew for sure there was someone inside and wanted to let them know they weren't about to give up. I got up and stood in the middle of the room. I stood there in my nightgown and stared at the door, unable to make myself open it. They knocked even harder, and I heard someone say:

"Open up, Mrs. Bjerre, please Mrs. Bjerre, open up!"

I opened the door a crack. It was one of Klaus's neighbors. I'd never spoken with her, but I knew she lived on the seventh floor together with her daughter. Klaus called her "that nutjob." She was as poorly dressed as I was, or maybe even worse, because the bib of her nightgown was stained with coffee, or maybe it was marmalade.

"Yes?" I asked through the crack.

"You have to come with me," she said. "Regina's locked herself in the bathroom and is saying swear words."

"Regina?" I said.

"My daughter."

"I don't think I can be of any help," I said.

"But you have to," she insisted. "Regina might die in there."

I wanted to say that I had a lot to think about, today in particular, and besides I don't usually go out this early in the morning. So I did, while trying to shut the door. But then the woman began to panic.

"*No, no,*" she shouted. "*You don't understand, Mrs. Bjerre, Regina might die in there, you have to come out and help me, otherwise she might die in there!*"

I don't know why, but I opened the door and joined her on the landing. All was silent. It was like we'd been completely cut off from Copenhagen's hustle and bustle, like the two of us, without knowing it and in separate apartments, had cultivated something all our own, something unpleasant and frightening. Our own vacuum, or our own sick universe. That's what I thought, and then I thought that I shouldn't have to know anything about vacuums or sick universes.

"What do you want me to do?" I asked.

"You have to help get her out of the bathroom," the woman replied.

"I'm sick," I said, not knowing why.

"What kind of sick?" she asked.

I tried to come up with a disease and said the most contagious one I could think of, that I'd caught some sort of pox.

"But I don't see any spots," she said. "What kind of pox is it? Impetigo?"

"No," I said. "Regular pox."

"Regular pox?" she wondered aloud.

"What do you want me to do?" I repeated.

"Help us," she said. "We have to help each other."

"Isn't there anyone else you can ask?"

"You're the only one who's free around this time."

She was right. I was the only resident of that building who wasn't busy. The rest of the doors were shut and locked, and would be until six or seven, when people started coming home from work. I was the only one free around this time.

"I guess I'm coming, then," I said.

I went into the apartment, got my key, went out, and followed her.

Her place was stuffy and messy. There was almost no daylight, and the rooms were lit up with lamps. There was a small shaft in the center of the building, probably an old garbage chute, that now served to let light into the apartments that didn't have windows facing the courtyard or street. So from certain rooms in her apartment, you could see into other rooms, and from the kitchen you could see into the bathroom. I stood there, looking through the shaft at a woman staring out of an open window. She was motionless, sitting just a few meters away from me. A pair of thick glasses distorted her eyes, and her expression was hard to read. Her mouth was set in a thin line, and she too was wearing a baggy nightgown through which you could see two oblong, sagging breasts.

"Can you show me the door?" I asked.

We walked through a narrow hall.

"Here it is," she said, showing me the bathroom door. "She's in there."

I grabbed the handle and rattled the door. Yes, it was locked. I knocked.

"Hello?" I said.

"Is that Mrs. Bjerre?" Regina asked.

"Yes," I replied, even though I thought this Mrs. Bjerre business sounded silly.

"You'll have to kick down the door," the mother said.

"Yes," I said. "I'm going to kick down the door now."

I bunched my nightgown up around my waist, tucked it in the waistband of my underwear, and stood there for a few seconds. The neighbor's eyes wandered up and down my body slowly, with displeasure.

"I'm going to kick down the door now!" I shouted to Regina on the other side. "Stand as far away from it as you can! Got it? Watch out!"

I backed up. Then I kicked. It was the first time I'd ever kicked down a door, and I didn't hold back like you do with a sparring partner. I put my weight on my left leg, lifted the right, and kicked straight ahead so the sole of my foot would meet the door. But right then, as I'm about to kick, I hear the mother say in a quick, weak chirp, like a little bird:

Think of someone you hate.

And before I had a chance to think, before I could process what she'd said, I saw Klaus Bjerre's face in front of me. I saw his face, his bloodshot eyes, and I caught a whiff of his sick breath. That face smiled crookedly at me as the full force of my foot hit the door. My heel landed right in Klaus Bjerre's mug. The hinge was exposed, the door swayed back and forth. Finally, part of the frame fell to the floor. And inside, on the toilet, sat Regina. Cross-eyed, heavy-breasted, and scared stiff. The woman beside me let out a whoop of joy:

"Mrs. Bjerre opened the door!" she shouted. "There you have it, Regina, no need for a man!"

Regina got up from the toilet seat, came over to me, and draped herself around my neck, and soon the mother did the same thing. There we were, enveloped in the soft smell of their armpit sweat, and maybe mine, too – I don't think you smell your own sweat in the same way. They dragged me into the kitchen, offering me liqueur and cookies.

"Come now, Mrs. Bjerre, sit down and let us show you our appreciation."

Their bare feet shuffled beneath their nightgowns, back and forth across the linoleum. Their heels were dry and cracked, their toenails long, and their feet left prints on the floor, which seemed to be slick with grease.

"I have to go back down to my place," I said. "Mr. Bjerre will be home soon."

They nodded. As I went down, they waved goodbye to me in the stairwell. I opened the door to the apartment, walked in, and was confronted with Klaus Bjerre's odor of despair. I stood there for a while, looking around. The breakfast table. The heater. The brick wall across the way. The bottles we were supposed to pour out that night. Our little life, the existence we'd managed to create.

Then I went into the bedroom, took out my bag, and packed my things. I walked out of the apartment, through the side streets toward Hovedbanegården. I spent a while watching the flurry of people under the glass roof and someone selling flowers nearby. A few minutes later I was on the train home to Skåne.

People on the site liked sending pictures of themselves. Some had cars and sailboats, big fancy TVs facing their living-room couches. Some sent pictures of their genitals. All of them said something nice about my picture. I wasn't used to flattery and it's true, people who aren't, people like me, really are the most easily flattered. So I sat there and smiled, thinking that maybe I wasn't so bad after all. Then I thought there was no reason to feel flattered. This was about something else, something that had nothing to do with me. I responded to one of the people who'd reached out:

Thank you for your reply, but don't have any illusions about me. I'm thirty-six years old, the picture is taken by candlelight . . . Here's a real photo.

I sent a photo of myself as I was right then, wearing panties and a bra in plain daylight (I edited out my head). Without going into detail, I can only say that the picture wasn't as flattering, and I cracked up thinking about the cooling effect it would have on the man in question. But he responded within a minute:

Other than the fact that your age suggests you and I will be able to engage in many interesting conversations and you in all likelihood can cook a very good dinner (I will, however, choose the wine), I'm convinced that your body, which I assume has already been enjoyed by many, contains a wealth of possibility. And your sex must be a cache of dirty acts in which I too can enjoy.

You devil! I wrote back immediately.

But I stayed at the computer. And in all honesty, I was curious. Curious about the man, but also the masculinity. Masculinity works like this: the more you find out about it, the less you understand, and your fascination keeps on growing. I don't just mean sex. For whatever reason, I definitely thought I'd keep emailing this man. What he wrote was a testament of sorts, an ugly realness that he was unashamed of. Maybe I could arrange a date with him. During the dark season we were now in, this kind of adventure would be beneficial. I always feel down when it's dark out.

When can we see each other? I wrote.
In three weeks, he replied.
What's your name and where do you live? I wrote.
My name is Ruben and I live in Stockholm, he replied.
OK, I wrote. *So I'll book train tickets and a hotel.*
You're welcome to stay with me, he wrote, but I said no.

The day I was supposed to go see Ruben was in early January. Two days before I was meant to travel, the TV said there was going to be a snowstorm. It was going to come in from the south, and then sweep up over the country like a broom, dragging everything along with it, and the spruce trees would rain down on the power lines like pick-up sticks. That's what the TV said. People out in their cabins would be without electricity for days, maybe weeks. I compared my train's timetable with the forecast. If I traveled north around lunchtime, which was when my train was supposed to depart, I could get there before the storm. When it finally rolled in across Stockholm, I'd be sitting at some bar. Probably a little tipsy, probably with Ruben.

I took the train as planned. First I took the bus from my village to Malmö. I've always liked getting away, as soon as the bus starts driving through the fields toward Lund it feels like anything can happen, like I'm some sort of funnel and things are about to start pouring in. The train left the station and traveled up through Skåne. The deciduous forest ended, and after that we traveled through spruce and pine forests, which parted for the long, dark lakes that flanked the rails. Everything in the train was peaceful. I sat in my seat and wondered what it would be like when I arrived. How Ruben would look, what his job was, if we were going to have sex and if so, how. I was nervous, but I was going to do what I always do when I don't feel at home: keep quiet until I understand what's what. I've always thought the man should take the initiative. I'm not one to walk on over and fan the flames. I've always thought that the hardest part is just before you take off your clothes. After that I usually feel completely calm, actually.

I fell asleep and only woke up when we were passing through the tunnels south of Stockholm. My ears were blocked and outside the window, a wall of granite flew by with dizzying speed, only a few decimeters away. Suddenly we rolled out of the hills and into the city. I'd never been to Stockholm before so I wasn't prepared. It was dead silent in the carriage, and when I looked around I saw that everybody was gazing out the windows. In the twilight, the sky was orange fading into blue. We traveled over bridges surrounded by water, cliff faces, and buildings with copper roofs. Bodies of water part-covered in ice wove through the city, and in the distance was the open sea. Everybody here must be happy, I thought. Healthy people. Generations of ice skating and jumping off the rocks for a swim. They must be drinking good coffee behind those large windows. Over a mix of hills, city, and sea that would be surreal for the rest of the world. When I'd finally gotten off the train I felt that the people looked hard-set and perfect, a little like they'd been cloned from a film. I felt uneasy. I longed to go home, if not to my village then at least to Copenhagen. In Copenhagen the Ferris wheel spins right next to the train station and everything has a whiff of urine, smoke, and waffles.

I'd booked a hotel in the center of town, and I checked in. It turned out that my room was in the basement and didn't have any windows, but there was a sauna out in the hall. I sat in it for a long time and then showered, switching between hot and cold, went back to my room, crawled into bed, and fell asleep. When I woke up it was nine in the evening and inside the windowless room it was pitch-black. I got up and put my makeup on in the bathroom, where the floor was still wet. I was doing quite a heavy face until I realized that women who wear a lot of makeup often look insecure, so I wiped most of it off with a piece of toilet paper. Then I texted Ruben saying that I'd arrived and showered and was now ready to meet him.

See you at Pharmarium, he replied after barely a minute. *Take a seat in the bar and look like you're for sale. That's how I'll find you.*

I asked the hotel receptionist what this Pharmarium place was. Directions in hand, I wrapped my scarf around my head and went out.

Since the sauna and my nap, the wind had really picked up. The winters up there are cold, and outside the hotel the wind was creeping along the ground only to spiral up into the air, taking with it fistfuls of powdered snow. I walked across a bridge and over to another island. There were tall brick buildings with green copper roofs. Everything looked grand and picturesque. In spite of the cold and snow in the air, there were a lot of people out and about. I arrived at a square with a church and four places where you could get a drink. One was Pharmarium. It sat on a corner of the square and its entrance was unassuming, but when I stuck my head in I saw that it was a place I probably would've chosen myself. The ceiling was low and it was hot inside. People sat in groups at low tables and colorful fabrics hung from the walls. Otherwise it resembled an old pharmacy, with dark wooden drawers that gave the place an occult feel.

Take a seat in the bar and look like you're for sale. That's how I'll find you, Ruben had written. I hung up my coat and scarf and sat in the bar. Then I ordered a drink, told the bartender I wanted "his best," and was given a smoky, sour job that I gulped down to kill the insecurity in my gut. After ten minutes, a man came over and introduced himself as Ruben.

"Are you Ellinor?" he asked.

"Yes," I said.

"I'm Ruben."

"Hi," I said.

Ruben was overweight, had dirty hair, and was obviously intoxicated.

"Maybe you didn't expect me to be so fat," he said after a spell.

"No," I said.

"Are you disappointed?" he said.

"I've never had a problem with fatness," I replied.

"Good," Ruben said and ordered a beer from the bartender.

We sat in silence as he drank.

"Will you come home with me now?" he said.

I mean, I couldn't have suggested the windowless hotel and even though I'd thought we might eat dinner somewhere before we, so to speak, began the next phase of our encounter, I said it was OK. We walked back through the alleyways and soon came to a big street where Ruben hailed a taxi. Then we traveled far, out of the city and onto a large road that ran along the sea and into a neighborhood with large houses perched on slabs of rock near the shore.

"Wow," I said. "This is where you live? What's it called?"

"Saltsjöbaden," said Ruben.

"Are you rich?" I asked.

"Rich?" he replied as though he didn't understand what the word meant.

"I mean: it looks really swanky here," I said.

"Swanky?" Ruben said, looking out the window. "I don't think anyone uses that word anymore."

His voice had something new to it, as if the top of his throat was pinched together. Maybe he didn't like me as much as he'd hoped he would. All this reminded me of a job I had when I was young and got roped into selling phone sex.

There was a guy from Malmö who thought he had what he called "the idea of the century." People are so damn lonely, he said during the job interview. People sit alone at home and no one can actually be bothered to leave the house, but everybody wants to meet the One. People want to score, he added, but they don't want to work out and if they don't have to shower, well then that's another plus. One of my clients was a TV chef. It was pretty incredible for a beginner like myself to land a celebrity, a cultural personality, but that's how it was. He wanted someone who wasn't practiced, someone who was doing it for the first time, just like him. I remember what it was like when he came. He'd yell out loud, and the yell would echo in his apartment. You could hear it in the handset for a second after he'd gone quiet, as though the scream was lingering, first in the room, then in the phone. The echo made him seem even more alone and it felt like I was sharing that loneliness with him, but it wasn't the kind of loneliness that ends when it's shared, no, it seemed to double, as though talking to each other was making us even lonelier. We kept talking. After a few weeks he asked me to dominate him. I told him I'd never done that before and I didn't know how. "Treat me like a dog," he said. "I've never had a dog," I said, "but if I had one I'd probably treat it well, better than I treat myself, actually. I can't stand to see animals suffer," I added, and then he became impatient. "Treat me like shit," he said. "You've treated someone like shit before, haven't you?" he added. I had a think, took a breath, and with a shaky voice I said: "Shut up and do as I say." First he went quiet, then he became submission personified. I'd rather not go into exactly what I mean by that because even though a lot of years have passed it's still embarrassing to think about how his personality took a turn there. Back then I didn't know if I thought the whole thing was really cool or really gross. But what I understood was there are different ways to exert power over people, and one way is to treat them like shit. And if you can do that, if you can take control of another person and see to it that their greatest wish is to follow your orders, then all of that person's energy is at your disposal, plus your own. It's like running in the same direction as a treadmill, you have incredible power even though you're making minimal effort. I felt different after having dominated him, if you can say that people can be dominated over the phone. As if I'd grown, as if I'd become a bit of a man. So this is what it's like to be a man, I thought. It really was a different kettle of fish. I think I fought better at practice after that. It's hard to explain. Later I saw him baking cookies on TV. There he was, bossing people around: check the oven, make sure the batter doesn't get too thick. I put my feet up on the table, leaned back on the couch, and laughed at the picture-perfect cookies, which didn't reflect his inner self at all. Sometimes he looked into the camera, and sometimes he smiled. I wondered if he was thinking about me. If he knew that somewhere out there on a couch was someone who could see right through him like no one else, who knew who he was and who understood that the cookies and cameras were just padding, props, and airbags around a wish he couldn't reveal to anyone.

So I was looking out from the taxi, at the houses passing by, grand and somehow stubborn, their large windows like eyes staring out over the water. The taxi pulled onto a smaller road that cut into the forest. It was moving more slowly, and we sat beside each other in the back seat not saying a word. I thought about what he'd written in his messages and noticed that his confidence and calm felt quite distant now. Had he been pretending? I glanced at the meter, but Ruben didn't seem to care. The taxi stopped and he paid by card. We got out of the car and he took a key out of his pocket and unlocked a big gate. Beyond it was a house made of dark wood. It was pitch-black everywhere, except for some muted lighting in the garden. Around the property was a tall, dark spruce forest and the sea suddenly seemed far away even though it was really only right behind the house.

"Having second thoughts?" Ruben asked.

"No," I replied.

"What if I'm a cold-hearted murderer?" he said and laughed.

"The bartender saw us leave together," I said.

"They see so many people," he said. "When it comes down to it, they wouldn't remember."

I grinned at him, because Ruben was the type of person who at first glance doesn't seem able to hurt a fly. We went in, took off our shoes, and he showed me around the house. It was obvious that all those kilos made it difficult for him to get around. The house was sparsely furnished and all the walls were white. When we left a room he'd turn the light off behind us. I wondered if he had a wife, or if he'd had one. Not that it mattered. It shouldn't have been hard to ask, but the question was out of bounds with Ruben, as though both he and his home demanded respect and distance from all who were let in. As if this were his terrain, and only he knew the way. When we came to the living room, he suggested we get a little alcohol in our bloodstream and opened a bottle of something strong, pouring us each a glass. After that he said it was "a bit chilly," and so he lit a fire in the fireplace. Then he laid out a pelt.

"You can get undressed and wait for me there," he said.

"Excuse me?" I said.

"Take off your clothes and lie down on the pelt, and I'll be with you soon," Ruben said.

I laughed.

"Do you think I'm a whore?"

"No," he said. "I don't think that. But we both know what's going to happen. And, shall we say, I'm not a fore-play man."

A gust of wind struck the window and we both looked outside. But the darkness was close and compact, and we only saw ourselves. I couldn't help but laugh.

"We look so small," I said.

"Yes," he said. "Are you going to get undressed now?"

I took off my clothes and lay down on the pelt. Ruben watched, arms crossed. But just when I thought he was going to lie down with me, he turned around and went out into the hallway. I heard the lock on the bathroom door turn and, after that, water flowed through the pipes for a long time. Then it went quiet. I lay there, staring up at the ceiling, then I turned on my side and watched the fur on the pelt move with my breath.

The heat made me dozy and I must have nodded off, because I woke up to Ruben standing in front of me naked. Like a mountain at my feet, his arms loose at his sides.

"There's something I have to tell you," he said, making eye contact. "Maybe I should've said it right when we started corresponding, but I was afraid you wouldn't give me a chance if you knew."

"What?" I asked.

"In recent years, the only sex I've had is sex I've paid for."

"What?" I said.

"It's been a long time since anyone's wanted to be with me of their own volition. You see what I look like. It's not just the weight, it's everything."

He gestured at his body and suddenly looked small in spite of all those kilos. Small, and in some way impotent.

"I've forgotten what to do when you're with someone who actually wants to be with you," he said, giving me an apologetic look.

I wished he hadn't mentioned it. I didn't know him well enough to feel compassion, and what we were about to do called for an ease that couldn't follow a disclosure like this. But Ruben seemed to be moving past his blockage, because he came over and lay down next to me on the pelt. I caught the scent of him. It was strange, but I didn't dislike it.

"Can't we just lie like this?" he said. "Get ourselves accustomed to the situation."

We lay like that, on our stomachs, feet toward the fire. The heat ran along our legs and our sexes and it was a nice contrast to the oceanic swells of hail pummeling the windowpanes. I asked what he did for a living.

"I'm a literary critic," he said.

"Ah," I said.

I had hoped he wouldn't be too intellectual. I didn't want to talk about literature before having sex, that wasn't the type of experience I was after. I wanted to clarify that for him, but Ruben had already started talking about an unusual thing that had happened not long ago. He had, he said, like most people who work with literature, a strong admiration for one particular author. He had been the driving force behind almost everything Ruben had done, both in literature and in life. But now Ruben was over forty and had been feeling like he'd reached an end with this author. He wasn't discovering anything, feeling anything new, wasn't entering new dimensions. And Ruben wanted to discover new things because he was, he said, the kind of person who thinks that life without development is insufferable. He could take anything on, and all kinds of highs could be swapped for all kinds of lows, but stagnation: never. And he wanted, so to speak, *to be youthful* in his discovery. Young, naive.

"Do you understand?" he asked.

"Yes," I said.

He kept talking about this naivety, like somebody going out into the forest for the first time, *seeing* the pines, *feeling* the air.

"As in Neruda," he said. "Do you get it now?"

To put a long story short, he wanted another author to admire. He read lots of things that all tired him out after just a few pages. Everything seemed corny and idiotic. But a few weeks ago he'd been invited to an event and the author in question was there, too. This was an author who is seldom seen out and so Ruben had never gotten to know him personally. But now he was right there, in the middle of everything, glass in hand, chatting freely and openly as though he were a socially competent person and the knots and darkness apparent in his books were just pretend. And out of nowhere, the author approached Ruben, put his hand on his shoulder and said:

You're Ruben, aren't you? I really admire your approach to cultural journalism. Unlike some people, you actually have something to say.

At that moment, Ruben couldn't remember much of what he'd written. All he could remember was an article of his on burned-out buildings in Västmanland, and when he told me this, there on that pelt, he looked perfectly confused, because when standing in front of the author he couldn't remember what burned-out buildings had to do with him, but he kept going on because it was all he could think of and this, he said, said something about how captivated he was in that moment. Blushing and stuttering, Ruben described his admiration for the author. The author, still with his glass in hand, looked like he pitied him. Within five minutes, they were friends. After ten minutes, he'd said he needed a pair of smart, sober eyes on a manuscript he'd finished a while ago and he'd be ever so grateful if Ruben would read it.

"Sometimes luck gets you close to the mystery," Ruben said, sprawled out on the pelt. "Sometimes everything just opens up."

"Have you read it?" I asked.

"Half," he replied.

His voice was shaky.

"I can show it to you," he said. "Come."

I could tell that this was a big deal, and the closest I'd been to anything like it was when Johnny and I were on the hunt. Some things can stop when you're standing in the midst of them, and it's as if you were meant to be right there, but in that moment you can't understand how or why because everything is in front of you, like fine-spun threads leading elsewhere, and not necessarily to anywhere good. We left the pelt. Ruben lit a candle and I followed him through some dark rooms until we reached his study. Like the rest of the house, it was clean and tidy. The desk was in front of an open fireplace, and a strange sound was coming from the chimney.

"That's the wind," Ruben said.

"Yes," I said.

The desk was clear except for two piles of paper. But they weren't neat piles. Some pages were folded and one of the papers was wrinkled, as though it had been scrunched up and someone had done their best to smooth it out.

"There it is," Ruben said.

He set the candle on the desktop.

"I hardly dare keep reading," he said and placed a hand on one of the piles. "I'm afraid the spell will break."

"What spell?" I asked.

"Sometimes," he continued, running his hand across the paper, "I don't want to read it because that means I have to touch it with something as banal as my hands."

"Yes," I said.

"This is the only copy," he said. "The author hasn't made a copy. He uses a typewriter and this is the only copy."

"Why?" I asked.

"Because . . . " Ruben began.

"What?" I asked.

"I can't explain," Ruben said. "But it's about respect, and material. The combination. The combination of respect and material. You have to respect what you do, its substance."

"I don't understand."

"Respect," he repeated.

"Respect for what?"

"For the inimitable."

I walked over and read the page Ruben was holding.

Male madness, it said, can almost always be traced back to dementia, or genius. It follows certain patterns of elevation, which originate in vanity and often become monotonous in the end. Female madness, on the other hand, is another matter altogether. Its domain is extensive, and seems capable of assuming countless forms. There is an elasticity to it, an elasticity reminiscent of the female body itself. The darkness that can take possession of women is far more demanding than the darkness that lays claim to men. And many women seem to be in some way willing to birth this darkness! It must relate to the ecstatic aspects of birth. In their flesh, women know the joy that suffering can conjure, and so they are more open than men when confronted with liminality. It is as though they trust in the positive power of suffering. Female madness is of incredible interest to me. It might have something to do with a "women's language." Luce Irigaray said that there is no female God, and so there cannot be a female language. For women everything is a compromise — isn't that the ultimate denigration? Jung said that he always spoke his patients' languages. If they were hysterical, then he spoke a hysterical language, if they were neurotic, then he spoke a neurotic language. I would have liked to see Jung speaking a hysterical language! How I would have liked to see Jung, with his white hair and his composure, speaking a hysterical language! Hysteria and intuition, the backwoods of women! Hysteria, and intuition. Intuition, oh, intuition . . . Everything can be explained. But an explanation of intuition is beyond reach in our time.

"I don't understand," I said.

"He's interested in women," Ruben said.

"Aren't all men?"

"Not like this," he said. "He's trying to do this properly. *Inhabit it.*"

"How's he doing that?"

"He's doing his best. But he's not succeeding."

"Is he going crazy?"

"I don't know," Ruben said. "I've only gotten this far." He waved a sheet of paper. "But I don't think this is going to end well."

"Why?"

"Because no good books end well. Now let's go back. Would you like another drink?"

We went to the living room, our glasses filled. I walked ahead of him, aware that he was looking at me, his eyes running along my body, appreciating the degree of pleasure I was capable of giving him as he gathered his strength in anticipation of what was to come.

"The manuscript is all very well," I said when we arrived at the fire. "But I haven't come here to talk literature."

"You are so very right," Ruben said and lay down on his back on the pelt. "I want you to straddle me."

I did what he told me to, but I was tense and the whole manuscript situation wasn't really a turn-on. I couldn't stop thinking about what it said about suffering and women, and all of this felt a little vile. But Ruben didn't seem to feel the same way, or he'd managed to get over it, because he whispered:

"Say you're my whore. I need to hear it, say it."

I shook my head. I didn't want to say I was his whore. I have nothing against games, but the problem was that it wasn't a game for Ruben. I leaned over and kissed him. Ruben's lips parted, barely, but then he pushed me away.

"What is it?" I asked.

"I saw a film once," he said. "In Italian. A woman says to a man: *Sodomizzami*. Sodomize me. And he wanted nothing more, he'd dreamed about it forever, but he doesn't understand what she's saying. He's too uneducated. He doesn't understand, do you understand?"

We looked at each other, the two of us chuckling. I thought that maybe this was what it was like when intellectual people went to bed. Elegant and stiff, like someone with good posture eating mussels with a knife and fork, discussing film and quoting things in different languages even though you know you're facing ruin, a flood that is about to roll in and ravage everything all at once, a kind of flood of the flesh. This whole situation had lost its charm.

"You know, I can fight," I said, getting up.

"Fight?"

Ruben got up, too.

"Are you suggesting a catfight?" he said.

"That, too. I could poke your eye out, quick like a weasel when you least expect it."

"No shit. Where'd you learn that?"

"In a basement."

"I like that," he said and ran his hand across my mouth. "You seem different inside than you are on the outside."

We must be really drunk, I thought, but something was already in motion and couldn't be stopped.

"I definitely like that," he said, moving toward me. "You make me angry, but in a good way. Poke out my eye, then. Come on."

"I can't fucking poke your eye out," I said, turning my back to him.

"Come on. Do it. Get your claws out and I'll drop my gloves."

"I should go back to my hotel," I said.

"Why?" he asked.

"Because you . . . I don't know. Actually, you kind of disgust me."

"I disgust you? Is it because I'm fat?"

"No, but I don't want your squished eye on my finger."

That last part was supposed to make him laugh, but apparently it hit a nerve, because his eyes changed. I'd started walking toward my pile of clothes when out of the corner of my eye I saw his body in motion, gearing up, and the very next second it was hurtling toward me. I managed to weave out of the way so that he kept moving straight ahead, but drunk and dazed, I tripped and fell against a table and crashed into a mirror on the wall. *This isn't happening*, I thought as I was falling, *nothing can end like this*. The mirror fell to the floor, and large shards covered the space between the wall and the pelt. Ruben had also crashed into something, maybe he'd stubbed his toe, because he was red with pain and rage like people get when they stub their toes. The moment was so full of pathetic subtext that I tried to laugh it off, but it sounded like a scoff and he turned around superfast and charged at me. I remember having enough time to think that he looked like a walrus about to maul another walrus. And I also had enough time to think that I was too drunk to stand up in time, and it was stupid that when you trained as a fighter no one ever talked about the intoxication factor. Right then I also remembered what my sensei once said (these kinds of situations can be like that, so much can come to you even though you only have a microsecond to spare): if you're a girl who's ended up on the floor, then it's curtains for you. That's why girls should study karate and not judo, because once you're underneath a two-hundred-kilo lump it doesn't matter how flexible or fast you are, a hundred kilos is a hundred kilos, and we have yet to overthrow the laws of gravity. I felt the glass shards under me and Ruben's body landing on top of mine. The incredible pain when the fragments pierced my body. There goes a kidney, I thought. In some situations you just have to hold still and not do anything, however much it hurts. Sit still in the boat. But somehow this situation had already slipped out of our hands, and pain made me sink my teeth into Ruben's shoulder while grabbing his hair and pulling his head backward and searching for his eye with my thumb, but all I felt was his hard forehead against my fingertips. The bite seemed to drive Ruben mad with pain. He roared in my ear, and I let go. Ruben reeked of sweat and our bodies slid against each other unpleasantly. He held my hands behind my back and a sort of calm arose, and we lay like that, looking each other in the eyes as though we were trying to fathom something. We smelled bad, were sweaty and bloodied, and Ruben was smiling crookedly.

"All right then," he said. "Let's begin."

I'm not about to say that he raped me, because I'm not the kind of person who gets raped. That's the way it is and that's how it always has been, I didn't learn to fight so I could end up a victim. Somewhere, somehow, I must've given it some thought, and I must've concluded that to get something to change, you have to do it yourself. And Johnny had said that people aren't angry because they get attacked, it's because they can't defend themselves, which was clever of him, maybe one of the cleverest things that had ever been said in our village. So then I went down into that cellar. If I'd actually been raped I'd never have mentioned it. I'd have smothered the secret inside me until it died and then, one evening when I was stone cold sober and wearing my black sneakers and my soft black sweatpants and my black Michelin man jacket, then Johnny and I would have gone out, and we would have found the fucker, strangled him from behind with a strap and cut him into pieces, which we'd have buried down by the pond where the seagulls gathered outside the village. So no, I can't tell you exactly what happened in the house by the sea that night, but I knew already that nothing could end there, and this was actually the beginning and something must have been set in motion, a chain of events that would turn us against each other but also, in a way, unite us.

It took about five minutes. Then he slid off me and fell asleep. I turned to vomit on the floor. Then I fell asleep, too. After about half an hour we both woke up. Ruben sat up, saw the glass, vomit, and blood, and looked unsettled.

"My God," he said and looked at me with concern. "What the hell . . . "

He put his clothes on and went into the bathroom. Soon he returned with a toiletry bag and took out a pair of tweezers. He asked me to sit with him on the couch and picked glass from the wounds, at least that's what he said, and then he disinfected them. He didn't seem to care about the blood staining the couch. I looked at him as he sat there, his face sweaty and bloated and red. He kept giving me guilty looks. I thought about getting him back, and how I'd do it.

"You have to let me pay you for this," he said.

I laughed and Ruben must have misunderstood the laugh, because he laughed, too.

"I must have flipped out," he said, shaking his head. "I should probably go talk to someone."

"Yeah, maybe," I said.

"Yes," he said. "Completely mad, I promise that I – and of course I'll pay for your taxi home. But you have to wait until they start driving again, until the roads have been cleared. We have to make sure that the wounds aren't too deep . . . But they don't seem to be . . . Only scratches . . . Little scratches, nothing more."

He was avoiding my eyes.

Soon we were sitting in front of the fire. Ruben had opened a bottle of mineral water and made a salad that we ate straight from the bowl. We both had a wash and Ruben spread a white throw over the couch to cover the stains. Everything seemed to be resting under a deep calm, as though only peaceful, slightly melancholic events had taken place in the house. I was lent a pajama shirt that reached all the way down to my ankles. At some point Ruben fell asleep. That large body, passed out on the pelt. I could never kick a sleeping person, and yet I imagined myself standing up and kicking him. A firm, swift kick right in the gut. My foot disappearing into his fat. And when he opened his eyes, I'd be raising my knee and planting my heel right in his face, while letting out a high-pitched yelp of rage that would echo between the white walls. If you do something like that, you have to do it quick. Rage is a perishable commodity and if you don't get rid of it in time you have to carry it around, and that's like walking around a party with stinking dog shit on the sole of your shoe. People catch a whiff and so do you. It really isn't one of those smells that disappears with exposure.

But then it occurred to me that there was actually a much better way of hurting Ruben. I got up, cautiously, without waking him, and went into his study. I turned on the light. There it was, the manuscript. A bit like the crown jewels in the inner sanctum. Candle in hand, I reread the passage about madness. Looking around the little room, I realized that standing in Ruben's study in front of the author's manuscript was like standing inside Ruben's heart with a pair of pliers. I could sever any vein I wanted. I laughed to myself. I merged the two piles and saw that the manuscript was titled *The Polyglot Lovers*. I wondered what "polyglot" meant. The papers were stiff and looked dirty and damaged by damp, stained as though they'd been out in the rain and a cup of coffee had spilled across them. I carried the pile to the living room. The fire had almost gone out and I had to blow on it to get it going. Then I burned the pages. One by one I let them fall onto the fire, starting with the end in case Ruben woke up and threw himself over what was left. The fire flamed as though it were hungry for more. I fed it page after page, and I noticed that not all the pages had been written in Swedish, some were written in other languages even though I didn't know what those languages were. Sometimes there were different languages on the same page, the same sentence might even begin in one language and then switch to another only to go back to the first again. It looked funny, Swedish words popping up in the middle of everything, and other words popping up in the middle of Swedish. But I didn't have time to think about it. I kept going until all of it had burned up and only one satisfied, happy ember remained, glimmering in the ash. Behind me lay Ruben and his stomach, spread out over him like a fried egg. His mouth was half-open and drool ran down his jaw. Now we're even, I thought. Now balance has been restored. I can go back to the windowless hotel.

I lay down next to Ruben and looked at the large, dark windows. Then I fell asleep. After a few hours I woke up because Ruben moved. He sat up, spooned me, and pulled me tight. I caught his scent and felt his hot breath on the back of my neck.

"You wanted me without being paid for it," he whispered. "That's incredible. And I hurt you. Can you forgive me, Ellinor?"

"It's already settled," I said.

I fell back asleep. I kept waking up during the night, hearing the hiss of the snow against the windows. The whole time Ruben's arm was around me, and he was breathing against my neck. Even as he slept, I was clutched in his embrace.

Around seven, a new sound woke me. Cracking and slamming, and the room was filled with a hazy, gray light.

"That's the ice breaking," Ruben mumbled.

The last thing I saw before I drifted off to sleep was long, dark cracks that began out at sea. They were running through the ice, toward the perfect city.

The next time I woke up it was almost ten. Ruben stood over me and his face was dark as coal.

"Where's the manuscript?" he said.

"Which manuscript?" I said.

"I went into the study, and it was gone. So now you're going to tell me where it is. Now you're going to say where the manuscript is."

"I burned it," I said. "As revenge for the glass splinters."

Ruben stared at me. The whites of his eyes were bloodshot and the hair across his forehead looked wet.

"What did you say you did?" he said, and his voice sounded like a gasp. "Did you say you . . . ?"

"Yes," I said. "I burned it. It's gone now."

"You fucking . . . Are you insane?"

I stood up but didn't look him in the eye. He was facing me, breathing heavily.

"Calm down," I said. "It was just a manuscript."

"You're crazy," said Ruben. "Completely fucking – "

I held up my hand.

"I know what you want to say. I was considering kicking you to death for what you did, but instead I burned a pile of paper."

"A pile of paper? You're calling the manuscript *a pile of paper*?"

Ruben sank into a chair and buried his face in his palms.

"The author is going to hate me," he said.

"I don't give a shit," I said.

I felt a flicker of something like compassion. I saw him as I thought he was: Ruben in the big house. Ruben sitting in a tidy office, reading a manuscript. Ruben having to pay for sex and Ruben lugging those kilos through the house and not understanding how you can go so long without feeling anything. Ruben as the only flawed person in this cold, perfect city. Like me. Alone and flawed, but in a completely different way.

I got up and got dressed. All the while Ruben was watching me. When I went to get a glass of water from the kitchen he followed me. I put on my shoes and got my bag, assuming I wouldn't be getting any money for the taxi now but who cared, even a place like this must have bus stops. I opened the door to walk outside. The wind had stopped and the trees around the house were tall and straight. Now he's going to push me out and shut the door behind me, I thought, but that's not how it went.

I've always thought that when I finally find a man it will be someone who comes from the same place as me. Someone you can go out to a cabin with on a Friday, light a fire, and cook a meal. That's how I've always pictured it. Sitting around a table in a cabin, a crackling fire, the surrounding forest tall and quiet. You know you're going to eat, drink wine, have sex, and sleep, and that everything is going to be OK, because this is exactly how life is supposed to be and if it could just be like this, then everything would work out in the end. I've always pictured Johnny with me there. But by the time I met Ruben, Johnny had in fact been married for years and was living on a farm outside the village with a wife who'd had work done on her lips, breasts, and genitals after giving birth to three children. I was friends with her on Facebook and from her pictures, I thought she looked like a ditz, but a happy ditz, and that was at least partly to Johnny's credit.

There we were, in the hall, me and Ruben, the morning after. I was wearing my boots, my bag in hand. Ruben's face was tense – tense and very dark. I had no idea what I was supposed to say, so I said:

"It's really cold up here. In Stockholm, I mean."

"Yes," he said. "Perhaps you'd like to extend your stay? Until the cold eases?"

"But what about everything that happened?" I asked. "And the manuscript?"

"I hurt you, you hurt me," he said. "Everything follows a natural logic. As you said, we're even now. I'll have to come up with something. An excuse, or simply say it disappeared."

He shrugged. I looked out the window.

"Stay at least until the worst of the cold passes," said Ruben. "Then go."

He carried my bag into the bedroom. I hung up my coat on the same hanger it had been hanging on and tidily arranged my shoes inside the door. Ruben brought me a pair of white wool socks, which turned out to be too small when I tried to put them on. I wanted to ask who they belonged to. Was there a wife in the picture? Or were these the socks he offered the women he paid? I didn't have a chance to ask, because Ruben scrunched up his forehead and took the socks to the bedroom. He returned with a pair of his own.

"Use these," he said.

"I probably won't be staying that long anyway," I said.

But the cold held fast. The temperature sank lower and lower down, the TV was on in the living room, and throughout the house you could hear the people on it, talking about new records. The couch was still covered with the white throw, and you couldn't see the stains underneath. Through the large windows in Ruben's house was a clear view of the sky. Behind the pines at the back of the house lay the open sea, where sheets of ice floated on the blue-black surface. You could see holes out there opening up like icy mouths in the white.

We ate lunch and then dinner. In the evening we fell asleep without having sex. Two days passed, then three, and soon the weekend was over.

"Ellinor," Ruben said when Monday rolled around, "if anyone comes to visit, could you lie low?"

"Who's coming?" I said.

Ruben shrugged.

"No one special. Just friends, maybe some acquaintances. People I know."

"Are you asking me to hide?" I said.

"Not at all, but perhaps you could keep to one of the other rooms."

"Are you married?" I asked.

"Married?" Ruben said as though he hadn't understood the question.

"Yes," I said. "Or on some TV show so everyone knows who you are?"

Ruben shook his head.

"No, I'm not on some TV show. But it would look odd for me to be hanging around with just anyone. And you know, we met on a – "

"We met on a dating site," I said.

"Please," he said holding up his hand. "Don't say that."

"I don't understand," I said. "Almost everyone who meets nowadays meets like that. At least you're matched according to some sort of algorithm, that's more than you can say when you meet someone in a bar."

That's not how it works at all," Ruben said.

"How do you know?"

"I've spoken with someone who works for that site. He says they just push people together willy-nilly, the only filters they use are age and height."

"What else did he say?" I asked.

"About what?" he asked.

"About the dating site."

Ruben shrugged.

"Not much else. But he could go in and see everything, and sometimes he read people's messages to each other. And it would make him so sad he'd be useless for the rest of the day. As though his heart was enlarged and misshapen, its edges jutting into his chest, and all he wanted to do was cry. The whole day would be ruined, he said, because it was impossible to walk with your head held high after you'd scrolled through all those hopes. You see how one person writes to lots of others, keeps writing, gets canceled on, breaks down, and cries out in desperation: Why didn't you come and how am I supposed to find anyone? The guy at the website said people know at first glance. As soon as their eyes meet, they know, everything is decided on the spot. If the other person is too attractive and you're too ugly, if you put on your newly ironed shirt in vain, if there's a whiff of cirrhosis under the cologne, fat peeking out from a gap in the blouse, if the photo was a lie. Most people use photos that are a decade old. Idiots. And the money they pay! Hopeless, the guy who worked there said it was. Damn hopeless. And he said an undergrowth emerges, a depressing forest of loneliness growing below everything else."

I wondered if the person in question had read our messages to each other, but Ruben didn't know.

"But you understand, don't you, Ellinor?" he asked. "Keep a low profile if anyone stops by."

I should've kicked him right then and there. Landed the kick, and then a few more, until he was on the floor coughing up his spleen. Then I should have put on my boots and walked right out the door. Squinted at the bright snow, braced myself against the wind, and taken the train to Skåne. When you realize that something is sick you're supposed to pull your hand back real quick, otherwise what happens is your whole hand starts to rot, too, and then you're done for.

But I stayed. You could say my brain was no match for my body. My flesh wanted, for some absurd reason, to know more about Ruben, and my flesh might look like it's on the verge of giving up, but it's stronger than you'd think. Strong and stubborn, like a hill full of furious red ants that will come out in droves if I try to resist. Resistance would be much more painful than simple obedience. No one can just lie there and be eaten. The body is driven by instinct after all, everyone knows that, that's the reptile in you.

And it was only the first week, and our routine was still taking shape. The next day Ruben left the house at seven, turned as he walked out the door to say, "Goodbye, Ellinor," and I said, "Goodbye, Ruben," as though I were a little wife, or doing my best to be one. Then I had a look at his books. There was only one bookcase in Ruben's house, and it was in the bedroom by his bed. It was a slim and well-organized bookcase, not at all what you'd imagine for someone who works in literature. Most of the titles meant nothing to me. Or more rightly put: none of the titles on Ruben's shelves meant anything to me. But on that first day I took a book out to flip through it and saw, as I was about to put it back on the shelf, that behind the first row of books was another row of books. I pulled up a stool, climbed atop, and yes: behind the front row on every shelf was another row right behind it, just as well-organized. The titles in the back rows were all by the same author: Michel Houellebecq. The name meant nothing to me, but there were two versions of every book, one in French and one in Swedish. I took one out and sat on one of the couches in the large, bright living room. I seldom read books but I knew there was something special about these ones, or they wouldn't have been in Ruben's house and they wouldn't be in their own row behind everything else. I opened the book and read the first page. I read it three times before I got up from the couch and put it back on the shelf. Then I sat in the living room and looked outside. Sometimes it snowed a little. The light made the contrasts razor-sharp and the pines looked black, so did the gate and the tall fence. I wondered about the responses on the website. I thought about the man who worked there reading all the messages. I wondered if anything was going on in my village and if so, how I'd find out. I thought about having come here to find the One. When the sun was at certain angles, "sun cats" would leap from the icicles, bright reflections of light stalked by yellow spots that danced in your field of vision if you looked at them for too long. Sometimes you could hear a great tit, and sometimes the tit itself would come skipping along, clinging to the window ledge with its bird feet and looking in at you, turning its head as if it were kindly trying to understand something incomprehensible. And that's when I'd feel nauseous. I don't know why, but sometimes when it's cold outside I feel like I'm going to die.

In the following days, I unpacked the rest of my bag and put my things in a drawer that Ruben had emptied out and said I could have. I had three pairs of underwear with me in addition to the ones I was wearing. I washed my underwear every night. Ruben always put a load on in the evening with the shirts and underwear he'd used that day. I had no desire to shower but every morning and evening I washed my armpits, sex, and face with cold water. It was as though the cold, which was kept at bay by only half a centimeter of glass, and the strange environment inside the house made me hold on to what was mine, and my smell was all I felt belonged to me. Ruben had nothing against it. In fact he seemed to need to ingest my bodily fluids and smells in a way that, at first, made me blush all the way up to my scalp. Johnny had been animalistic in his way. Deep down I think all men are, even if some are animalistic in the way of a hedgehog or a kitten. And then it's like Johnny said: the body absorbs everything. I still remember the way Klaus Bjerre's pillow smelled. And Ruben had no problem with my odors. He used his tongue in every imaginable way and when I shouted at him to stop, he said he wasn't doing it for my sake, but for his own. Just fantasizing about pushing his tongue inside me could make him come. That says something about something. Lots of men think they're like that, but actually only a few have it in them. As a woman you can't possibly understand until you've been with someone like Ruben and after that everything else is unworkable. In part because of all the other men, in part because it ruins you somehow. You have to watch out with men like Ruben. They take everything you give them, use it, and then they grow. Gain self-confidence, lose weight. Crop their hair. Get another woman on the line, and another. In the end they realize they've become someone else, they can be choosy, and then they distance themselves. So you're left standing there. You've created the man, and yet you're the one who has to figure out how to survive.

One evening over dinner, Ruben brought up the manuscript:

"Where books are burned, in the end, people will also be burned," he said.

"I don't see how I could burn a person," I said.

"You can't always see everything," Ruben replied, "and things don't always burn as you expect them to."

"Are you afraid of the author?" I asked.

"He's tried to get in touch," Ruben said. "He calls, but I don't answer when I see his number."

"He must be wondering," I said.

"If he comes here you'll have to deal with him as best you can. After all, it was you who . . . "

The sentence was left hanging.

"Take it easy," I said, thinking I'd be heading back to Skåne any day now. And then that would be that with the manuscript.

But it wasn't exactly possible to be carefree, because the next day when Ruben was at work the phone rang. Several long rings broke the silence. I was standing just a meter from it and when seven signals had sounded I went over, picked up, and said:

"Yes?"

There was no reply, but I heard breathing.

"Yes?" I asked again. "Who is it?"

The person still didn't say anything, just breathed. After a moment there was a click, and the line went dead.

After that I started thinking more and more about the manuscript. One day I tried to go into the study, just to look at the desk it had lain on, which I'd remembered was painted a pale yellow with the woodgrain shining through. But when I pushed down the handle, the door was locked. Standing there, holding the handle, I couldn't understand why he'd locked it. I wanted to ask him when he came home. But it was like everything else about Ruben, while he was gone you imagined asking him a bunch of things. Where his parents lived, what kind of education he'd had and if he'd mostly had long or short relationships and if he wanted to have children, the usual things you ask each other when you're a couple, but once you were sitting across from him it was impossible. It was like there was a force field around him. When I realized this, I also realized that if you wanted to get to know Ruben, there was only one way to go about it, and that was by spying. But I'd never spied on anyone. I may have done bad things in my life, but I'd never spied on anyone.

The telephone rang the next day, too. And the next, and the next. I answered it those first days, and it was always the same breathing on the other end. Then I stopped answering. After a while I'd pull the cord out of the jack and only plug it in again when Ruben came home in the evening.

Ruben was, like many overweight people, extremely thorough with his hygiene. After breakfast he showered and washed himself thoroughly, a deep and painstaking disinfection – unlike me who only used water. He soaped up his entire body, his head, his face, and all the rest, including his feet, and then he got out of the shower and took care drying himself off with the towel, after which he sprayed himself with various scents. One for his armpits, another for his sex, then a cologne (Ruben always shaved thoroughly, but never nicked his face), and then a serum for his hair which, before he cropped it, lay slick and dark against his head. Then he got dressed and went out into the hall and put on his shoes and coat. He would stand there, fat, worried at first but increasingly calm. Then he would close the door behind him. Even though the house was silent, it seemed to be buzzing in my ears as I'd watch him go. His coat was black as coal, like his boots, and he trudged toward the gate and onward down the plowed road. I considered shoveling the snow. I considered calling my people back home and telling them where I was and about the turn everything had taken. But no one seemed to miss me, because my phone was always fully charged and silent on the couch.

When Ruben disappeared around the bend I watched TV. I would watch anything, often binging on shows. One show in the morning and another in the afternoon, and always several episodes in a row. I thought those series were teaching me something. I couldn't tell Ruben that. He could be incredibly contemptuous about certain things, but I thought what I was watching made me smarter. There was, for example, a very good scene somewhere in season four or five of *Breaking Bad*. Walt, the amphetamine cook and main character, is waiting for a round of cancer treatment. He is bald and gaunt and wearing a grim expression, and he's had that expression from the start so it's nothing the cancer brought on, but it has intensified. And next to him there in the waiting room is another man who has just received his cancer diagnosis and is waiting for his first treatment. He tells Walt about the shock of it all. That he was in the midst of living, and had planned on having a wife, house, child, a company, and all the rest, and now this. He's talking about how he's trying to relax and take each day as it comes. In short, he's spitting out those statements like a living dispenser of empty rhetoric, and you understand how he's been conscripted into that mode of thinking by welfare officers and doctors and others who have an interest in you being calm and not panicking as you face death. So they sit there. Walt and the man awaiting his first treatment are both wearing long sick gowns, white with green polka dots, which tie behind the neck. They look ridiculous from behind: two men in polka-dot gowns. Walt's cell phone rings, he answers, and when he starts talking it becomes clear that he's got a thousand other things going on besides his cancer. He's in that spotted sick gown telling people what to do left and right, the phone rings again and he continues talking and saying what needs to be done for this or that drug deal, and the other guy is just sitting there next to him, gawking. It's nicely done. Because you understand that Walt hasn't retreated from life in order to hang around waiting for the illness. You understand that he's marching on, that he has retained his authority and cred in life. And so he starts going off at the guy beside him about the importance of taking control of your life, and I think it's a very good monologue. I don't remember exactly what he says that's so good, but it's something about preferring to keep living as usual until he's actually dead, and that he's been near death so many times already, but has never actually died. And even if at this point in the series Walt has become cynical in a way that's hard to sympathize with, that speech of his is still a good one. Otherwise the one I sympathized most with during this part of the series was Pinkman, who seems to have gone crazy after shooting a man in the head while looking him in the eye. I don't mean that I sympathized with Pinkman because he shot a man in the head while looking him in the eye. I sympathized with him because he couldn't handle it, because he broke down and went crazy.

At times I thought that instead of watching TV series I should watch documentaries. That would've given me something to talk to Ruben about over dinner. But when I browsed the available documentaries, they were all about the ocean, animals, environmental devastation, or pornography, and I chose the last. One of those documentaries was about a bunch of has-been porn stars talking about their lives. One by one they talked about what they'd done and then we were shown clips from films they'd been in. In particular I remember a man who was large and hefty with white hair on his head and chest. He said that he didn't have a wife and nor did he have any children, but once he'd fallen for his female costar in a movie. He said that she wasn't the most attractive porn star, but there was something immensely desirable about her. That's exactly what he said, he used the word "immensely" even though it's not a word you imagine a porn star using. So they'd been in a few films together, earned a good amount of money, and one day after a few months they ran into each other in town. She'd been shopping and was carrying a bunch of bags, and he offered to help her with them. They walked together through the city. He said that walking around like this felt different, because they were wearing clothes and no camera was circling. Passersby didn't recognize them and they weren't attracting any special attention. They were just walking along. He said that's when he realized he wanted to get out of porn and do something completely different. He wanted to stop fucking on film. Stop being a marionette in a lustful, sordid establishment built on filthy lucre. Instead he wanted to start a life together with this woman. They could move, he said, to some country where people didn't watch much porn and where no one would know who they really were. They didn't have any children or any other ties really, just plenty of money, and were free to do exactly as they pleased. But then it occurred to him, walking along with his colleague, that men probably asked her out all the time. She was probably tired of guys swarming around her like flies as soon as the opportunity presented itself. So he decided to hold off. Not ask her out right away, but wait a few days. They didn't have any shoots scheduled together, but they'd surely run into each other in the studio and when they did, he'd try to be polite and pleasant and not pester. He'd ask her out in a week, he thought. And he stuck to it. He carried her bags home, set them on her kitchen floor, and looked around her apartment, which was as clean and cool as she was, like the part of her that was her soul, which, as he put it, sort of floated above everything else. As he left, he felt her watching him go, her gaze lingering on his back and this, he thought, boded well. He held off for a whole week. He did as he'd planned and talked to her when they ran into each other, but didn't take any initiative. After a week he rang her bell. She opened the door wrapped in a sheet. Her hair was mussed and she smelled of sweat and sex. He'd wet combed his hair and bought a bouquet of flowers that the woman in the flower shop had wrapped in lots of cellophane, and now it all seemed excessive: the flowers had grown into something enormous and plastic-wrapped expanding between them, really it was like the flowers weren't even there, just all that cellophane (he didn't say as much, but you get that it was like that). He held them out, and she accepted them, but was confused.

"I didn't think you were interested in me," she said.

"I am," he said. "I just wanted to wait, so you didn't think I was out for sex."

"But we fuck all the time," she said.

"I know," he said. "That's why."

She looked sad, shook her head, and then from inside the apartment a male voice could be heard calling her name. They stood there a while, staring at each other in the doorway, like they both understood that everything was going to hell and there was nothing they could do about it, that's how things went, sometimes, it was a part of life and there was nothing you could do. Then she shut the door, he said in the interview, sadly.

"But that's how it goes in this old life," he added. "If you don't take what you want, someone else will come along and snatch it."

The camera lingered on his face and for a split second it looked like he was going to cry, and I think that was kind of the point of the whole documentary, for the camera to wring tears from that porn wreck. But he didn't cry.

"A lot of the time I think porn is more exciting than real sex," he concluded.

His chin jutted out as he said it, as though he were bracing himself against something undefined.

After the porn documentary I started reading the books from the second row again. You couldn't put them down, even though you didn't like them. There I sat for several days reading Michel Houellebecq's books in Ruben's living room. I took a TV break for a few days, and every day when Ruben left for work I went into the bedroom and took a book from the back row, and sat down to read. Outside it would thaw, only to refreeze at night. The sea was as it always was, even though its colors changed with the sky. When it was time for lunch I helped myself from the fridge. I ate at the dining table while reading. I cleared up, washed my hands, and went back to reading on the couch. Every evening, about fifteen minutes before Ruben came home, I wrote down what page I was on in a notebook I kept my bag. Then I shut the book and put it back on the shelf.

I also watched documentaries on YouTube where Houellebecq was being interviewed by journalists. In many he was sitting with half-shut eyes, taking a drag from a pretend cigarette (until you see it for yourself, you can't believe people like that exist), seemingly uninterested in everything they were asking. I don't think anyone can look as uninterested as Michel Houellebecq does when he's being interviewed by the BBC. In one documentary, a woman says the biggest problem with Michel Houellebecq is that he's not interesting. That didn't seem true. The biggest problem with Houellebecq can't be that he's not interesting, because then everything would have resolved itself. The biggest problem with Houellebecq is that he's a creep, but he's an interesting creep. I wanted to tell Ruben this, but it was impossible. Eventually I'd seen every documentary there was on YouTube. Then I went back to the TV shows and got into a rhythm where I would switch between doing some reading, watching series, and poking around in Ruben's things.

I still felt all alone in the house. Especially after the thing with Mildred, I'd find myself on the couch at twilight, and I'd look into the dark and get the feeling that someone was out there, looking in. *It's just a feeling*, I'd think – it's the only natural feeling to have when you're sitting in the light, looking into darkness. I saw my face in the glass and smiled at myself, trying to draw comfort from the smile. But I couldn't.

One day I called home, a friend I hadn't spoken with since I came to Stockholm. She said people in the village were talking about me, and someone had said I'd met someone from Stockholm on the internet. "Has anything happened in the village?" I asked. She said nothing special had happened, except that the ditz had thrown Johnny out. "Where's he living now?" I asked. "In a trailer behind the farm, a few hundred meters into the forest," she said. "How's he doing?" I asked. She said she didn't know, no one had seen him in a long time, he didn't come down to the village in the evenings anymore, and no one had seen his Subaru driving around. She also said she hoped I wasn't thinking about losing my dialect. Speaking a new language was like adding a ship to a fleet, but changing dialects was akin to treason. "You can cut off your bunions, toes, and heels to fit into a shoe," she said, "but the shoe is still a shoe and the foot, a foot. Don't forget that, Ellinor: whatever you do, a foot is still a foot."

What I liked best about Ruben was the everyday, the routine we managed to create. When Ruben came home from work, we ate, but before he sat down at the table he'd usually go into the bedroom and change before moving on to the bathroom to wash his hands. Then he'd come into the kitchen. We'd sit down and he'd pour the wine and I'd carry the plates from the kitchen to the table. Then we'd eat in silence. Ruben didn't look at what he was eating. He didn't see it, and he didn't taste it either. And that was a shame considering I spent a big chunk of the afternoon fixing dinner. Often it took me a full two hours to prepare it. When I cook, I always think carefully about what I'm doing. For instance, I always let the vinegar soak into the salad before I add the oil, because once the oil is on nothing else can be absorbed, right? Still it would take him barely five minutes to eat it all up. He ate in silence with an absent look, as though instead of thinking about his food or the company he was in, he was thinking about his day, the meetings he'd had and what he'd write tomorrow and how he'd end up arguing with various people, and whether it was worth the trouble. Sometimes I'd ask about his day and his replies would be monosyllabic.

"Have you written anything fun?" I might ask.

"Fun?"

"Yes, or interesting?"

He never responded to stuff like that, he just sat there chewing, his fork dangling above his plate. After a while I gave up and joined him in silence.

After dinner he said:

"Put the dishes in the sink, I'll take care of them later."

But I never put the dishes in the sink. I always cleaned up after dinner. Sometimes he came over and held me from behind as I did the dishes. Sometimes he pushed himself against me, and whispered in my ear: "Will you lie with me on the couch when you're done, and we can watch a movie?"

I finished the dishes, dried my hands on a kitchen towel and went into the bathroom to moisturize them with a Clarins hand cream. My hand cream is the only thing to do with my appearance that I pay good money for. Ruben said that my hands were the most beautiful part of me. Someone else might've taken that as an insult, but I didn't. I knew what he meant when he said that. My hands are strong and soft. They might look a little useless, but they can grab hold and pitch in when needed. That's what he meant. When I was done moisturizing my hands, I went over to the couch. Ruben was holding the remote and for the first time since he'd come home he'd smiled at me.

"Lie here," he said, patting the space in front of him. I did, and he held me from behind.

"What do you want to watch?" he whispered.

"I don't know," I replied.

"A porno?" he asked, and when I didn't reply he put on a porno.

After he came, he took the remote control and turned off the film, which was now really disturbing. And then he said he was sorry.

"I'm sorry Ellinor, for everything."

"For what?" I asked.

"For everything. Because I'm so tired. Because I come home and fuck you in front of a movie and then fall asleep. I'm sorry. I'm just so damn tired, but also so damn horny."

"That doesn't matter," I said. "You're tired and horny, that's all. Just eat, sleep, and fuck then everything will be OK."

Then he went to bed and I sat up for a while longer watching TV. And this is how the days and the weeks passed.

I'd been at Ruben's for a few weeks when the thing with Mildred happened. Soon after lunch a car stopped at the gate to Ruben's house. I went to the living-room window and looked out. Nobody ever visited us. But now there was a car. I thought it might be the author, but no author came out. Instead someone who looked like a chauffeur got out and opened one of the back doors. A woman wearing a short white fur coat appeared. Large black sunglasses hid her face and the fur had a thick, high collar that reached up to her ears. The driver gave her some sort of short white stick. He leaned forward to speak in her ear, and she nodded. The man got back into the car, started the engine, and parked a few meters away on the shoulder.

I stared out the window. My heart was racing. The sun was shining from the south. It was almost unnaturally clear out and I had to squint to see anything in that sharp light. The woman was still on the other side of the gate, but was now facing the house. The pines were tall and silent. She glanced to the right, at the slope leading down to the sea. Then she leaned her head back, apparently to look at the sky. Her dark, flame-red hair tumbled over her shoulders and down the white fur. She unfolded the stick the man from the car had given her, and it became a support cane. She moved it along the ground in front of her as she made her way to the gate. There she stopped and fished a key out of the fur's pocket.

My first impulse was to call Ruben, and I did. I dialed his number, hands shaking. It rang and rang, but no one answered. I stood there, holding the phone, watching the woman walk through the gate, fold up the cane, and close the gate behind her. She was making her way toward the house. Easy now, I said to myself. I'm not a person who gets scared, and anyway she's blind. She held the cane in one hand like a baton or a rolled-up newspaper. And her steps were effortless, not at all how you'd imagine a blind person walking. I realized that she must know the exact distance, because she slowed down as she neared the door, but without reaching for it. She moved the key toward the lock.

From where I stood, there was no doubt that in a few seconds the woman would be inside the house. And the next thing you knew, the lock turned and the woman walked into the hall. I was trying not to breathe. I read somewhere that people can feel it when you look at them and if there's anyone who's refined this ability, it must be the blind. That's why I looked out at the garden. A few lonely snowflakes glittered in the air. The black car was still out there and faint, wispy clouds had dulled the sunlight. The winter birds seemed to have stopped singing. Then I snuck another glance at the woman, who was listening through the silence.

"Hello?" she said.

She said it softly, and I could tell by her voice that she knew she wasn't alone. But when she didn't get a reply, she cleared her throat and took off her coat. I thought I saw a flicker of a smile, as if her entire being was saying *I know somebody's there, even if I can't prove it because I'm blind.*

She took off her shoes and arranged them neatly with the heels to the wall. She also took off her sunglasses, folded them, and set them on the small table right inside the door.

She was wildly attractive, I could see that now. People can be kind of attractive or attractive and then there are those who are wildly attractive, so attractive that just looking at them makes your whole body ache. That's what she was like. Her body looked mighty. Her long, shiny hair was worn in a perfect center parting. It was as though everything inside her was working with the aim of perfection wholeheartedly and in unison, and as though perfection was all that was programmed in her DNA. When she turned around I saw her large, muscular rump. A hot meaty ass, Johnny would've called it. Her white pants clung to her in a way that made them seem sewn on. I couldn't understand how a blind person could be so attractive. I don't mean that blind people can't be attractive, I just mean they can't look in the mirror and fix themselves up like the rest of us. But of course this wasn't about looking in a mirror and fixing yourself up, this was something else.

She ran her hands along her hips. Her hair was charged and static around her head, like those lamps that have bolts of lightning moving around in them. Her eyes were looking straight ahead, in my direction. I also remembered reading somewhere that in familiar environments blind people can navigate with the same sureness as those who can see. They create an exact copy of reality inside their minds, then they move inside that copy. There are lots of things about blind people that we have no idea about. They only need their cane when they're out walking. At home they're like anyone else, they just can't combine colors like we can. That's what I was thinking, and my armpits felt wet. Ruben had never mentioned a blind woman. Ruben had never mentioned any woman. He'd also never said there was a wife in the picture, but of course this woman was his wife. That was crystal clear from where I was standing. Ruben had a wife, a blind wife, and now she was here. There was only one positive in all of this: she couldn't see me. I repeated the thought twice, as you do when you don't actually believe what you're thinking. Something inside me knew that her blindness in this context was meaningless. If the woman standing in front of me wanted to hurt me, then she'd do it, and she'd do it just as assuredly as she'd come up the path, unlocked the door, and hung her jacket up. As a blind person, she'd know exactly how to hurt someone, because if you're blind you think these things through, like you think through how to move around inside the copies, where things are, and how far it is between you and everything else. You could say, I thought to myself, that blind people were actually totally tuned in. I tried laughing to myself at that sentence, an attempt to lighten things up, but I couldn't. There was no way to get traction. Take it easy, Ellinor, I thought. Don't worry. When it comes down to it, well, you can kick anyone in the head.

The woman made her way to the kitchen. She stopped at the threshold, her hands on the doorframe as though she were familiarizing herself. I got up from the couch and snuck after her. My pulse was still beating in my temples, but since she'd turned away from me my curiosity had somehow grown stronger than my fear, or was at least equally strong. This thought ran through my head: If you want to get to know Ruben, you have to spy on him. She went through the kitchen and down the hall to Ruben's study. Her hands searched the door panel and pushed the handle down. To my surprise the door opened. She went inside. At the doorway, I crouched down and craned my head so I could see. She was at the desk. She stood in front of it for a second before placing her hands on top of it. Then she stiffened. She stood dead still, and started searching the surface. She's after the manuscript, I thought. She knows it's supposed to be there, and she's come here to get it. It was the only possible explanation. She stood like that for a full thirty seconds, searching across the desk with her hands, as if she couldn't understand that what she was looking for wasn't there. Straightening, she crossed her arms and turned her head. From where I was standing I saw her head in profile. Her nostrils seemed to flare, even though it was impossible to see both of them. She started turning around, and her movements were very slow. My armpits were soaking wet but I got up and left the doorpost and snuck back into the living room because I knew the woman was heading my way, and I couldn't have held back a scream if those eyes directed themselves at me. I sat on the couch and pulled my knees to my chest, trying to tell myself that she would be out of the house soon, and that would be the end of it. Someone had stopped by, but they would leave again, that was it. I sat with my back to her, aware that she was moving around in the hall behind me. I didn't want to turn around, because I didn't want to meet that gaze. She walked very quietly, and there was nothing strange about that, someone like her has to walk quietly, anything else would have been odd. Finally she arrived in the living room. I'd hoped she'd head straight for the door, put her shoes on, and go to the car. But right when she was in line with me, she stopped. Again she turned her head. She did it slowly and self-righteously, those steel-gray eyes on me. Her dark red hair fell over her face. I wanted to scream, but instead of a scream I let out a mix of a hiss and a squeak, a ridiculous sound, but more than enough to confirm that somebody was there.

"Who are you?" she asked.

I wouldn't have been able to answer even if I'd wanted to.

"Who are you?" she repeated. "Are you one of Ruben's sluts?"

I still couldn't get a sound out. She went to the entry and stuck her hand in the pocket of her coat, took out her support cane, and unfolded it. Then she came my way. I stood on the couch, climbed over its back, and headed for the hallway. She came after me, the cane tapping the floor. I went into the bedroom. There were no good hiding places in there, so all I could do was crawl under the bed. It would've been better to have stayed on the couch, I thought when I'd done it. It would've been much better to stay there, and to have said, all cool and collected: *I'm no slut. I am Ellinor. And who are you?* But it was too late for that. The dust under the bed stuck to my neck and my damp arms. I lay still, taking in the smell of sweat and dust. My ears were buzzing, and meanwhile I heard footsteps and the cane hitting the floor, rhythmically, like a metronome. *I'm-coming-for-you*, it seemed to say. *I'm-coming-for-you-you-lousy-tramp.* I saw her socks. They looked fancy, a deep emerald green, fine knit with a reinforced toe. Once she'd arrived, she bent down. First all that long dark hair swayed to the floor, then I saw her face. She was a few dozen centimeters from me now, and her steely-gray, blind eyes were staring at me. Her nostrils flared.

Clear and crisp, she said:

"I've come to pick up the manuscript."

It felt like a fistful of loose change was stuck in my throat.

"Which manuscript?" I whispered.

"To my knowledge there is only one. Where is it? If you tell me where it is, I'll leave."

I swallowed, but my mouth was dry and there was no saliva to swallow.

"I don't know about any manuscript," I whispered.

The woman stood up.

"Get out here."

Without thinking I crawled out and faced her. She reached out and lay her hand on my head, ran it over my hair, along my throat. There it spread flat, before squeezing my breast.

"What are you doing?" I asked.

"Confirming that this time at least he didn't humiliate himself with some rack of lamb."

I swallowed the insult, though there's never been anything wrong with my breasts. Not as ample as hers maybe, but not stretched out or drooping, if that's what she meant.

"Shall we sit?" she said and turned around as if there were nothing strange about any of this. "Have a little chat, woman to woman?"

She could have spared me the tone because it was clear this was not a question. I followed her to the couches. We sat across from each other. She said:

"What's your name?"

"Ellinor," I said. "And you?"

"Mildred," she said.

"Are you Ruben's wife?"

"Yes. But don't worry. I've always left him in peace with his sluts."

"Aha," I said.

"Anyway, we're getting divorced," she said.

I didn't understand how a man could divorce someone like Mildred.

"How long have you been here?" she asked.

"A few weeks," I said.

"Do you hate him?"

"Huh?"

"Do you hate him?"

"Why would I hate him?"

"Because he's mean to you. He's always mean to his mistresses."

"What makes you think I'm only a mistress?" I said.

She laughed, and the laugh was loud and sincere.

"Ruben isn't a mean person," I said.

"No," she said. "He's just very damaged. But now I must know about the manuscript. Where is it?"

"Why do you want it?"

"I feel responsible," she said.

"For what?"

"For its genesis."

I didn't understand.

"Are you the one he's writing about?"

"No. But without me it wouldn't exist. And the man who wrote it isn't particularly strong, if that's what you think. He has known great loss. Toiled, hoped, suffered, is still suffering. He should have his manuscript."

My first impulse was to tell her there was no manuscript anymore, but then again if I played my cards right this could be an opportunity to find out more about Ruben. Suddenly everything felt easier. It occurred to me that I'd been alone for a long time, but now something was finally happening.

"Even if I knew anything, what makes you think I'd tell you?" I said.

"Because you must," Mildred said, now with a hint of impatience.

"Make me," I said.

"I'm supposed to *make* you?"

"There's a saying in my village," I said.

"Is that so?"

"You catch more flies with honey than you do with vinegar."

"And what is it that you're trying to tell me?" Mildred said.

I shrugged. She seemed smart, and yet you had to explain the obvious.

"You have to make me want to."

"OK, Ellinor," Mildred said, leaning back into the couch. "I see what you're getting at, and I respect that."

"Good," I said. "And?"

She thought for a while. Then she grabbed her ring finger and pulled off one of the rings.

"See this ring?" she asked. "It's mine and Ruben's. I'll give it to you as proof that I'm handing Ruben over to you. You can have him. Here, take it. You can have the man and all that comes with him. Just tell me where the manuscript is."

I took the ring from her outstretched hand. It looked expensive and fancy.

"Is that enough honey to please your flies?" she asked.

"But what am I supposed to do with it?" I asked.

Her smile vanished.

"Have you never heard of *symbolic value*?"

"Symbolic value?"

"When a thing means something other than what that thing is."

"I'm not really one for things that mean other things," I said. "I want Ruben, not some secondhand ring."

"Oh," Mildred groaned. "He used to choose his mistresses with care, but you, you're just . . . "

"What?" I asked.

"I don't know. So *prosaic*."

"Prosaic?"

"Let's take a practical view," she said and cleared her throat. "You should be able to get at least 50,000 kronor for that if you cash it in."

"Fifty large?" I asked.

"Yes," she said. "That should cover your trip home and then some, shall we say."

I looked at the ring. Inside was inscribed *Mildred Ruben 2000.* I handed it back to her and said:

"OK. Here. Give it to me when we're done."

"Good," she said and took the ring. "You'll tell me where the manuscript is and get 50,000 richer. Not bad, is it?"

"Yes," I said. "It's alright."

And it was alright, even if her Stockholm dialect bothered me. She sounded like someone who thought they were on television. There's this thing with Stockholmers that bothers me: they don't like us. They think we're just hicks and racists. And maybe we *are* hicks and racists, but not as hick and racist as they are.

"The ring isn't enough," I said.

"You're telling me *the ring isn't enough*?" Mildred said.

"No," I said. "The ring is only money, after all, and I've never had money and I can live without it. I want one more thing."

"What?" she said.

"I want you to tell me about Ruben."

"About *Ruben*?"

She sounded like I had asked her to tell me about the train schedule, or Eslöv Cemetery.

"What do you want to know?" she asked.

"I've been wondering lots of things," I said.

"What exactly, Ellinor?"

"Who he is. Who he really is. And how you get him to fall in love with you."

"Some days he's a bull in the bedroom," Mildred said. "An asshole outside. In the long run it gets heavy, carrying around so much shit. If you want my advice, find yourself another man."

"I'd gladly make do with Ruben."

"He's only been in love with one woman, but she no longer exists."

"What do you mean she no longer exists?"

"There was a woman who . . . " Mildred began. "Oh, never mind."

"How about we do this," I said. "You tell me about the woman he loved, and I'll tell you about the manuscript. The whole truth about the manuscript, not just where it is."

Of course I was fishing with fake bait, because what more could I say about the manuscript other than it no longer existed? But the thought must've been enticing, because Mildred opened her bag and took out a cigarette, then a lighter. She lit it, took a deep drag, and blew the smoke at me.

"All right," she began. "It's like this, Ellinor. Ruben has only loved one woman in his life, and that woman is dead. That's why he's wandering around. Like a restless phantom. Looking here, looking there. Most likely you're his latest hope. I'm sure he picked you up online. That's what he does. But watch out. Ruben isn't a whole man, and broken people break things."

She paused. The cigarette's end glowed in the half-light and the cigarette paper crackled as she inhaled. Outside, thick, dark clouds had formed in the sky. Mildred's blind gaze rested in the space between us.

"I knew her," she continued. "The only woman Ruben ever loved sang in the choir where I played cello, and one evening when he picked me up, they met. That's how it goes sometimes. This was before the eye sickness, so I could see everything happening between them. You can't imagine it. From the very beginning to when lust dug its claws into them and past the point of no return. And the agony that followed. With certain psychological mechanisms one should . . . It was all so unfortunate. He didn't want to hurt me. She didn't want to hurt her husband. Nor did she want to hurt me. All those people who people don't want to hurt when the flesh wants what it wants. It's such a shame when you think about it, because the flesh doesn't care who gets hurt. The flesh doesn't give a damn about anything. It takes, if you didn't already know, enormous self-control to rein in true lust. And you shouldn't fool yourself into thinking that doing so makes you any stronger. Or maybe you do become strong, but you also dry out, dry as a sheet of paper. You lose the intimacy, and intimacy is the stream leading to the spring of life. Do you get it, Ellinor? Certain people can live without it, like certain people can live an entire life archiving paper in underground corridors or stamping documents at customs. Others wither away. Ruben is among those who wither away. Without intimacy, without its dark rooms, he dies like a vampire in the sunlight. That's what Ruben is like. That's what I'm like, and that's what Max Lamas, who wrote the manuscript, is like. And perhaps you're like that, too."

Suddenly I hated the blind woman sitting across from me. She was too perfect to bear. Sure she was blind, I thought, but she seemed to have made something of her blindness, maximizing it, so to speak. She was like a different species with that light coming from her eyes, and that hair. I don't understand how Ruben could agree to a divorce, I thought again. No one could want to divorce such dignity. An enormous armored dignity, a dignity that nothing can beat. No man, no time, and no other enemy either.

"But didn't you hate him?" I said. "For the betrayal and the lie?"

"Women you have to watch out for, but there's little more harmless than men's lies. Men lie to protect. They think they're protecting the world around them by keeping the truth of themselves from it. And considering their true nature, you can't blame them. They often have a muddy kind of self-knowledge that occasionally aligns with their protective instinct. You can't hate them for that. To hate the man for his lies is like hating a scorpion because it has a stinger or a fish on the bottom of the sea because it's ugly. It's utterly futile, and you're the only one who risks dying from that hatred."

"But a lie is still a lie," I insisted.

"Please, spare me your rural sensibility. Open your eyes. Kind lies pose no danger in this world. We simply need to believe what they're saying. They, on the other hand, must live with the agony. And then lying isn't that easy, not if you want to turn it into a *modus vivendi*. You need a good memory. You have to be smart and you have to be lucky."

"What happened next? With Ruben and the woman he loved?"

"I saw everything one of those afternoons with the choir. Everything that was to come was already in their eyes. It was there to be read, like an open book. I saw the lies and sneaking. The joy, the shame, the fear of the consequences. His guilty conscience about me, her guilty conscience about her husband. The mire they were about to sink into. And I wondered how to handle it, whether I should confront him, leave him, or simply ignore it. Some wives ignore infidelity. Ones who know that if they just wait, they'll win. Patiently, day after day. A long wait, but also the knowledge that in waiting they can only become stronger. A mistress can be exactly what's needed for a couple to find its way back to each other. The man's masculinity grows, the wife can take pleasure in this, the spark returns. And when contented domestic life reigns, the mistress is thrown out like used blotting paper. And then she's lost everything. That's why wives and mistresses must be strategic. But I never needed to be strategic with Ruben's love, because one day she died in a car accident. Right into a tree trunk, just like that, bam. She wasn't sober, and she was driving with the music turned up. The man who found her said that everything by the tree was dead and silent, but the radio was blaring at full volume through the forest. You could hear the music from several hundred meters away, he said. I think it was Gyllene Tider, or Europe. In any case it was the kind of music no one wants to die to. The fire department came and had to cut open the car to get her out. Somebody said her whole face and head were so mangled . . . well, it doesn't matter. But Ruben wasn't told, because not many people knew their secret and so no one said anything to him. The accident was in the papers, but the names were left out. And the days passed. Ruben went around like a worried dog. She wasn't answering phone calls or text messages. Then I got a note from the choir. It said that a funeral was going to be held and we were going to sing and play. First I thought: Damned slut, just you try and get me to play. Then I thought: How am I going to tell him? I stood there holding the card. My body began to shake. *In sympathy.* Yes, that's how it was. Life isn't always what you think it will be. But it doesn't matter now. I should've hated him, but I felt like someone witnessing an execution. I shouted through the house: *Hanna D. died in a car crash! I'm going to play at her funeral!* After a long while he shouted back: *Oh!* A few minutes later the front door slammed. He must've drifted through town. Pacing around with all that despair. I sat on a stool in the kitchen. Just sat there, peeling an orange, which I put on the table and didn't eat. And where was he going to go? There was no one he could call, no one he could talk to or seek support from, he was no one in her life. He wasn't even invited to the funeral. But I was. And a week later I went to the church to play my cello. At the altar there was a closed casket. In the first row were the closest surviving relatives, her son and husband. The priest was speaking and it was a typical funeral – some people were nodding off, others were crying. Suddenly the door at the back of the church opened. And in walks Ruben. He just stands there at first. Everyone turns around. What's he doing here? they're thinking. Isn't that *Ruben Rondas, the critic*. What is *he* doing *here*? He makes his way up the center aisle, until he's at the first row. The priest has stopped speaking, and Ruben's footsteps are the only sound in the church. He sits down with Hanna D.'s husband and son. People stare, then it dawns on them. But he stays put. Not caring about the looks he's getting. Not caring about the heads leaning toward each other, or the dismay. My husband just sits there, with his red-rimmed eyes. Because he loved Hanna D., and he knew that if there was anyone in this church who had a right to sorrow, it was him. Everything was sullied and confused, yet clean. And people stared at me. I was the betrayed, and there is shame in that, as well. They put two and two together there on those pews, people aren't stupid, and now everyone was a detective hot on the trail. Me, I was seized by calm. I sat with the cello in my arms, the dark wood hot from my body. I looked at Ruben and his flaming face. I wondered: What is life doing with us? The conductor raised his hand. The choir began to sing. I lifted my bow and began to play. And I've always played like you talk in a crowd. Without any ambition to have your own voice, just part of the din. But now I was playing for *Ruben* and *Hanna*. The pain ran through me, but I was on another track. I played for a love that is pure, even though

I've never believed in that, and nor do I now. The feeling was among the strongest I've ever felt. And even though it would go on to fade and be replaced with humiliation, I can still conjure it. I can still feel what I felt as I sat there. I can still remember exactly why I thought right then that I'd always loved him."

She fell silent and looked out the window. Neither of us said anything for a long while. Then I said:

"Do you think I can make him love me for real?"

She straightened.

"With all due respect, Ellinor, with his baggage and at his age, to begin the long and arduous journey into another person: he'll never have the energy for that. No. He'll never have the energy."

She stubbed out her cigarette in the ashtray on the table.

"Well then," she said. "Now it's my turn."

"Can we take a break?" I asked. "I have to think."

I got up and went into the kitchen, screwed the coffee maker together, and put it on the stove.

"Would you like coffee?" I called to Mildred.

"No thank you!" she replied. "But if there's an open bottle of wine somewhere . . . I'd very much like a glass!"

I found a bottle of white in the fridge and poured a glass. The coffee was almost ready, but I stayed in the kitchen. I'd never heard anyone share so much all at once. It was a little like sitting in the sauna for too long, you go mushy in the head. I'd never met people like this. Never met anyone like Ruben, never met anyone like Mildred. What other kinds of people were out there in that snowy city? I glanced out the window and there was the sea, ice cold, and the sky too, that was just as ice cold. Then I went into the living room with the glass. Mildred drank the wine like water, in big quick gulps. She put the glass down on the coffee table, burped, and laughed, displaying an even row of white teeth.

"OK, Ellinor," she said. "Try not to be contrary now. I only give people *one* chance."

"Yeah, yeah," I said. "The manuscript is not in this world."

"*Not in this world?*"

"It went up in smoke."

"Did he burn it?"

"I burned it."

"You . . . *what?*"

Mildred shook that red hair and laughed in disbelief.

"Hold on," she said. "Hold on, Ellinor. You burned the manuscript. Why?"

"To avenge something Ruben did to me."

"What?"

"It doesn't matter. There's no manuscript anymore, that's all there is to say. And I don't know anything about it either. I lied so I could find out about Ruben. I'm sorry."

Mildred's forehead furrowed and a wrinkle appeared between her eyebrows.

"That wasn't good, Ellinor," she said. "The manuscript you burned was all he had left. I think it was the only thing that could save him at this point."

"Save who?"

"Max Lamas. The author."

"Save him from what?"

She shrugged.

"Some sort of disintegration. Age. Disillusionment. Disappointment."

"Oh," I said.

"There are books you write for others," she said, "and there are books you write for yourself."

"I don't understand," I said.

"Of course you don't," she said. "How could you?"

I didn't know how I was supposed to reply to that, but I didn't need to say anything because Mildred kept talking about things I'd never heard anyone talk about before. She said almost no men write about women, so when one finally does you should appreciate him and not set fire to his efforts. She also said that in these times, it was important to imagine how life could be if things were different. That was the world's biggest task right now: to try to see how everything could be if things were different. And that's when visionaries were needed. People who took their eyes off the rearview mirror and looked ahead. And that's what Lamas had done in *The Polyglot Lovers*. He'd done his best to go outside himself and visualize something completely different.

"And why'd he do that?" I said.

"Because I told him to," she said.

"And who are you?" I asked.

"His medium," she replied matter-of-factly.

I wondered if this was the kind of thing you could say in the snowy city. Maybe it sounded perfectly natural up here with the sea, the rocky slabs, and the big sky. A cinematic city demands cinematic people, and it sounded like something straight out of a movie.

"His medium, you say?"

"Yes," she said. "He's cursed, and I'm trying to help him lift it."

"Ah," I said. "A curse."

"The problem is, the woman who cursed him has killed herself," Mildred said. "Making it hard to lift."

"Yes, it must be," I said.

"But I thought that if he wrote something for her, then it might work anyway. If he, so to speak, atoned for his crime."

"And what was his crime?"

Mildred made a strange gesture with her head, as if she suddenly understood that she was talking with someone who had no idea about polyglots, curses, or manuscripts. She got up, went out into the hall, and put on her shoes and the fur. Outside, it had stopped snowing. Everything was still, and the dark clouds lingered behind the tops of the firs.

She was leaving, but it seemed like she had more to say. She stopped mid-step and turned around with a finger raised.

"One last thing, Ellinor."

"Yes?" I said.

Then Mildred did something quite unexpected. She let the door shut and took two steps toward me. She put her arms around me and pressed my head to her neck. My first impulse was to push her away, because I've never been like that with a woman.

"Easy," Mildred said and pressed me to her harder.

I felt her heat, and the scent of her hot neck and the luxurious oil in her hair. I don't know how long we stood like that, but it felt like minutes. Finally she let go of me, took my head in her hands, and put her lips to mine.

"Everything is going to work out," she whispered so that the air from her words entered me. "Everything is going to work out, but in a way that's unimaginable to you right now."

Something frisky, almost happy, overcame her.

"So I guess you've seen into the future?" I said.

She didn't reply. Instead she took the ring off her finger, searched for my hand, placed it in my palm, and closed my fingers over it.

"He's yours now," she said. "But when you have the chance to get out of here, take it. Grab hold of it like a castaway grabs hold of driftwood, because that's what's going to save you."

Then she laughed, turned, and left. The man who'd driven her got out of the car and held the gate open. Soon the car door shut behind Mildred Rondas, and the engine started. I watched her go. My lips and face felt hot. From the window in the living room I shifted my focus, from my own reflection to the firs, moving toward the last of the daylight and the car slowly disappearing down the hill.

At the bottom of Ruben's property was a dock. It appeared to be wedged between two rocks and reached far into the water, and you could see it from the kitchen window. On one of our first nights, Ruben had talked about it, said how lovely it was in summer when you could walk right through the terrace doors and down the slope and onto the dock and fling yourself into the sea. One evening when I was cooking I wondered if Mildred had done that when she lived here. If she'd walked down to the dock as confidently as she had inside the house, wearing her bikini. I imagined her in a silvery, sort of slutty bikini with a Brazilian cut.

Ruben came over and stood behind me. Out on the sea, a large ferry was idling by. After a while Ruben said:

"Ellinor, did you know a people can be read in their local water?"

"How do you mean?" I asked.

"As is the water, so are the people. That's always true."

He talked about the water in Stockholm's archipelago. Rocky islands, islets. Saltwater bays, Lake Malar and its outflow into Saltsjön. Sweetness and salinity, fresh air and freedom.

"Stockholm is one of the most beautiful places on earth," he said.

"Yes," I said.

"What's the water like down where you are? Do you have a pond somewhere? A puddle for the farmers to splash around in when it's hot?"

I set the knife on the cutting board and remembered the lake outside our village. People used to call it *the pearl of Skåne,* but it lost that name over the years because too much fertilizer seeped into it from the surrounding fields. For several summers it was a pale green, foul-smelling soup. Once Johnny asked: *Ellinor, wanna tag along and go fishing?* I replied that the lake smelled of old shit. And Johnny replied that maybe it did, but that didn't mean there weren't any fish in it. Even as he was speaking, it felt like that sentence was crucial and would stay with me for a long time, even though the sentence didn't really say anything. *It might smell of shit, but that doesn't mean there are no fish in it.* We went down. Johnny pushed the boat out and jumped in. He floated a few meters away from the shore. I stayed there, watching him. The oars hung from the boat and down into the water. He sat in the middle and moved them like two spoons in nettle soup. *Are you really going to go out in that?* I asked from the beach. We didn't need to speak loudly at all. It was dead silent and the water carried our voices. Insects buzzed above the surface and I could see he was concentrating on hooking a worm. I repeated my question as the boat glided further out into the green water. Across the lake the sky was turning red in the evening sun. And it was like the silence had crawled into my head, like I might be losing some sort of interface with the world, or like there might be something seriously wrong with my ears. It was like everything was going straight in. The splashing against the boat. Johnny's face as he handled the worm. The green algae bloom and the heat. I put my hands over my ears and looked at the ground. I stood like that for a long time, until the sounds started to feel more normal. I felt relieved, almost happy in a way that I couldn't remember feeling in forever.

"Johnny?" I said.

Even though he was a way from the beach he heard me perfectly.

"Yes?" he said and raised his head.

"I love you."

As soon as I saw his expression I regretted saying it. He kept his mouth shut, like a child pressing its lips together so that nobody can shove in food. Taking hold of the oars, he rowed out to the middle of the lake. All I could see was the sky and his back there in the rowboat. He sat with his bait sunk in that soup for hours, not saying a word until nightfall, when he came gliding in again and needed help pulling the boat ashore.

"No," I said to Ruben. "No ponds. Just inland lakes where the water is soft, warm, and dark."

"Soft, warm, and dark, Ellinor . . . Do we have time before we eat?"

If we had sex now it would end with a heavy, cold, and irrevocable orgasm. An orgasm that, so to speak, would be impossible to get out of alive. Like a fork in the road. If you go in one direction you'll never get anywhere. If you go in the other you won't get anywhere either, but you'll get nowhere in a completely different way.

"Is it true that you've only loved one woman in your whole life?" I asked.

For a moment he looked puzzled. Then he took my hand and dragged me out of the kitchen.

"Who said that? That's not the sort of thing you go around here thinking about, is it? Poor Ellinor. Tell me about someone who liked you instead. Someone you've been with.

Someone who used you. I want to hear, tell me everything, and don't leave anything out. Make me hot because I don't have it in me to do it all by myself."

My first impulse was to tell him about Johnny. But I felt like I couldn't tell him about the fights, the cellar, the pickup or the cabin with the bead and butt paneling. Nor did I want to talk about the lake or the thing with the interface. I couldn't really figure out what it was about Johnny that I couldn't offer up, I just couldn't. That's why I told him about Klaus Bjerre in Copenhagen.

"What a sorry fucker," said Ruben when I finished the story. "You really cooled me off. It's impossible to fuck after hearing a story like that, Ellinor."

"Not everything is about sex," I said.

"No," said Ruben.

"There are other things. In life."

"Yes. I know some people can be satisfied with only having sex twice a year. Or maybe that doesn't satisfy them, but they also understand that their lives don't hinge on sex."

"With Klaus Bjerre it was something else," I said.

"Yes," said Ruben, "with Klaus Bjerre it was definitely something else. You weren't able to hide the monster inside you."

"What do you mean by that?"

"You should've helped him. But you left, fled the field. And now you have a guilty conscience, because you don't want to acknowledge that part of yourself."

"I don't think that I – " I began.

"My favorite author," he continued, "the French author who's what one might call *un enfant terrible*, he tries to articulate exactly that. That you can evade the monster. You can be evasive your entire life, without anyone noticing, not even you. But it's there, and it wants to eat. He knows that most things in humans are monstrous, but somewhere in the midst of all that shit there's something."

He took a deep breath and said:

"Now and then you can catch a glimpse of the *heart of the monster*. Do you get me, Ellinor?"

I looked at my feet.

"I've read all your Michel Houellebecq books," I said.

"What do you mean?"

"I found the row on the bookshelf. The one behind all the other books. And I read them, one by one, while you were working."

Ruben stared at me.

"Are you joking?"

"No."

"Hold on, Ellinor. Hold on."

He stood in front of me. Raised his hand and let it drop again.

I looked out the window behind him.

"There's an animal outside," I said.

I kept staring at the window, and meanwhile Ruben stared at me. For a long moment all I saw was Ruben's reflection and my own. I brought my hands to my nose and smelled the cream.

"There's something out there," I repeated.

"Ellinor," he said and came closer. "I don't think you're feeling well. I'm going to pick up a takeout so we don't have to cook. Both of us are tired. I'll be right back, and then we'll talk about what you read."

He took his jacket and walked out the door. I heard the gate shut behind him. I went closer to the windowpane, saw my face get bigger. I knew what I would see if I put my face to the pane, blocked out the light with my hands, and looked out. I would see the path with the snow, the pines, and the gate. The air would be high and still, as it is in winter up north. *At his age, to begin the long and arduous journey into another person: he'll never have the energy for that.* I took a breath, and felt fortified somehow, as if my nails had gotten stronger or my nasal passages had cleared. I would go into the bedroom, take my things out of the drawer and then get my bag. Open the door. Open the gate. See a bus stop. Walk to the bus stop and wait. Then I would take the train home, and find Johnny in his trailer. I wondered if you could get to Johnny's trailer without passing the ditz's house. If there was a back road of some kind, or if you had to pass her house, where she might be sitting on the porch with the child and the dog and the whole circus, her man in a trailer in the forest. If that was the case, I'd walk right by without a word. If she shouted anything, like *hello who are you and what are you going to do in that trailer*, then I'd say: *I'm Ellinor and I'm going to see if Johnny wants to come to Copenhagen with me.* Then I'd say to Johnny: *I have 50,000 kronor. You coming to Copenhagen?*

I thought I caught the scent of the sea. I'll soon be on a train, I thought. I'll soon be looking at the forest and the long, deep lakes along the tracks.

Then I put my hands to my temples, pressed my face to the glass, and stared out into the darkness.

II. MAX

"Life debases," Henri de Régnier once noted; life wears you out, above all — there doubtless remains in some people an undebased core, a kernel of being; but what weight does this residue carry, in the face of the general decay of the body?

MICHEL HOUELLEBECQ

Back then I was already tallying up the women I'd had, quietly and to myself. I still do, and when I do I don't remember them individually, but like those seaweed forests that spring up from the bottom of the sea in warm waters, the ones the Spanish call *posidonias*. The seaweeds sway with the currents and when you swim over them, they appear as a harmonious whole – an ocean forest, the canopy of which reaches longingly for the surface. Certain women's bodies merge in my memory, as do faces, names, and voices. I might assemble new bodies by piecing together parts from some with parts of others. I make women of women. Pleasures of pleasures, and, at times, perfections of perfections. Once, I pieced together my ideal woman. In my fantasy she was dark, short, curvy, and wore her hair in a wavy bob. She was a mélange of eight women I'd been with. The fantasy woman spoke a language I didn't understand, and so all possibilities of and demands for communication were rendered impossible. It gave me the deepest sense of calm. If she was sad, I wouldn't be able to console her. If she was happy, I'd notice nevertheless. I christened her Lolita, a name I found base but beautiful.

My wife's back was, on certain nights at the start of this story, an unvoiced rejection made of skin and vertebrae. One night I thought: With a back like that, who needs words? A very small back, on a very small person with a very large desire to take practical care of her husband.

"Your day will come," she'd say.

Each day she wedged her flesh-colored folders under her arm and walked to her job at the plant. There she sat, week in, week out, month in, month out, and yes – year in, year out. When she came home each day her face was paper-white. On the twenty-fifth of each month her salary arrived in our account.

Once upon a time my fingers would descend the staircase of her spine, feeling her vertebrae until they gave way to the soft cleft of her buttocks. The bones meant nothing to me then, except that they were part of the back of a woman I loved. That was then. That was when we'd be in the car and I'd glance at her sideways and when my eyes met hers she'd spread her legs. I'd put my hand on her and I can still recall the heat. The heat of her sex as she sat next to me in the car. Looking straight ahead, as though she were the one driving, as though she were the one who had to focus on the road. Maybe that's how it was. Maybe she'd been the one driving all along, and I was merely sitting beside her. With my hand against her hot, damp stockings. Mute, mixed-up, and imagining myself blessed. Until the sun disappeared behind the clouds. Until the moisture vanished. Until the heat vanished, too. Then there was nothing left. Only her cold sex and an open, juddering window, a night sky in gray, with a view of the void.

I pictured another woman. A very young polyglot lover with enormous, white, milk-scented breasts. Someone who spoke the languages I myself spoke, someone you could speak to in each language simultaneously, one word in one and another word in another. I pictured the intimacy that seamless communication could yield. I also imagined that the woman would know the simple art of the game, and so would switch between being a high-end French prostitute and a maternal Mexican. And yet, in spite of years of celibacy at my wife's side, and even though her body had begun to undergo a decay as apparent as it was merciless, for rather a long time it was to her alone that my lust was chained. All other distractions in which I would occasionally allow myself to indulge were perfunctory and dwindled into nothingness right after orgasm, leaving only an insight into something distant and lost, something that had slipped one's grip and could not be taken back. In the end, I stopped picturing the polyglot lover's physical and verbal superiority. It all reminded me of an overripe mango, the sweetness of which had almost given way to the intrusive taste of alcohol. Only at my wife's side could it regain the flavor of wholesome fruit.

But the *tristesse*, oh, the *tristesse*! No one can be saved from it!

"Do you remember how much we've done together?" I asked one morning at breakfast.

"What have *we* done?" my wife replied.

I wanted to say that we'd traveled to Vienna and gone to the opera. Or that we'd seen a musical in London. Or that we'd gone hiking in the mountains and made love four times a day even though our bodies were forty-eight years old. I couldn't say any of this, because we hadn't done any of it. We had done other things. Lovely things that I couldn't recall right then. Once we'd gone camping together. She'd complained about the "devastating smallness" and "the tyranny of tiny details." The caps that hung in pairs on the inside of open trailer doors, the hierarchy among the trailers, the smell of shit in the communal toilets (where someone had made a habit of spreading feces on the mirrors at night). Her complaints were pointed: Is this where you take me? We made the decision to come here together, I replied to her unspoken accusation. With that I was lost, because if you respond to an unspoken accusation, you are of course at fault. We kept walking through the campsite's pines.

"Not exactly a place to be happy," she said. "I work in dreary corridors all year round, and when I go on vacation it's like walking into another."

"Look up," I replied. "Don't you see the crowns of the pines? The sea? Doesn't it make you want to go for a swim, then sit on the terrace drinking cold sangria and write an Alessandro Baricco novel?"

She chuckled. Crow's-feet appeared by her eyes. Beautiful, sprightly crow's-feet by her eyes. I felt elated and kept talking.

"Moleskines are overrated," I said. "I prefer school note-books for €1.30 apiece."

Again, the *tristesse*, like a fog over her gaze.

"Yes, yes. You don't say. To an outsider, paper is paper, it seems."

"Have you thought about how everything is different here?" I said. "The pines are different. The crowns spread out as if they want to provide shade. At home they're more peaked."

And she replied, distracted, slowly:

"Haven't you ever wished that everything, and by that I don't just mean the pines, could be different? History, everything, life?"

The pines stood tall as though nothing had happened. And beyond the pines: the sea.

There are events that act like nodes in our lives, that definitely and irrevocably alter us. There are people who trigger these events and who might be on the periphery, blurred faces in the background of a photo, until one day you realize they've always played a central role. It's rare to notice the tremendous weight of certain moments as you're living them. How they rise up like towers and cast other moments in shadow. The light of retrospect reveals so much. And in retrospect lies nostalgia. You imagine it was better then, you wish you could leave everything untouched and return. To remember without nostalgia?

I'll try, really I will.

It began in April. Stockholm was still cold, but when you looked out over the bay you could see greenery. It wasn't there if you looked for it tree by tree, but from our apartment a pale verdant gauze clung to the groves on the far shore. The sea was cold, the cliffs dark. On the street below our apartment people were sitting at outdoor tables, wrapped in blankets and holding cups. We would stand by the living-room window with the light in our eyes and look out over it all. I say "we" as though my wife and I comprised a harmonious whole. But as I've said, it wasn't like that at all. I didn't like the loneliness. I would get the feeling that something was missing, that neither I nor my life had found our bearings in this insufficient state. But as far as coupling went, there was never any doubt: frankly, it was unfeasible. My organs seemed to stop working. My face sank in on itself like a deflated pastry. With disappointment, I might ask myself: Why are you so weak, why can't you handle this? My admiration for everyone who could handle coupling up was endless. I imagined them making epic sacrifices so they could handle playing the game, enduring the strain with a smile. My inability to do the same was a personal failure.

The morning everything began, the alarm clock rang as usual and I got up and went to the kitchen, where my wife was having her coffee at the table.

"Good morning," I said.

"Good morning," she said.

I continued to the bathroom, where I showered and shaved. Then I went back to the kitchen and poured myself a cup of coffee.

"Are you writing today?" asked my wife.

"Yes," I said.

"Were you thinking about writing at home?" she said.

"No," I said.

Did I hear a sigh of relief?

At this time, I was writing a collection of short stories about Stockholm. My intention was to mimic Söderberg's walks through the city, but with a modern eye. How blind I was to this tired concept! A city is a city, *una cittá è una cittá, une ville n'est qu'une ville* – and one can't endlessly wring from it its essence. My wife had always been my best and biggest critic, but this, my lack of originality, had gone undetected – on the contrary, she thought the project was "brilliant." Often, I put what I'd written during the day on the kitchen table before I went to bed. When I got up in the morning, those same efforts were there but with corrections and comments in the margins. From this perspective, our marriage was perfect and I couldn't wish for a better woman at my side. But a man is not his efforts alone. A man is also a predator, and no predator can live on paper.

So, the day had begun. I would put myself at the disposal of the stories for five hours. I looked forward to flâneuring, my 10:30 a.m. coffee, the pleasing introspection and calm that it bestows, like a storm's eye in the unending swarm of life. I stuffed my computer into my bag and rode the subway into the center of town. You find the best stories where no one is thinking about stories, where no one is aware that stories even exist. Harbors, train carriages, construction sites, Italian suburbs, or changing rooms in communal swimming halls. With time, I've refined my ability to catch the scent of such possibilities. And now I was randomly getting out at Central Station and heading toward Vasagatan, Kungsgatan, and Cityterminalen. Right before I got to the airport buses, three women crossed my path. They were lively, young, and their hair swished in the cool spring air. They were wearing short skirts and high heels. Their legs were wrapped in silky stockings that shimmered in the morning light, and they were redolent with youth and perfume. A lover? I wondered. Destiny helps those who help themselves. I followed them.

The women walked through the doors of the building immediately in front of the airport buses. It was the first time I'd noticed this building. It floats impersonally in the city. If it catches your eye at all you might think it's a hotel, part of Central Station, or an office complex, but you'd never imagine what's inside or how it exists. Now I could see that here too was a hidden world. A world of light, greenery, and order. The building was called something pretentious like *World Trade Center*. You walk into a spacious lobby, from which escalators roll up to other floors. The stairs are lined with tall, dark green potted plants, which, combined with the vaulted glass ceiling, creates the impression of rising through a tropical jungle. The women were a few steps ahead of me on the escalator. Their legs were pillars of soft skin and sturdy flesh holding their bodies up to the sky. The legs, the greenery, the space and light thrilled me. The feeling did me good – as if the hardening arteries in my chest had dilated, allowing the blood around my heart to flow freely.

When the women reached the top of the stairs, they hurried off. They cut a well-worn path through men in suits and receptionists in dark jeans and sparkly earrings. Everyone seemed to stop to clear the way for these women, a sea parting for the chosen ones, then closing behind them. Myself, I bumped into people carrying coffee cups, briefcases, and papers. For a second I lost sight of the women, and then I saw them further ahead, just past the cafeteria on the second floor. They took a left into a small room where a receptionist greeted them by gesturing toward a door. The women disappeared inside and the door slammed behind them. I lingered in the waiting area with the smiling receptionist behind the desk.

"May I help you?" she asked.

I fumbled for something suitable to say. I hadn't prepared an excuse that would give me a reason to be here, so I ended up standing in silence for a second. The woman tilted her head, as though she thought I was a very shy person who needed to see unlimited kindness in the listener's face to dare say anything. I noted that she was not as young as the other women I had seen in the building. She wasn't young at all in fact, and for a moment I wondered how she could be allowed to work here, being neither young nor pretty.

I corrected myself immediately, for even if such thoughts merely flutter by, they say something about you, and what they say is not good. So, instead I thought that she must be a highly experienced receptionist. She knew things no one else knew, was what the ancient Spanish would have called an *ama de llaves* — a mistress of keys — a woman who has access to everything and can decide who is granted access to which spaces. Perhaps she could speak Chinese or something else invaluable?

Finally, she said:

"Are you attending the SKF conference, or Novartis?"

Her face was grooved, her nose pointy, mouth etched with thin lines. She was wearing too much black around the eyes and her hairline had crept up high on her forehead. Her hair was styled well, but dry at the crown. She had a glazier's gaze. Empty, clear, and delicate — like crystal not yet crushed. Did I know then that I would be the one to crush her? Of course I did. The brain might not understand, but the body surely knows.

"Novartis," I said.

"Then go back out into the hall, and it's the third on the right."

She reached across the counter and angled her hand to the right to clarify the direction I was supposed to take. I could see the cleft of her cleavage. It too looked dry. I took in my surroundings and noticed that a few meters from the reception was a waiting area.

"My lecture isn't for another few hours," I said. "Do you mind if I sit here and polish my presentation?"

"Be my guest."

Lifting up a panel in the counter, she came out from behind the desk. She led the way to the waiting area and gestured toward one of the sofas.

"Please," she said. "Would you like a cup of coffee? Tea?"

"No, thank you," I said. "If I can sit here and not be of any trouble to you, then I'm happy."

"You're no trouble at all," she said. "No trouble at all."

She went back to her desk. I opened my laptop and started reading my story. I did my best to concentrate on the text, but my thoughts drifted. For a good while I contemplated how the World Trade Center was built, how big it was, and its position in relation to Central Station. I also thought about the people walking around here. Their jobs, their tasks that day, their papers and their smiles, and the closed conference-room doors. I thought about how lonely writing is, compared with this sea of planned and random encounters. I thought about the women, and I thought about the men. You might think men are in the driver's seat, but you'd be wrong. Or maybe they are in the driver's seat, but they can't have their way. As I write this, I'm remembering the time my wife read aloud from a slim book, the name of which I can't recall, but it was by Stephen King. She was smoking in bed as she quoted:

"Men are not so much gifted with penises as cursed with them."

She nodded to herself, and I raised my eyebrows. A good sentence. At least for someone with a reputation of not being able to write.

"I agree," I said. "Just because you're holding the rudder doesn't mean you can set the course."

"What do you mean by that?" my wife said.

"King put it well," I said.

I recalled this as I observed the woman standing behind the wide, glossy reception desk. Behind her was a potted plant that had somehow outgrown its proportions. The pot in which it grew was small, at least compared with the plant's stalks and leaves, which spread out across the wall.

The more I looked at it, the more confounded I became. There seemed to be an absolute affinity between the woman and the plant. At the same time, it was so clear that neither the woman nor the plant belonged in this milieu. When I'd understood this affinity and concurrent contradiction, I couldn't stop thinking about it. It was as though there were a conclusion to draw, something to be deduced below the surface. The wall the plant was climbing up received little light, and this lack of light was probably the reason it had taken on such a wan and washed-out hue. But the plant kept on growing. It hadn't given up. Undernourished, depleted, and mighty, weaving its way across the wall. Sad people have sad plants. Angry ones angry. Angry vegetation, something unstoppable. *Una vegetación furiosa!* I jotted the thought down in my notebook.

Eventually I put the flâneur story aside, and drafted a short story that would take place behind one of the doors around me. I imagined a married man giving a PowerPoint presentation at a conference and he's forgotten to turn off the chat function. Suddenly sexual messages from his lover start popping up on the screen. Scabrous, depraved sexual messages, messages that attest to the fact that nothing is as it should be with either of the lovers. I wrote them in French and Spanish and Italian, unable to decide which language was best suited. All Latin languages are extremely well suited to perversions; Swedish alone is impracticable. In Spanish and Italian certain crass words for genitalia can in certain contexts sound incredibly arousing, while the same sentence in Swedish, if you're lucky, is hammy. Other Latinate expressions have a nice ring to them, whereas in Swedish they become flat and vulgar. For example, the Italian *brutta testina di cazzo*. I once heard a man say that to his girlfriend right before he kissed her. *Brutta testina di cazzo.* You ugly little dickhead. Then they met in a tender kiss. Every aspect of Italian is as intoxicating as it is inscrutable – this also applies to the innermost nerve of the language.

I'd been writing for a few hours, and even thought I'd come up with a pretty good ending, when I was overcome with fatigue. I leaned back into the sofa, shut my eyes. A bit later I was woken by the receptionist's voice:

"You look happy."

I looked up, and there she was, right in front of me. Now she was smiling at me, and her smile looked so sincere, as though I'd pleased her with what must have seemed like a happy snooze. I imagined her behind the reception counter, seeing my face and being unable to resist the temptation of coming out and standing in front of me, waking me up. This spontaneity, somehow lost and confused, made me feel a pang of sympathy for her.

"Were you dreaming?" she said.

"Yes," I said.

"What were you dreaming?"

"I don't remember," I said. "But I think . . . I think I was dreaming of the sea."

"The sea . . . " she said and turned her head. "It's been a long time since I've dreamed of the sea. I wish I could. I think everything would be very different, if I could dream of the sea."

"One can always dream," I said.

"Dream of dreaming," she said.

I could see her eyes clearly now. Iris and pupil. Her gaze radiated warmth. A dull nausea moved along the bottom of my stomach. I recognized it: it was related to intimacy. I feel nauseous when I get close to new people too quickly. I need time. Aloof drinks at stiff networking events, circumstances that allow me to observe undetected and form my opinions in peace, like a spider in the cellar's calm slowly weaving a web. Opening up too quickly is like going down a slide in the dark: security is imaginary and you end up free-falling. People who do this inexplicably enrage me, as if someone had suddenly pressed their body against mine, hard and unbidden.

"I intend to write a novel about women," I said.

Why did I say that? It wasn't true. I was still living with the idea about the flâneur stories, and the brief moment we'd shared didn't invite this type of confidence.

"Oh?" she said. "A novel about women in which sense?"

"About the dream of forgiveness. Between lovers."

"Oh. The dream of forgiveness. Between lovers."

She looked down at her hands and smiled dreamily. Then she shrugged and rubbed her palms together, as though she suddenly felt distressed.

"Coffee?"

"Yes, please," I said.

She turned around and disappeared. I stayed put, feeling the nausea spread in my gut. I was about to leave when the woman returned with a mug and a vanilla heart cookie on a plate. She placed it on the table in front of me. Then rested the tray on her hip, as if she were waiting for me to speak.

"Do you have anything against me keeping you company?" she asked.

"Not at all," I said.

She sat down and crossed her legs. They were long and shapely.

"So you write alongside your work at Novartis?" she said.

"Yes, exactly," I said.

I drank my coffee and took a bite of the vanilla heart.

"And you work here, at reception?" I said.

"Yes," she said. "And for much too long."

"Have you thought about finding something else?" I said, continuing to eat the heart.

"No," she replied curtly. "But I have considered taking my own life."

"Excuse me?" I said, thinking I might choke on the bite of cookie.

"Yes," she said. "I've considered taking my own life."

The nausea was now rising up my throat so insistently that I had to concentrate on swallowing the bite of cookie to ease it. I felt ashamed that at the start of our conversation I had briefly brushed up against the idea that this woman could be my future lover. My polyglot lover. I often do a quick mental scan of women when we first meet, swiftly assessing the possibilities: whether she speaks to me physically and whether she knows my languages, or has the ability to learn them. And that's what I'd done this time, too. Now I understood that she couldn't be the polyglot, because how can a man out of his own free will desire a woman who wants to kill herself? (It didn't occur to me that such a desire could have constituted salvation.)

"I see," I said. "Is there a particular reason you want to take your own life?"

My words were calm and collected, but I didn't know where the calm came from.

"Unhappy love," she replied.

"Oh. Unhappy love."

I knew that I was supposed to ask her about this unhappy love. How it had infiltrated her life. How it had broken her down, and how it had finally crushed her. A cynical man who had trampled her life force. But I didn't ask. Instead I said:

"Unhappy love is in fact all that can motivate a suicide."

"What do you mean?" she asked and gave me a confused look.

"I mean that everything else you can sort out. Money, betrayal, illness, you can fight most things. But there's no antidote to unhappy love, no cure. You're full of wounds that never heal, and you have to learn to live with them. And learning to live with wounds, when all is said and done, is nothing less than learning to live as a cripple."

Something in her face twitched as I said this. There was a near imperceptible spasm in the corner of one eye, and a tremble in the corner of her mouth. Inside, I felt a strong but serene dismay over my words. I didn't understand why I'd said that. First and foremost, I knew it was cruel, and it did not reflect my conception of pain and its potential. All pain can occasion growth, if an individual is capable of handling it correctly. Shoots can be grafted into wounds. Nutrients can be extracted from pus and blood. Growth then leads to something otherwise unimaginable. For those who know how to make use of the pain, how to use it as fuel, there's no limit to the proportions that growth can achieve. But I didn't say this. Instead I continued down the same bizarre track I'd set out on.

"Think of all the magnificent people who've taken their own lives, precisely because of unhappy love. Victoria Benedictsson, Virginia Woolf. Hemingway, Dagerman, Philip Seymour Hoffman, Plath, Cobain. Had there been a solution to the problem, these people would've come up with it."

"I'm not sure the people you're listing killed themselves because of unhappy love," the woman said with disbelief.

"Ultimately everything is about unhappy love," I said. "For people, ideas, or life itself. And suicide is a refusal of sorts when faced with the knowledge that you have no choice but to live with compromise, that you have to be resigned, walk on bended knee."

I drank the coffee cooling in the cup.

"What's really strange isn't that people take their own lives," I continued. "It's strange that people *don't*. Personally, I have far more reasons to take my own life than to keep living it."

"For instance?" the woman asked.

I laughed.

"I don't know where to begin. But you're saying you're unhappily in love. I, on the other hand, am not even in love. I haven't been in love for several years. It's like my heart can't take it anymore, as if it's gone and gotten too shrewd. It sees through everything right from the start and wonders 'why should I crawl out of my den just to be tormented?' One of the shortcomings of age. Not being stupid anymore, quite simply. And that's why you don't get to experience that pure true pain. The pain I'm enduring is like dirty water. All that muck swirling around. You can't see, you can only glimpse, just barely, a swell of confusion. No real order, even when it hurts. No, I've lost that ability. It's like a herd of donkeys is galloping back and forth across my heart. Back and forth, back and forth. Muddy hooves and common braying. That's all I can muster."

As I spoke, I felt a drop of cold sweat slide from my armpit down my body. I put the cup on the table and thought I felt the room around me moving.

"I'm sorry I said that," I told the woman. "I'm clearly terrible at being comforting."

But the woman didn't hear me, because she'd gotten up and was walking to the entrance. A portly man dressed in a suit, his white shirt hanging over his waistband, had entered the space. The receptionist paused, then hesitantly proceeded toward the man. He gestured dismissively at her. She stopped at a few meters' distance, as though she didn't know what to do. Apparently, he wasn't somebody you could direct into a conference room. Nor did the man seem to know what his errand was, precisely. He slowly scratched his near-bald head. Finally, his eyes landed on me. The woman turned and looked at me too, and with sudden relief she said to the fat man:

"Why don't you sit down and have a chat with this gentleman? He's going to Novartis in a bit and is polishing up his lecture. Why don't you have a seat, and I'll get more coffee?"

The man looked at me. His gaze was like that of an ox. His cheeks were two drooping sacks and his mouth was like an upside-down half-moon between them. He walked hesitantly toward me and the sitting area. We introduced ourselves to each other. He said his name, which I no longer remember, and that he was the one who "was the boss of all this." *I'm the boss of all this*, he said when he opened his arms, *I'm the boss around here*. I've got to go home now, I thought as I squeezed that spongy palm. The truth could suddenly come in handy and that's why I told it like it was: I'd lied to the receptionist, I didn't work at Novartis, I was just sitting here, on a sofa meant for conference participants, without purpose. Surely, he was going to escort me out of the building, because a place like the World Trade Center can't be a hangout for wanderers in search of inspiration. But the man didn't seem to want to throw me out at all. He stared at me for a few seconds, before breaking into a large, fat smile.

"That's ingenious!" he exclaimed. "You're a damn genius! You come here and . . . You come here looking for inspiration. Inspiration! Yes, that's what I've always said! Is it the light, you think?"

He gestured to the glass ceiling outside the waiting room.

"Or is it the palms?"

He swung his arm toward the escalators.

"They came here by boat from farms in the Canary Islands."

"Yes, it's something," I said and got up. "It's certainly something."

"Wait," he said and reached for me. "Wait. Don't run away. You're more than welcome to sit here. I'm going to sit down too, take a load off."

I sat back down on the sofa. Five minutes, I thought. I'll give him five minutes. The woman from reception came out with the same tray as before, now with a cup for the man and a fresh one for me. She took my old cup and set the new ones on the table in front of us, and said, "Here you go." The man didn't say thank you. The woman left. The man fixed his gaze on me, and leaned toward the cup so that his enormous gut was squeezed between his upper body and his legs.

"What do you do with an old Potemkin that doesn't understand it needs to be scrapped?" he whispered and nodded toward the woman.

I'm sure she heard him. From where I was sitting, I could see her stiffen and look up, only to fix her eyes on something beyond the waiting room.

"I think those who've lived and have defects are more interesting than the new and flawless," I said, more loudly than necessary. "But you also have to know how to *see*."

The man looked at me blankly as he sipped his coffee.

"*See*?" he asked. "Did you say *see*?"

"Art is also in the eye of the beholder," I said.

I was ashamed of my platitude, but comforted myself with the thought that to him it probably seemed like great wisdom. But I was mistaken.

"What a load of crap," he exclaimed. "What a load of pretentious crap. You know how long I've been trying to get rid of that old wreck? But she *sinks* her teeth in. She knows she could never find anything anywhere else. That's why she sinks her teeth in."

As he said that, his upper lip lifted in a quivering, predatory motion. The half-moons parted to reveal a yellow row of teeth between his jowls.

"That's probably what you and I, and probably all of humanity, would have done in the same position," I said.

Again, he fixed his ox eyes on me.

"She sinks her teeth in," he repeated. "Like a leech. You have to *cut* her off if you want to get rid of her."

"I have to go now," I said.

"She cursed me, you know," he said.

"Excuse me?" I said.

"Yes. She said: 'I curse you.'" Like she was right out of some old Bible. She's cuckoo. One hundred percent cuckoo. Should be locked up. Or shot. Locked up or shot, doesn't matter which."

"I have to go now," I said.

"But you needed inspiration," said the man.

"I've just gotten some," I said.

"What do you do?" he asked.

"I'm an author," I said.

"Author!" he exclaimed. "You're an author! So am I!"

With a jolly grimace, he got up and took a small notebook out of his back pocket. A sweaty, flattened notebook. I couldn't not picture it being pressed against his giant hams and impregnated by his bodily emissions as he rode the escalators up and down the World Trade Center. The nausea in my stomach intensified. He opened the notebook, flipping through it with a smile plastered across that big face, glanced at the receptionist, and then began to read. The poem was sickeningly bad. I sat as though petrified before him. The woman at reception was now standing with her back to us, but there were mirrors on the wall and in them I could see her face. As her superior read, a mocking smile crept across her face. She held out her hands to examine her nails, all the while wearing that smile. He finished reading and sank back down into the armchair.

"Phew," he said and wiped his forehead. "What an effort it is to catalyze poetry."

"Catalyze?" I said.

"Catalyze," he said. "From *katharsis*. Don't you know the Greeks? You shouldn't be writing books if you don't know the Greeks."

I thought to myself: I'll count to ten and then leave. But by the time I got to seven the man said:

"I think I have a worm."

"What?" I asked.

"Yeah, I think so. I think there's a worm inside me."

"A *worm*?" I said.

"Yes," he said. "I know it sounds strange, but I'm almost certain. It lives inside me and is feeding on me."

He glanced at me and I thought I noticed him blushing slightly. What kind of day is this? I wondered. People come to me, telling me they want to kill themselves, and that they have a worm. What kind of day is this, and what is the World Trade Center *really*?

"You should probably have a doctor take a look at that," I said and closed my bag. "You have to watch out with parasites."

"Not that kind of worm," the man said and lowered his voice. "Not the kind of worm a doctor can help with. I have a different kind of worm. It's in my head. Do you get me? I wake up at night and see it. It's large and white and it feeds on me. I can hear it chewing in the silence. I tried to research it, but I can't find any information. I haven't told anyone. I'm telling you because I don't know you."

"Maybe you should see a psychologist?" I suggested.

"I'm not crazy. Just sick. I'm suffering from a sickness of some kind."

"It sounds like a neurosis," I said. "Something in you seems to be suppressed and is manifesting in this way when you relax."

"Yeah, yeah," the man said with a dismissive wave. "Whatever I've got probably has some fancy name. If I thought a doctor could help me I'd have gone to one. But now I'm talking to you, and you're an author. Authors know people's dark sides. You must be able to imagine why a thing like this would happen inside a person, to be of some help."

He leaned over and took hold of my arm.

"Writing is one thing," I said. "Cures are another."

"Reading can be a cure," he said.

"If you can find the right book," I said.

A fog rolled over his gaze and for a second it looked like his head was in a glass jar. A large, disproportionate human head, preserved in formaldehyde, with half-open eyes forever staring through the glass.

"Don't pretend," he said slowly. "You know about the darkness of the soul."

"All I know is that it can get very dark," I said.

The man leaned forward.

"I'm afraid it's going to spawn," he said in a low voice. "I'm so fucking afraid of that. What will I do if the worm starts to spawn?"

"Worms don't spawn," I said and leaned back against the sofa. "That's frogs."

"So what do worms do?" said the man.

I didn't know what worms did.

"They procreate," I said.

The idea of the worm procreating must have seriously frightened the man, because terror spread across his face. My budding nausea had grown stronger, and it took monumental effort to resist grabbing my bag and rushing out. I felt like I was sitting in front of a monster, an absolute zero of a man.

"If you're sick in the soul," I said, "and don't know how to get in touch with your sickness, then you should go for walks. Just like light and fresh air does the body good, so too can it soothe the soul. Everything is about oxygenation."

The man's glare was cold.

"Why are you being banal?" he asked. "I opened myself up to you. You're pushing me away."

"Not at all. I'm just trying to give you advice."

"You haven't understood a word I've said. You say you're an author, but you seem to be an idiot. Do you really think the worm can *breathe*? This isn't the kind of worm that will get some air if I go for a walk. All this worm does is eat."

I got up, grabbed my blazer and my bag. Then I turned toward the man.

"Keep an eye on your masculinity. Don't let it consume you."

"What are you getting at?" he said.

"Be nice. Just that. *Be nice.*"

I nodded toward the receptionist.

"No, I can't be nice. Not to her."

He shook his head violently.

"I've paid her salary for so many years, without her providing any value in return. I hate her. I see no solution."

"Some things are only resolved in death," I said.

"What do you mean?"

My disgust with the man was now so potent that I felt I had nothing to lose by speaking my mind.

"Some people think the wrong thoughts for so long that in the end death is the only possible solution for them."

The formaldehyde head seemed to sink in on itself.

"For some people the only solution is sex," he replied. "Sex remedies everything. I'm going to go find someone to get with. There's lots of sex in this building. All you have to do is wear the pants, and everything sorts itself out."

I continued toward the exit. I had the feeling that the man was considering running after me to hurt me. I pictured how bullfighters, when they turn their back on the bull, don't actually get attacked. Cattle don't attack from behind, I told myself. When I'd taken a few steps, I turned my head just far enough to see him out of the corner of my eye. Right I was. He was like a fallen soufflé on the sofa. I wanted to ask one last question before I went. *Have you read Michel Houellebecq?* But I realized there was no point to it. The man was the essence of everything Michel Houellebecq has ever wanted to say.

"Try to find another job," I told the receptionist when I reached the counter. "You'll be poisoned if you stay here."

"But what should I do?" she whispered, and there was a streak of suppressed desperation in her voice. "Do you really think I'm employable? Who would want to hire *me*? I'm doomed to remain here. I can only hope that one day he'll begin to hate me a little less."

"You don't understand," I said. "His hatred of you is the realest thing he has. You can't touch it."

Something about her eyes changed, and she leaned toward me and whispered:

"Not unless we kill him."

I held out my arm.

"Who *are* you people in here?" I said.

"Please help me," she whispered.

I shook my head and continued on my way to the exit.

"I was thinking about killing myself anyway!" she shouted after me. "I said so. I said that I was thinking of killing myself anyway!"

Her words echoed throughout the white space, and I thought everybody had stopped to look at us. Leave, I thought. Leave and forget about these people. Something isn't right here. I was almost at the escalator when I heard high heels hurrying behind me. I turned around.

"Can we see each other again?" she asked, out of breath.

I gave her an unsympathetic look.

"But why?"

"To see each other," she said.

"I'm married," I said.

"If the position of wife is occupied, then I can satisfy myself with that of a mistress," she said.

She smiled as she said that, and the smile made me want to smile too. Mistress, I thought. That heart-rending state.

"Here, take my number," she said, and handed me a scrap of paper.

A little later, when I walked into my and my wife's apartment, the two people I'd met in my short time at the World Trade Center felt both fictitious and illusory. I poured a glass of wine from a bottle in the fridge and chuckled to myself. Then I sat on the living-room sofa for a while, staring out at the sky, which was unnaturally clear that evening.

How old was I then? Fifty-four. How did I imagine my future? That there would be islands. Michel Houellebecq wrote a book called *La possibilité d'une île*. *The Possibility of an Island*. Think what you like about Michel Houellebecq, and the majority of the world's population has the right and the duty to hate him, but *La possibilité d'une île* is one of the most beautiful titles in the history of book titles. Writing about love is difficult. You have to have special filters, and so much is about finding these filters. Then you have to wait for a kind of eclipse, when everything stops, the light vanishes, and that eye looks at you. Stephen King has written about such eclipses. The eye that looks at people, and the eye that looks out, from inside a person. As I said, for someone with a reputation for being a bad writer, sometimes he can really write.

The receptionist stayed with me in the following weeks. Her face came to me when I least expected it. Some nights she was the last thing I saw before I fell asleep. Those heavily lined eyes and that downhearted gait when she brought over the coffee. That mocking smile when her superior read his poem aloud, and the stern pattern of wrinkles around her mouth, her dry cleavage. And I saw the haughty young women gliding around her, like fancy fish in an aquarium where she no longer fitted in.

125

My sleep got worse. Some nights I woke up and saw the receptionist's boss in front of me, and the white worm that was feeding on him. I broke into a sweat when this image came to me. It caused uneasy swells in my body and made it impossible to fall back asleep. My heart seemed to refuse to obey my breath and fluttered in my chest like a plastic bag caught on a post in the wind. I writhed in my damp sheets, doing my best to keep from waking my wife. But nocturnal worry is like stale air, stifling a room, and the lack of oxygen will wake even a tranquil partner. One night she sat up in bed, sighed, and glowered at me. Then she took the pillow and the blanket and went to sleep in the guest room.

"I don't know what's happening in your life," she said, standing in the doorway, "but you have to snap out of it. Is it your flâneur stories?"

Flâneur stories? They felt so far away.

"There are agonies you can't escape," she said. "There are agonies you have to enter, in order to get out the other side. You have to figure out what needs to be done. When you know *why*, then you also know *how*. It's all about finding the deeper nerve, the underlying artery, the clear water in which everything becomes apparent."

I recognized the words. They weren't my wife's, but Nietzsche's. It's funny that someone like my wife – an administrator at a governmental plant with corridors full of flesh-colored folders – can love a philosopher like Nietzsche. You'd think that someone like her should be reading crime novels and watching reality TV. Instead, in recent years she'd spent her evenings reading Western philosophers. And her conclusion was that there was only one who encompassed everything. I envied her this love. I also wanted to be fulfilled, I also wanted to believe that

I'd found the philosopher who encompassed everything. If I'd found one such philosopher I would have entered his work, never to emerge. But where wisdom had moved in with my wife, tenderness had moved out.

"When are we going to have sex again?" I bluntly asked one evening.

"I don't have the energy to talk about it now," was the answer. "Close the door behind you, will you please?"

At the beginning of July, we went out to the archipelago. We took the boat from Strandvägen, water foaming at the prow and seagulls shrieking in the air. We thought we were heading for a period of happiness and rest, but Swedish beauty has always made me melancholy, and I can't enjoy a deep forest or the view over the Baltic Sea without sensing that my days are numbered. Why doesn't the same feeling of desolation arise when I look out over the Atlantic from the Costa da Morte or stand in the steep hills of the Basque Country? There I feel freshness, venture, strength, vitality. An eagle's eminence, an eagle's need for wind beneath its wings. Now, here, I was high up on a Swedish island in the white house my wife had inherited. The curling ornamentation on the gable ends, the wooden floors polished to a shine. But I couldn't escape the feeling that I was in for a long and insufferable summer.

From the kitchen window, I could sit and watch her. It was so clear that she felt at home, that this was her place. She tended to the overgrown kitchen garden and filled baskets with berries that she boiled into fruit syrup. The paper-white hue left her face, and the days at the plant seemed to be wiped from her memory. Sometimes, when we socialized with friends from the city, I felt ashamed of her. When people sat there with their glasses of rosé, telling us about who they were, what they had achieved in their lives, which places they'd visited and which dishes they could cook, it was like she disappeared from the room. I'm sure people wondered: How can someone like him have a wife like her? When asked about work and careers she told it like it was: I'm an administrator at the plant. She didn't say anything about ending up there by mistake, or that she was going to find another job soon, the type of reservations people have when they think their job is beneath them. My wife didn't even say she *worked* as an administrator, my wife felt she *was* an administrator. But if that's what made me feel ashamed of her, it was nothing compared to what made me ashamed of myself. Being supported by someone whose work you're ashamed of – who can fathom the self-loathing that can cause in a person? How many more books would I write while she supported me with her time in the corridors? With each passing year she seemed to sink deeper inside herself. She became all the more insignificant, gray, and mute.

But now – in the house in the archipelago – she was humming. She glided happily across the floors in her muddy boots. In our apartment in the city, wearing your shoes past the doormat was strictly forbidden. In the city she was cleaning-mania incarnate, and it occurs to me now that it must have been a symptom of confinement, some sort of "keep-your-cage-clean" neurosis. But now the floors were dirty, and there was dirt under her fingernails at dinner. I don't even think she washed her hands before she cut the salad. Doors and windows were left open for days, and the smell of boiling berries, wind, and brackish water wafted through the house. Insects flew in and out. In the evenings, she read her Nietzsche. She had brought along all of his books in her wheeled suitcase, and they were stacked in high towers on her bedside table. Every evening before I went to bed I knocked on her door.

"Yes," she'd say.

"I just want to say good night," I'd say through the door.

"Good night," I'd hear her say from inside the room.

I'd push the handle down, open the door a crack. There she'd lie, on the feather bed with a book open on her chest.

"Are you having a good time?" I'd ask.

"Very good," she'd reply.

I'd want to say more, or wish that she would say more. Pretending that all is well when you're off to bed is nice. It helps you sleep well, and I needed, so to speak, a little assistance into that delusion. But she'd just lie there, looking at me attentively.

"I presume a dead old philosopher is a better bedfellow than I," I'd say.

"Are you calling Nietzsche a dead old philosopher?" she'd reply.

I'd close the door and retreat to my room. There I'd sit by my window in the bright summer night and look out over the comfortless Baltic Sea with its islets, rocky islands, and long-legged seabirds. Once again, I'd wish that I could enter something. Find a protected place, like the island my wife had found in Nietzsche. Me, I couldn't seem to work up an enthusiasm for anything. No book seemed interesting enough, no TV series worth following, no idea enticing enough to write a story about. The calm that should hang inside a person like a lead weight on a string was as tangled as yarn. Eventually I started dreaming about the polyglot lover again. A hotel room by a salt-rich sea like the Mediterranean or the Atlantic, and a book. Long, intense hours in bed by an open window. Making love, a lace curtain waving in the night breeze. I was convinced that would have made even the melancholy of a Scandinavian summer night bearable. *Le spleen d'un été scandinave. La inexorable melancolía de una noche de verano escandinavo. Vemodet i en skandinavisk sommarnatt. A mistress, un'amante, Oh, un'amante.*

One morning in the middle of July, I started wandering around the island. I've never doubted the curative power of a walk, so I set out in the morning, taking the paths by the sea, looking at the water all around us, and tried to feel like the privileged person I was. I walked and walked, stopping now and again to swim in small bays that cut into the island. I took off my clothes, laid them on the slab of rock, and swam out. When I stopped to tread water, I felt cold currents against my legs. I'd float on my back and look up at the sky. I'd see the receptionist's and the fatty's faces. They'd flash before my eyes like a spliced-in sequence in a film, a hidden snippet of an ad that you barely register but know is there, affecting you. It happened when I least expected it, and I hated it, I had the feeling there was something out of order about these flashes. One night I was woken by a dream in which I was standing very close to the receptionist; I'd looked at her face and every wrinkle had appeared as clearly as if through a magnifying glass. And when I was floating out there in the sea and she happened to appear before me, it felt like the water was deeper, the undersea currents colder, and like this wasn't a slow, shallow, northerly water at all. Sometimes my temples would be pulsing as I swam to shore, convinced something in the deep had caught the scent of me.

*

One morning, as I dozed on the sloping rocks on the other side of the island, I woke up to someone walking on the path above me. It wasn't unusual for people to swim from the rocks, but it was odd for them to be down here so early. Whoever had strayed from the main path leading to the water crossed the slab right behind my head, and when I became aware of their steps, the person in question was only a meter or so away. My first impulse was to throw on my clothes, but I stayed put. I opened my eyes, propped myself up on my elbows, and squinted at the figure approaching the not entirely deserted swimming spot at the end of the slope. The morning sun was in my eyes, and at first I couldn't tell if it was a man or a woman approaching. But soon I saw. There was a lapping in my chest; never before had I seen such a body. I sat up to get a better look. I felt a shiver of gratitude for creation, as you do when you encounter a certain type of perfection. At first you wonder how it's possible for a woman like that to have been created at all. Then, when the possibility sinks in, you wonder why all women aren't created in this image. Why do anything different? It would have been so much easier for women and men if all women had been created like her.

She made her way down the slope, stopped a few meters away from me, and pulled the short cotton dress over her head. The perfection was confirmed. I didn't dare move. Didn't dare risk breaking the spell. I turned my head slowly and saw that, though she wasn't wearing a stitch, she was now navigating the rocks, carefree and natural, natural in a way one seldom sees in women today, because this quality relies on an unbounded indifference to the perceptions of others. I looked away again. Out of the corner of my eye, I watched her twist her long, dark red hair and fasten it atop her head with a rubber band that she pulled off her wrist.

Then she closed her eyes and turned to face the morning breeze. She stood like that and put her hands on her chest and started to sing a melody, a melody I recognized, and I soon realized it was an Italian lullaby. I felt a burst of joy when I recognized the song. My nanny used to sing it for me when I was little, and I hadn't heard it since. I was violently overcome by memories. My childhood outside of Trieste. My Spanish-Italian roots, our nanny's soft voice. I wanted to stand up and announce my kinship with the melody she was humming, indirectly informing her of the kinship we shared, too. But of course, that would have been madness. It was a small mercy to know that already. I stayed put, heart pounding. The lullaby ended, ebbing from the woman's lips as she seemed to turn her attention to the sound of the breeze and the water lapping at the rocks. She took a few steps toward the dock and dove into the dark water. That powerful body met the black surface and white foam closed around her. I got to my feet. For a few seconds, the water was calm. Then she surfaced a bit further away, snorting and frothing. She swam around, arms and legs splashing, and I thought I heard her laughing out there. I sat down and tried to swallow the elation, which was like a glowing orb bobbing in my throat. She began her swim toward the beach. She swam past the dock and straight toward the rock on which I was sitting. When she was a few meters out her toes found the floor, and she rose from the water.

When I wrote at the beginning of my story that there are nodes around which our existence turns, moments that cast shadows on unrelated moments, I meant this sort of moment. That heavy, strong body rising from the water. Her pale skin, the freckles on her face, shoulders, and arms, the water droplets rolling down her, and her hair, like black seaweed draped over her shoulders. Everything inside me halted, definitively and irreversibly. This, I thought, is the ultimate endgame. Of all efforts, all words, and all intentions. The thought made me euphoric, as though my circulatory system had opened up, my arteries had widened, and the oxygen in my body – long stifled – now awakened every pore. I saw her face, but she was looking down and I couldn't see her eyes. She picked up a towel from the rock and dried off. There was only a meter or so between us again. Her way of ignoring me while exposing herself was incredibly alluring. I thought I understood. She was challenging and inciting me. In other words, I could expect her to be complicated and deliciously intriguing. Irrational. Which can be disadvantageous in everyday life, but at least a woman like that doesn't see sex as a treatise of equality. All the years I've spent up here! I thought. I must go back to Italy.

She bent down to pick up her dress from the slab. I looked the other way, because the level of intimacy was shocking even for a relatively hardened man such as myself. She let the dress fall over her body and ran her fingers through her hair. She grabbed her towel and walked back up the path. I looked out over the sea. Waiting for the moment when it would feel appropriate to turn and watch her go. But when she passed by me on the path just above my head, she paused. I held my breath. She was still there. I turned my head and looked up at her. And only then did I see her eyes. By her luminous, fixed gaze I understood that she was blind. Shame hit me like a club. Why hadn't I said anything when she'd come walking down? Something like "what a nice day," or "the water's warm"? The woman hadn't moved from the spot, and her childlike confusion suggested she'd just become aware of my presence. Her confusion was, if possible, even more attractive than what I'd interpreted as her boldness. But even now I couldn't bring myself to stand and address her. Face flaming, I stayed on the rocks, and the seconds felt like minutes. Finally, she began walking, slowly and hesitantly. I watched her disappear up the hill and into the pine forest.

I closed my eyes and breathed. I could picture myself sitting on the rock, and the woman disappearing behind me. I saw the island, the forest, the black water all around. I heard my breath, and the sea moved with the same rhythm, like some sort of observant eternity. And then I remembered a line from *Thus Spoke Zarathustra*, something like *I am the godless Zarathustra and I cook each opportunity in my own kettle*. I got up and followed the blind woman down the path. It wound into the pine forest, first over stones that were still cool, then on across the soft earth where the long pine needles made a soft and still-wet rug for my feet. The path narrowed and wound tighter the higher up we came, but the blind woman took quick, assured steps over the roots and stones jutting from the earth. After one hundred meters the path gave way to a well-mowed lawn. In the middle of the lawn was a small white house, typical for the island and not so unlike ours, but not as big. Smoke was billowing from the chimney and the wooden shutters were half shut. The blind woman took her quick, assured steps across the lawn, whereas I stopped at the edge of the wood. I looked out over the property. Everything seemed desolate and deserted. The blind woman went to the veranda, opened the door, and entered the house. A window was ajar, and I waited for her to shout "hello!" or whatever you might shout to your partner when you get home. But I heard no such call. The house was still and quiet. Maybe there's no man? I thought. Maybe she's alone? If she's the only one there and is singing an Italian lullaby, then maybe she too is longing for a soulmate, a lover, a polyglot like herself? I laughed. *È buffo che il cuore non si fermi mai*, I thought. Yes, it's funny that the heart never stops, *que el corazón no se para nunca*. Well. It stops in the end, but then you don't notice.

I jogged across the lawn, hunching forward, and snuck up to the house, possessed by curiosity. Soon I was at the veranda. There was a small birch basket, stained blue at the base. There was also a pair of rubber boots with tall slim shafts, and on a hanger on a hook on the wall was a yellow raincoat. The thought of the blind woman picking bilberries in the yellow raincoat filled me with tenderness. I pictured her among the bilberry bushes, intent but uncertain as she searched for the fruit. There was no trace of a man on the veranda either. I resisted the impulse to knock. Nothing can be that easy – you knock on a door and the woman of your dreams opens up – that much I knew. A cold gust of wind came in from the sea, and raindrops slammed against the windows of the house. A few seconds later, the heavens broke. The rain poured down as the clouds on the horizon eased. Strange sunlight filled the troubled air. Curtains of water seemed to stream around the pines, which were like a dark foreground to the sea. This, combined with the bright light from the gap in the clouds, made me want to compose a poem about something tremendous, but I restrained myself. I could tolerate being crazy, but not pathetic.

I continued to take shelter on the veranda. The rain stopped as suddenly as it had begun, and I snuck down the steps, toward the shutters on one of the short sides of the house. At the base of the wall was a protrusion where I could place my foot and heave myself up. I did, and spied through the window. It took me a moment to distinguish the contours of the two people inside. But when I saw them, it was like another blow to the head. On the floor, a man lay on his back with his head toward the window, and the blind woman was on top of him. The raindrops on the window cast blue, sliding patterns across their naked bodies. Behind them, in the open hearth, a fire burned. The woman's luminous eyes were half-open and directed right at the pane, and at me. I'll never forget that gaze, or the light that seemed to be streaming from her head. Part of me is still in that moment. It's like I'm stuck and can't tear myself free without losing a chunk of my own flesh. The man, who was grossly overweight, had his hands on her hips. I recalled something Houellebecq had written, that it is a human's bare, hairless skin that makes it hard for her to live without touch. I think it went like this: *The lack of caresses makes mankind's fragile, hairless skin unwell.* No, I thought. That's exactly how it is. The lack of caresses makes me unwell. And in fact, it's much worse than that. I can't bear to live without caresses. I'll put a gun to my head and pull the trigger if I can't have them now. I loosed my grip on the windowsill and fell backward to the ground. I lay in the soaking wet grass, feeling like someone was laughing behind my back. Destiny. Destiny was in the wings, smirking at how it had sunk its iron fist into a human's soft gut. It smirked at the longing, at the hairless skin, at the dream of hot hands. I got to my feet and ran across the lawn. Blood pounded in my temples and I couldn't get rid of the powerful, demented rage in my chest. But it wasn't because there was a man in the picture and the woman was clearly happy enough with him to have sex, but because my own meagerness was made all the clearer. I saw hands moving in the vegetable garden. Flesh-colored folders, joyless eyes. Gray skies and garments shrouding a body in decay. I had to forget it all. The rocks, the body, the veranda, and the bilberry basket. Some people can handle equations, some can piece everything together. Others have to make do with the backwoods.

But in my indignant state, I hadn't run back to the path I had taken. I was going in the opposite direction, toward the house's driveway. I stopped and turned around. There was the house, and beyond the house, the sea. Now the surface of the sea was glittering and glassy, as though nothing but gentle ripples had ever moved across it. A bewitching white mist rose from the lawn in front of the house. Next to me in the driveway was a red Toyota. From there, a small gravel path led down to the island's main road. I saw a mailbox where the gravel road met the main road and walked toward it. And indeed, there was a small sign attached to the top.

Ruben and Mildred Rondas
Cultural Journalism and Paranormal Phenomena

I recognized the name "Ruben" immediately. I was sure it wasn't the first time I'd heard it, and because the subheading said "cultural journalism," I understood that he was someone I should know about. And so, this woman was called Mildred Rondas and she worked with "paranormal phenomena." I laughed. Paranormal phenomena. I imagined calling a writer colleague of mine when I got home, a colleague who's also a close friend, and I could see us laughing together about this, because if there's one thing we don't believe in, if there's one thing we've never believed in and that we despise, even, then it's paranormal phenomena and people who believe in stuff like that. Airy-fairy pathetic people who've never heard of Darwin. OK, I thought. With a body like Mildred Rondas' next to you, you could probably put up with any old brain. An island is an island, and if you find one like that, you can't complain that the grass is too short, the ground too rocky, or the water levels too low. If you find an island, you're the king of the island and so you hold your tongue. Seized by a sudden calm, I walked back across the lawn, down the path, and on toward our house.

When I arrived home my wife was still sleeping in her room. I walked quietly so as not to wake her, and after I had changed out of my wet clothing, I went into my study. I called my colleague to get information about Ruben Rondas.

"Ah," he said. "Ruben Rondas. Don't you know him? He's written an entire thesis on your suite of novels from the nineties."

"Must be insufferable reading," I said.

"Not as insufferable as the suite of novels," said my colleague.

I knew I was supposed to laugh, but I don't laugh when people joke about my books. It's not because I don't have a sense of humor. I have a great sense of humor, but only if what's been said is funny. And the problem with a book is that a book is like a child to the person who made it. Is a mother supposed to laugh at her child? Make fun of it because it happens to be a little lame, because one leg is longer than the other, because it has an unruly whorl on its head? Is she supposed to clap when someone bullies it in the schoolyard? No. Likewise, an author shouldn't be expected to hold in esteem someone who's slaughtered his progeny.

Ah well. My novels were not the important thing now.

"Do you know anything about his wife?" I said, trying to sound uninterested.

"Oh, his wife . . . You mean the beautiful Mildred?"

"Yes, exactly."

"She's blind."

"Yes."

"She works with paranormal phenomena, or so I've heard. Which is interesting."

"Are you joking?" I said and laughed.

"Not at all," he said.

"So tell me, what exactly does a medium *do*?" I asked, skeptically.

"A medium does an analysis of your life path number, charts your horoscope, and reads your cards. Normally you get to ask one or two questions about something that's important to you as well, maybe about someone on the other side."

I couldn't understand why he knew about this. Was it general knowledge? Numerology and life numbers? Everything felt crazy and unfamiliar. I tried to get my colleague to admit that he was ribbing me. But he wouldn't be swayed, and when we finally hung up and I sank into bed, my confusion was absolute. I fell asleep and slept deeply and dreamlessly, long into the afternoon.

Three days passed before I decided to knock on Mildred and Ruben Rondas' door. Three days of curiosity, agony, and despair; three days during which my desire and hesitation over whether or not I could intrude was like a rash covering my body and soul. After hearing what my colleague had to say, I wondered if I might be the one who'd been missing something. Had I unconsciously been keeping something at bay my entire life? It's because of my upbringing, I thought. Rationality has always been foisted upon me from every direction. You couldn't expect me to see anything else. *Imagine if you experienced a miracle, but missed it because you don't believe in them?* I heard someone say in a movie. And a miracle might be just around the corner. This wasn't about miracles or rationality. This was about me and Mildred Rondas.

I was at the door, right where I'd stood a few days previously, and next to me on the floor of the veranda were the boots and the little bilberry basket. I raised my fist and delivered a few firm knocks. It was silent down to the wind in the pines. But soon the door opened, quick and firm, as though the person had been there the entire time. The blind woman was right in front of me.

"Hi," I said. "My name is Max Lamas, and I live across the island."

The blind woman nodded in reply.

"You were the one at the swimming spot," she said.

"Yes," I replied and was grateful that she couldn't see me blush. "I'm the one who was there. But how can you know that if you're . . . ?"

The sentence hung in the air.

" . . . blind?" she said. "How can I know that if I'm blind?"

"Yes," I said. "Exactly. How can you know that if you're blind?"

"There are many ways of seeing," she said. "Would you like to come in?"

She gestured behind her and I entered the hall. It was tidy in there. The window was open onto the garden, and the cold fireplace was silent and gaping.

"I assume you've come for a session?" she said.

"Yes," I said. "A colleague told me about you."

She smiled indulgently, as some women do when they know you're making up excuses to be near them.

"It costs 700 kronor," she said.

"I've brought cash," I said.

She showed me to a table at the back of the living room. Colorful cloths were hanging on the walls, and behind her chair was a tall bookshelf. I've always thought you can get a sense of someone by studying their books, and that's why I was wondering whether the shelf was hers or her husband's.

"Mine," she replied laconically. "My husband, who knows a thing or two about literature, thinks it's vile."

Books by Nobel prizewinners sat next to crime stories and Harlequin novels. There was specialist literature about psychology, astrology, astronomy, and Buddhism. I had a thousand questions. When had she read these books? When had she gone blind? What was her opinion of these authors? How did she read now? Did she move her fingertips across the pages of the books? Did she read books in dark rooms? I've always been fascinated by the idea that blind people can read in the dark. But Mildred's expression was anything but inviting, so I chose not to ask any questions. I sat there quietly and watched her concentrate. Several minutes passed. Eventually I checked the time and saw we'd been sitting in silence for almost seven minutes. I cleared my throat and asked if everything was OK. She lifted her head and said:

"You've come with questions of the spirit. But you can keep your money, because I can't see anything at all."

"See *how*?" I asked with trepidation.

"What surrounds you. In the fields. It's empty. It's like they're waiting for something, and meanwhile nothing can happen."

"Like the calm before the storm?" I ventured.

"Or a sandy beach before a tsunami."

"Excuse me?"

"When the water recedes and the sand is laid bare. Before the floodwaters roll in."

I tried to interpret her expression and thought that she looked exactly like you'd imagine a fortune teller would look if death were on the cards.

"But I still don't understand," I said.

"It can depend on various things," said Mildred. "Usually you see something. A picture of some sort. But all I see is a big cloud, of ash or smoke. There are probably lots of things inside that cloud, things that will happen. But unfortunately, I can't see them."

I took a deep breath. But her not saying anything didn't really matter, because I didn't believe in any of this anyway. I had come here to meet her, not to be read, and not seeing anything might have been irritating, but it wasn't in any way decisive. That's what I told myself.

"Do you think I'm going to . . . die?" I eventually said with a metallic laugh.

"Die?" she said. "It's something else, something that will happen, something that will change you. And you're going to write something, something I can't see either."

I thought: Maybe you're what's going to happen to me, Mildred Rondas. Maybe it's you who is going to happen to me, and you're going to get me to write.

"My husband is a critic," she said.

"Oh," I said.

A cool wind came in through the open window.

"When's he coming home?" I asked.

"He's upstairs, sleeping," she said.

I looked up at the ceiling.

"I write, too," I said.

"Yes," she said. "About sex, right?"

"No," I said. "I don't write about sex. I write about love."

"That's what all men say," she said. "But actually they're just writing about men. Men and sex."

I laughed. I took her point. Here it came. The bad man's dishonest worldview.

"The problem," I said, "is that if you write about anything but men, it gets political. I'd have been more than eager to write about something else," I said. "I'd have more than wanted to write about women, homosexuals, dwarfs, or the disabled. Or administrators, black people, communists, and fascists. I'd have more than wanted to write about all of these groups, if it would have done any good. The problem is that if you want to tell a story, then there's only one untainted perspective, and that is the white heterosexual man's. It is the only sheet of paper that doesn't, so to speak, have a history of oppression."

I was going to add that if I'd written about someone like her, too, I'd have been engaging in politics. But I could see in her face that my expounding had tired her out, and so I kept quiet. The purpose of my visit wasn't to be right.

So I said: "But who knows. One day I might write as if there wasn't any background."

"I might buy that book," said Mildred.

Then that's the one I'll write, I wanted to shout, if you want to read it, then I'll write it! But then I heard steps upstairs.

"Well then," Mildred said with a tight smile. "Until next time."

She got up and went to the door, and soon I was on my way across the lawn and down toward the path.

I went to the rocks the following days, too, but Mildred didn't show up. I suggested to my wife that we do something together, travel to another island or invite a few friends over, but she said she had lots to do in the garden and with the books, so if we could just "live parallel lives" she'd be grateful. I decided to take a trip into the city the next day. First, I imagined strolling around, sitting on some restaurant's patio and going up to the apartment to check the mail. But then I remembered the scrap of paper with the receptionist's phone number. Why not? I thought. The *tristesse* is so strong, that of life and of the island, and the way one loosens a knot means nothing. She was hardly my dream woman, but for want of anything else . . . The next day I woke up, showered, and got ready. I put on a white linen shirt and dark blue linen pants. I smiled at my reflection in the mirror. My cropped hair was graying, and from where I was standing I didn't think that was to my disadvantage. I put on a few drops of my Van Gils cologne. A bit later I took the boat, got off at Strandvägen, and went up Hamngatan. It was as though time had stood still in the World Trade Center. The same plants, the same light. The same escalators, the same elite guppies, and the same glass ceiling. The place had been a constant presence in my life because, in my head, I'd visited the building several times a day since I'd last been there. I went up the stairs. I rolled past the greenery from the Canary Islands. I smiled at the young women. Naturally, my smile was ignored, but I smiled anyway.

I headed for the waiting room and reception. When I came in, there was no one at the desk. The plant was still there, still stretching its stalks and leaves across the wall. But now everything had a brownish, desiccated tinge. I took a seat on the sofa and waited for her to return. After a few minutes the fatty walked by, and when he saw me, he stopped mid-step and came into the room.

"The author!" he shouted and came toward me. "To what do we owe this honor?"

"I intend to exchange a few words with your employee."

"You mean the old whale?" he said.

"Do you call her the old whale?" I said.

"Yes," he said. "The old beached whale."

"In what way is she beached?" I said.

"In every way," he replied.

He stretched, and his stomach stuck out over his waistband.

"You feel what you feel," he said. "And the body doesn't lie."

"The body alone does not lie," I said, "in all likelihood because it doesn't have a head with which to do the lying."

"Can I buy you a coffee?" he said.

I sat in the cafeteria with the man until I saw the receptionist pass by and return to her desk. I stayed put for a few minutes, then got up and said goodbye to the man. Out of courtesy I considered asking how it was going with the worm and his mental illness, but with a certain type of person courtesy is meaningless. I took my blazer, thanked him for the coffee, and went on my way.

The receptionist was behind the counter, as she'd been a few weeks ago. Alone, severe, and heavily made-up. Behind her that raging plant was spreading its pale, mighty leaves. She was reading a weekly magazine I had seen there before.

"Hi," I said.

She looked up, and a smile spread across her face. Clearly, she remembered me, and this made me – somewhat unexpectedly – hot inside. She lifted the panel in the counter and reached for me, as if I were a family member returning home after a long trip.

"Oh, you," she said. "I truly hoped you'd come back."

I wrapped my arms around her and breathed her in. It was a fine scent, like a pine forest – healthy and calming – but there was also a distinct sense of gloom and, yes, displeasure.

"I've been thinking about you so much," she said against my neck. "And what I said to you."

"But you're still here," I said.

"Yes," she said and opened her arms. "As you can see, I haven't killed myself yet."

We both gave a hollow laugh.

"Would you like a coffee?" she asked.

I shook my head.

"I've just had a cup with your boss," I said.

"Oh," she said.

She glanced at her magazine.

"Look here," she said. "I was reading a feature on Italy. I was thinking of you, actually. You're from around there, aren't you? Or is it Spain?"

"My father is a Spaniard," I said, "and my mother Italian. But I've lived in Sweden since I was seven."

"Well there you have it," said the woman.

She turned the magazine toward me.

"Look," she said. "Look at them. Isn't it like something out of a fairy tale?"

Yes, the picture she was showing me on the page was indeed fascinating. An older woman sat on a rococo chair, and next to her was a woman who must have been between forty and fifty, and another who couldn't have been more than twenty.

"Wonder where the man is," I said.

"The man?"

"I mean, there has to be a father somewhere."

"It says something about him here," the receptionist chimed. "About the marchese, the one who was married to the eldest. It says how he disappeared, do you want to hear?"

Without waiting for my reply, she started reading aloud from the article:

"The most peculiar family story must be the one about the marchese who traveled to Jalisco to learn Spanish, never to return. It's even more peculiar that the Marchesa Matilde Latini did not mince her words when recounting that, there, the marchese met the owner of the local bordello, a certain 'doña Eladia,' with whom he fell in love and stayed. Now the three women live alone in Palazzo Latini together with their staff."

The receptionist was all smiles.

"What's the magazine called?" I asked. "I'd really like to read more about these women."

"You can have it," she said, and pushed it toward me. "I'm done reading it anyway."

She seemed to be waiting for me to announce my errand. I said:

"You said we should see each other again. The last time I was here, you said you wanted me to come back."

She gave me a quizzical look, as though she didn't understand what I was talking about. I felt embarrassed.

"Do you want . . . ?" she then said. "Or am I interpreting . . . ? Do you want us to . . . ?"

I looked at her, in silence.

"Will you come back when I'm done here?" she added. "And we'll go somewhere?"

"I'll arrange the place, you finish your work in peace and quiet."

"Seven o'clock," she said.

I went to the hotel right across the street and booked a room for the night. While I waited, I settled in to people-watch from one of the sofas in the lobby. A little way away sat a man with a notebook on his lap, writing, brow furrowed. The lobby's speakers were broadcasting a program about Djuna Barnes. Someone said: *I wonder what Djuna Barnes looked like when she was writing* Nightwood. I tried to picture it. Then I wondered what Michel Houellebecq looked like when he was writing *La possibilité.* I imagined the desolation that spread around him, the lonely landscape around his villa by the sea. An austere face. But still something tells me that when he writes, a naive smile breaks out on Michel Houellebecq's lips now and then, and that smile does in fact light up his face. If someone happens to come in, he'll look up and darken into his usual cavernous self.

I opened the weekly magazine the receptionist had given me. The issue was mostly taken up by the feature on beautiful buildings in Italy and their inhabitants. One picture was of the Palazzo Latini in Rome. The caption read: *Claudia Latini Orsi: "Madness is my only defense against the world."* I imagined the woman in the picture saying it with a shrug. *My only defense against the world is madness. Which defenses have you built up?* Me, I had none at all.

When the clock struck seven I crossed the street to the World Trade Center. The receptionist was waiting outside. She was excited, and she smelled of liquor. Had she left the empty reception for some bar in the World Trade Center, to have a drink with her colleagues and tell them about her evening plans? Or did she have a flask in her handbag? The thought made me feel so low I worried about being able to perform. A lonely woman with suicidal tendencies and a flask, hopeful before a night with a strange man. My mood blackened at the thought.

Over the next hours I wondered if I'd made a mistake. Nothing about this sparked my interest. The receptionist and I had nothing in common, not even so much as to make the adventure feel meaningful. Except for forgotten school French, she knew none of my languages. She had read nothing, written nothing, nor had she lived anywhere interesting. After a few glasses of wine, she started talking about suicide again. When I told her about my background – my eleven languages and growing up in various countries – she said that she'd always dreamed of going to Provence. This is as deep as it'll get, I thought. We might as well get out of our clothes as quickly as possible.

We went up to the hotel room, switched off the lamp, and embraced each other.

The following morning, I woke up when the light began streaming through the windows. Snug in bed, becoming aware of the woman breathing beside me, I let my waking take its time. Then it came back to me, the night before. It filled me with unease. I had lived up to the situation's expectations, but her mouth had reeked of liquor and her hands were cold. Intercourse had been mechanical and lifeless, an act to honor the memory of something else, or to keep the hope alive that something else does in fact exist. You can't know what's inside a person before you, so to speak, have probed her depths, and that's what I'd just done. I'd been driven by my curiosity about the bizarre people in the World Trade Center, but now I knew that the story about the fatty, the receptionist, the glass ceiling, and the plants from the Canary Islands had reached its end and could be sealed up and relegated to the past. I was free. That's what I was thinking as I woke up in that stuffy hotel room.

I was in fact, without knowing it, in a precarious moment. Everything was still running along its particular track. Nothing had fundamentally changed yet. Nothing had become anything else. Everything was still intact and could be preserved. I had taken a step inside, but I could turn around and step right out. No gestures or statements had ruined anything. There was an obstinate overlapping of options, in which both were still available and both were intact, but soon one would begin growing unchecked at the other's expense. I could leave the hotel room. I could still gather my things and head for the door. The woman would not try to stop me. I could have opened the door and as I was leaving the room I could have paused to say:

"Goodbye. Maybe we'll see each other around."

Instead I lay there. I thought about what I would do when I got back to the island. Shower and take a walk, wash myself off and exhale the night that had been, do some reading, and talk to my wife about Nietzsche. I thought about all the women I had been with during my marriage, who, including the receptionist, now numbered fifteen. Then I felt a craving for coffee in my gut and the gentle headache that comes when you stay too long in bed. I got up, started collecting wine glasses, plates, and the bottle that had fallen over and stained the carpet. I carried everything down to the lobby, where I fetched two cups of coffee and brought them up. When I came back into the room, the sour smell of wine and wall-to-wall carpeting and stagnant breath hit me. I wanted to open a window, but when I tried it was nailed shut – as hotel windows often are, to keep people from committing suicide on the premises. The receptionist stirred in the bed.

"Good morning," she said.

"Good morning," I replied.

"Did you sleep well?"

"Very."

I handed her the cup, and she drank in silence. I tried not to look at her. Everything was so different now, here in the morning. Neither of us was what we had been the night before, especially not her.

"I've never been with anyone like I was with you last night," the receptionist said.

She looked up at me, and the stark light from the windows cut across her face.

"No?" I said.

I understood that this should have been taken as a compliment. It was supposed to mean that I was capable of giving pleasure, and isn't the ability to give pleasure one of the finest abilities you can have? Yes, it was, and I still believe it to be so. As a man and as a person, the ability to give pleasure is one of the best qualities one can have. Life is so short; moments and the intensity we are capable of giving them mean so much. And yet I wasn't grateful in the slightest for what she had said. I felt forced to return the compliment, and it roused in me nothing more than rage and an urge to wound.

"I really mean that," she said when I didn't reply. "For me it was something out of the ordinary."

"Is that so," I replied.

"What about me?" she asked.

Still I said nothing.

"And me?" she repeated.

"And you, what about you?" I replied.

"What am I to you in a starry sky of lovers?"

Of the many categories of repulsive people, I thought, it's the inarticulate ones who are the worst of all.

"I have to go," I said.

"Wait," she said and reached for me. "I have to know. Am I also among the best you've had?"

I turned toward her. And slowly, as if I were passing a sentence or letting an ax fall, I said:

"There's something about you I can't stand."

"What?"

Her anxiety was palpable. It froze between the walls, as if it and everything else were fixed in its form and nothing could move until I had replied. I let seconds pass. The woman sat at the edge of the bed with terror in her eyes.

"You're forgetting to breathe," I said.

"What?"

"You're forgetting to breathe. It looks like you're going to faint."

"Breathe?" she said.

And then:

"You're mean. You're like my boss. You men are all alike."

She hung her head and stared at the carpet.

"Your boss," I said, "is a creep and deserves to die."

"Help me kill him."

"How could I kill him? I've never killed anybody. And anyway, one could say you had a hand in creating him. Without compliant women like you, men like him can't come to be."

I looked at her. She looked at me. Then she blinked, and looked at the floor.

There and then, I felt possessed by a great power. Through the window I could see sky and rooftops. Birds flew through the air, and in the distance an airplane was preparing to land. But around us all was silent. I could see everything clearly. I was holding a woman's self-esteem between my thumb and index finger. Everything was within my power. I could show mercy. But I could also crush her.

"Don't you want to know?" I said.

"Know what?"

"What you're doing wrong in bed?"

"Well, yes. What am I doing wrong in bed?"

"You don't abandon yourself."

"I don't abandon myself?"

"No. You don't abandon yourself."

"So you're saying that I . . . " she began, and her eyes flitted as her finger rose to her mouth and her lips wrapped around its tip. Maybe it was a reflex from girlhood, biting her nails. She must have taken pains to get rid of it, because now her nails were impeccable, long and manicured. I laughed. Then I realized the cruelty in what I'd said. But it was as if the words were beyond my reach, as if I were not in fact participating in what was happening, as if the words were being spoken somewhere else by someone else. It was so very interesting to watch this unfold. And what was happening now was that this woman was being so obviously stupid – giving a stranger the power to define who she was. A cynical smile must have spread across my face when I thought that when all is said and done, some people, no matter how they refine themselves, are cattle. I wanted to laugh again, loud and thundering, like I never otherwise do, but I kept my composure.

"So you're saying I'm not good enough in bed?" the woman said.

Her throat seemed constricted, and the last words in the sentence were spoken feebly, almost in a whisper.

"Yes, exactly," I said. "That's exactly what I mean. You're *not good enough*. You're too old, too inhibited, and too boring."

There it is, I thought. The death blow. A few seconds passed. She got up and stood in front of me, crushed. The harsh light coming through the window made her body, with its loose, saggy skin and scrawny thighs, seem infinitely defective. She wore an ancient expression. She must have seen that I saw, noted that I noted, because her gaze dropped to the floor once again.

And there I left her. The receptionist from the World Trade Center. Her body and soul. Her face, her hair. The smell of souring liquor that lingered in the room along with what I'd just said. It was as though I'd managed to appropriate this person's full power and was now growing with it. And though time has passed, this moment is still so clear to me. It is as though the intensity of that moment, instead of fading, has amplified with time. I can for instance recall sounds I didn't register then. Someone walking in the corridor, a car roaring down the street. The steady whir of the fan, the ambient noise from the city. Part of me seems to still be in that hotel, never to escape. The woman, her eyes still averted, made no sound as I gathered up my things. She looked from the floor to me, to her handbag, and up at me again.

"I'm not paying you anything, if that's what you thought," I said.

It's not easy writing these lines, it's not easy giving an honest account of what happened. I wasn't thinking about anything. I was calm, tense, and expectant, like a researcher trying to deduce a guinea pig's next move.

What happened after I left the room? Did she sit on the edge of the bed, take a deep breath, and recover? Or did she cry? *Did she sit there, alone on the edge of the bed, in her aging skin, and cry?* Or did she go into the bathroom and sit still on the toilet seat with the door locked until her face was red and puffy? I suppose I assumed I'd never find out. Me, I left. Even though it was late summer, it felt like I was stepping into the spring, into a spring where everything was coming alive again after winter, where people on restaurant patios hid behind dark sunglasses in the early spring sun. I thought I'd left that place, and carried on into life. Set out on foot into life. Out among the streets and in among the alleys. Certain I'd soon find new women, new loves, new bodies to satisfy mine.

So, I took my blazer from the hanger and the elevator down to the lobby. I paid the hotel bill, for the dinner, and the wine. I passed through the doors. It was a fine day, the sun was shining and it smelled of the northern sea and the city, that smell you only find in Stockholm.

But out on the street, I become aware of something. I slow my steps and squint. Something isn't right; I see it out of the corner of my eye. Something isn't right at all, something is out of whack. Something should be elsewhere and different. But yes: out of the corner of my eye I've already seen her. She's pulled up the window in the hotel room and is leaning out. The window, I think. Wasn't it nailed shut?

"Stop!" she shouts.

And the shout is a command, the voice a voice that has lost every battle but has risen and knows that it will now be obeyed, because if you've lost every battle and can still get up, then you will be obeyed. I stop in my tracks. All the people around me seem to be stopping too, and they're turning around and looking up at the window and at the woman standing there. *It's nailed shut!* I want to shout. *This can't be happening, because the window is in fact nailed shut!* The building is a creature full of eyes. The windows glare at the street, but only one window has a person at it.

"Who, me?" I ask in disbelief, placing my hand on my chest.

"Max Lamas!" she roars.

I break into a full-body sweat. She is standing in a window in a building in the middle of Stockholm roaring my name. She's standing there. I laugh, looking around. No, I think. No. A semicircle has formed around me. People have retreated, as though I were enclosed in an invisible dome. Now they're standing there. Looking at me with disdain.

"But . . . !" I shout up at the window.

And to the people in the semicircle:

"I don't know who that is! I don't know her!"

But they don't believe me. And I see it, their disdain. Disdain has installed itself in their eyes, and will not yield. I suddenly understand: the people who happen to be on the street hate me. They know nothing about me. They've never seen me before, they don't even know what happened up in the hotel room. But they hate me. They believe the rage of a roaring woman in a window. She still hasn't said anything, and yet they fully believe what she's about to say.

"The madwoman in the attic . . . " I begin.

But the voice in the window interrupts me:

"*I curse you! I curse you, Max Lamas!*"

The people look at me, and the very traffic seems to have stopped. Everything is still and quiet; only the sky is darkly revolving, like a door to something unknown.

I laugh out loud. I laugh so loudly that I too am almost roaring. Then I fall silent. Look around. Look up. She steps back and pulls down the window so it shuts with a bang. I'm left standing on the street. My back is soaking wet, and the ocean breeze presses the thin fabric of my shirt against my skin. I turn around to leave. I scratch my head, I walk, but it doesn't feel like I'm getting anywhere. Is this really happening? I think. I mean, is this *really* happening? It has to be a fantasy, I must be overstrained. But a woman spits on the ground when I leave the semicircle and a large quivering gob lands a few centimeters from my shoe. So, this is in fact happening, I think. I increase my pace. I walk faster and faster, and still people seem to be stopping to look at me. I start jogging. Then I run. Finally, I tumble into the subway, right as the train hurtles into the station.

III. LUCREZIA

I tell you, Madame, if one gave birth to a heart on a plate, it would say "Love" and twitch like the lopped leg of a frog.

DJUNA BARNES

My name is Lucrezia Latini Orsi and I am the maternal grand-daughter of the notorious Marchesa Matilde Latini, who died of a broken heart in the summer of 2012. Therewith, my family was robbed of its soul. To an outsider, this might sound dramatic, but along with Grandmother the palazzo disappeared, and without its protective walls, without our world of endless rooms, our grand melancholic views of the Pantheon, and without our mirrors, furniture, and crystal chandeliers – without all of this we were soulless.

"Of course, you have a soul," our family lawyer Giuseppe Martini said. "The soul belongs to the person, not the trappings."

My mother gave him a vacant look, because with this statement he showed how glaringly little he understood of the nobility's inner essence in general, and ours specifically. Where one can separate the soul from the trappings, decay is already a fact. Where the face loosens itself from the skull, one can only expect the total decimation of the individual. But we said nothing of this. Giuseppe Martini was Giuseppe Martini and, as Grandmother used to say, one might be able to make a diamond out of coal, but never out of gravel.

For a few days in the summer of 2012, my grandmother's broken heart was for the sum of its entertainment value put on display in the southern European tabloid press. The event has had many consequences, one of the most serious for me being that I can no longer walk the streets of Rome without being recognized. I'm not one to disguise myself, nor do I enjoy the quality of attention that accompanies scandal. And so I've stopped taking my walks, walks that for the entirety of my life have imbued me with the indescribable energy that rises from the ground in Rome, and to the best of my knowledge is found only in Rome. I no longer experience the changing of the seasons in the trees along the Tiber, bar goers squinting into the first spring sun, or the lull in the cramped alleys when the August heat settles over the city like a glowing gridiron. I no longer look into the elephant's eye at Piazza della Minerva, and I never hear the violinist playing between the columns of the Pantheon on certain rainy nights in September. Our palazzo by the Pantheon has now been sold to a large hotel chain. I read in the papers that the hotel is exceeding expectations. So I couldn't resist venturing into the center and revisiting the building my family had raised and lived in for 400 years. Early one morning I took the tram, walked from an empty Trastevere across the Tiber and through the backstreets toward the Pantheon. I could only spend a minute or so at the entrance. It was far too painful that, in spite of the early hour, throngs of garishly dressed Americans were going in and out of the door, like a bubble of gum in and out of a mouth. The smell of the house, which had always been a mix of age, mold, and damp marble – which in a way is also the smell of us – had been replaced by a sharp, chlorinated smell. I can only imagine all that had needed to be torn out to rid the place of that old smell. We had been cleared away, aired out, made irrelevant – but perhaps we lingered in the building's ancient memory as faint reminiscences.

As for myself, I now live in an apartment close to the tracks that run between Trastevere and Fiumicino, a small two-room apartment of sixty-five square meters on the third floor in a nine-story building. It's quite different here. The trains to and from the airport pass through the area once every ten minutes, often not far at all from my balcony, which means that I occasionally see a surge of faces inside the cars, faces impassively regarding our building. I imagine the passengers cannot reconcile these areas in the outskirts of Rome with the image of the city they'd had when booking their trip. To them Rome must consist solely of frivolous neighborhoods where smiling, beautiful people wander around in cinematic settings. Rome is the place in Europe where the baroque *par excellence* finds its full expression in a framework of heathen, masculine steadfastness. In short, the people on the trains expect to see the environs in which I was born and raised. Instead, they see building facades that bear witness to a different Italy, a hostile Italy where people are worn out, vulnerable, and condemned to a lifetime of ugliness and misery.

As seen from the outside, there is no difference between my apartment and those surrounding it. My apartment is but one in a homogenous conglomeration, just as my face, during my years in the neighborhood, has also blended with the faces of my female neighbors. I can't say that I've ever been beautiful, but I have experienced a blossoming in certain periods of my life, and moreover I have a particular aura that has been constant throughout the years. But my facial features are of the sort that do not give way. My face does not move when put under pressure. There is no elasticity that allows it to yield, rather it holds fast like asphalt or a dry branch. And such faces don't age well, for something will come along and break them yet.

Seen from the outside, my home in the building by the tracks is identical to those surrounding it – however, inside, my apartment is the very image of me and my history. The two-room apartment is filled with items from the apartments by the Pantheon. When they were sold, they were partitioned into eight, of which none was smaller than 150 square meters and three were larger than 200. When it was all being sold off, the volume of furniture was vast. Most of the buildings' contents needed to be liquidated, and so they went to auction, but our family lawyer made sure that a fraction of everything remained, and that fraction is being kept with me. In my sixty-seven-square-meters I have household goods spanning 400 years of family history. There are rococo bureaus, velvet draperies, lion-footed chairs, chaises longues, and golden fabrics, old shoes made of yellowing silk with matching corsets, lamps with drops like crystallized tears which the headlights from passing trains illuminate at night. I lie in my ninety-centimeter-wide bed and see the tears being lit up by the beams, and then comes the tremble running through them that must be from the structural vibration that courses through the building when the trains go by. I also have mounted mannequins, maimed female bodies, on which Grandmother used to hang her best clothes because she thought ordinary hangers made them lose their shape. But the most eye-catching things in my little apartment are the mirrors, for mirrors are so clearly out of place when forced into small spaces. Most of the mirrors in my apartment can't stand straight because they are much taller than the ceiling. My provisional solution is to pull them slightly forward and slide wedges between them and the floor. This means that from my bed I can see the ceiling from below. There is something ominous about seeing the ceiling mirrored from below, even if I can't quite put my finger on what.

Each morning I drink black tea in the little kitchen and toast white bread. I listen to the trains below, and look across the mass of furniture at the living room. I always take lengthy showers in the morning. Long spells of water running over my body are the only luxury I can still afford myself. Sometimes I see cockroaches searching the mouth of the drain with their antennae. They don't disgust me. They have always existed in the environments where I have lived, and they are only doing what the rest of us do – seeking a place outside the misery.

But now to the point. Two years after that fateful summer with Max Lamas in Mogliano, I received a call from our family lawyer, Giuseppe Martini. He informed me that the assets I had until now been living on were nearing full depletion, and I would be forced to sell Mogliano if I couldn't be responsible for the upkeep. The surrounding land had been sold long ago, he said, now only the building remained, but because of the decay it was depreciating with each passing year. He said he had also spoken with Mother at the rest home and she was not opposed to the idea of selling it off.

"I'll come and see how it feels," I said.

"Feels?" said Martini. "Oh, Lucrezia . . . "

One week later I took the subway to Stazione Termini, and at Piazza dei Cinquecento I soon found the bus that went toward Le Marche and Mogliano. With that I began the beautiful journey across the Apennines. The sun shone on the mountains, and the bus had a modern spaciousness and was pleasantly air-conditioned as it made its nimble way along the winding road. The view of the long valleys, precipices, lakes, and rising forests was at times dizzying, and I looked out the window, thinking of all the times my family had traveled along this road. My maternal grandfather in old buses with heavy steering and engines that zipped up the hills, the type of bus that went between Rome and the Adriatic coast at that time. Since her youth my grandmother had only driven her Buick Riviera, and sitting in the bus I pictured her as she must have been then – perfumed and with skin as smooth as a stone from the bottom of the sea, the corners of her headscarf whipping at her jawline in the wind. And now me. The next in line, who because of the selling-off would mark the end of a story, closing the chapter on our family in Le Marche, and perhaps – it had just occurred to me – closing the chapter on our family as a whole. I felt remarkably indifferent about this. At the most, I would sign a paper, and then all would be gone. I traced a run in my stockings and drank from a bottle of water I'd purchased at the station. Sweat was trickling from my armpits down my sides and wetting my blouse. I could picture Martini hugging me and feeling the wet, cold fabric against his palms. He'd probably feel mild reluctance and subconsciously connect the wetness of my blouse with the demise of my family.

And so it was – upon arrival in Mogliano I was met by Giuseppe Martini. He embraced me in that cool, correct manner he'd adopted with me ever since my family's assets had run out. Nevertheless, for a split second before letting me go, I felt him press me to him harder, as if in spite of it all I contained a reminiscence of something he wanted to do his utmost to retain. He held open the car door without meeting my eye. I took my seat, and the door slammed shut. Martini drove his BMW hard and staunchly, as a man does when he expects trouble from the woman beside him, because his car, *that* he can dominate, it will never be contrary.

"I don't know if I'll sell," I said when we parked in the forecourt.

Why did I say that? To tease, I presume. To confirm his unspoken theory that nothing about us will ever be simple.

"You have no choice," Martini replied, ice-cold. "You can't keep it if you can't afford to take care of it and – "

"I understand," I interrupted, examining my nails. "I understand perfectly."

Out of the corner of my eye, I could see his fingers whitening around the wheel.

"Lucrezia," he said finally. "Listen. You must listen to me now. For once in your life you will listen to me."

Another deep breath.

"My contract with your family expired two years ago. *Two* years. Do you understand what it means to work for a family for two years without compensation? I have no reason to – "

"Please," I said and held up my hand. "You're free. I will be *fine*."

Martini let go of the wheel, turned toward me, and gripped my hand.

"Lucrezia," he whispered resolutely. "You know very well you won't be *fine*."

I pulled back my hand with a titter.

"Dying is the worst that can happen," I said. "And I'm not afraid to die."

"Dying *isn't* the worst that can happen," Martini replied. "At least not in your case. You'd do an excellent job dying, as did all who died before you. The worst that can happen to a person like you is to be forced to live in misery. True misery, Lucrezia. You'd never be fine with *that*. You are *not* a woman who can be fine living in misery. You are not a woman who can be fine *getting along*."

I smiled at the way he stressed the syllables. How long had he been carrying around this anger? I wanted to say one thing to him, one thing I'd read in a book, namely that "nothing is as dreadful to observe as a person brooding over an injustice."

Instead I said: "You don't know me."

"In fact, I do," said Martini with a bitter laugh. "I know you, Lucrezia Latini Orsi. I know you *far* too well. And I know that when it comes to practical living, you are equally as incompetent as your mother and grandmother."

I thought: Enough. And so I took my handbag, got out of the car, and looked around.

"Ah," I couldn't help but exclaim.

It was the best time of year in Mogliano. The smell of the Adriatic swept in across the land and lay heavy and salty over the rolling hills. Ripe figs hung in the trees down by the stream, and the hydrangeas dazzled in the flower beds. The pines at the bottom of the garden emitted a strong scent of sap that could be caught all the way up at the driveway. Like a natural pearl, the main house was set in the midst of it all, surveying the landscape. I walked across the gravel, took off my shoes when I got to the lawn, and then went around the garden, looking at the fruit trees bending with overripe fruit and the vegetable patches overgrown with wild lettuce.

Martini followed a few meters behind.

"Lucrezia," he said. "I'll give you one week. *One* week. If you can find someone who can help you financially, then I too will aid you. But if you can't summon the funds for the most pressing matters, well – then I'm afraid our ways part here. I'm not one to stay on a sinking ship."

I smiled at him.

"The rats are always the first to leave a sinking ship."

"I have been here," Martini said, voice trembling. "At least in the background. Watching over you, and keeping in touch with your mother. Now I've ensured that you are here. So yes, I have been taking care of you, Lucrezia. It's what Matilde wanted, and I have fulfilled her wish insofar as it has been possible."

I moved closer and touched his arm. Clearly the gesture moved him, for his gaze flitted from my hand to my face, across the hills, and then rested on my face.

"Give me one week," I said. "And I will do what I can. If I can't find anyone to help me, then I shall do as you say and sell."

I stretched up to give him a peck on the cheek and pressed my bosom to his upper arm. I don't know why. Martini wasn't my type, and after his self-pitying outburst in the car he was as attractive as a wet blanket. And yet a charge ran through me when I felt the heat of his arm against my bare décolletage.

Surprise bloomed in his gaze.

"Lucrezia," he began. "It would be improper of me to . . . "

"Oh," I said and took a step back. "Please. It's not you. The fresh air: it can be arousing."

"Would you like me to stay the night?" he asked.

What delusions were now dancing before his eyes?

"Carrying in my bags will do."

Martini lingered before returning to the car. He took my bag from the trunk, and the handbag from the ground, and carried them to the entrance. After that he strode angrily to the car, the gravel crunching beneath his soles.

"Seven days, Lucrezia!" he shouted after me. "I'll be back in seven days!"

His car unleashed a cloud of dust. The motor spun hard and the tires skidded as he turned onto the road. Then all was silent. I went to the house, took my key from my pocket, and unlocked the door. Inside it was clean, but stuffy. The mirrors were covered with white sheets. I put the bags down on the floor, opened the windows and the back door. Fresh, salty air filled the room. In spite of the heat, I lit a fire in the fireplace on the terrace and fetched the pillows for the set of chairs from the scullery. I took my computer and opened my email to see if I still had Max Lamas' address. I did. I started a new email, and wrote:

Dear Max Lamas,
It's me, Lucrezia Latini Orsi. I assume you remember me.

I didn't know how to continue, for how does one email *en passant* and breezily about the kind of thing that happened to us that summer? I ended up writing:

A long time has passed since we last saw each other. I hope you're faring better. It still saddens me that you crushed my grandmother. But I'm convinced that the women in my family also crushed you. In a way, it is what they do.

For a moment, I could picture my mother coming down the stairs, manuscript in hand, placing it on the table in front of me and Grandmother, and slowly saying: "Now let's see what that devil wrote about us." It was best not to touch on any of this, so I wrote:

As for me, I am now living alone and without assets, which is why I'm writing to you. Could you give me one hundred thousand euros? I need to secure the upkeep of the property in Mogliano. I do apologize for the bluntness of the query, but I don't know if it can be put in any other way. I need one hundred thousand euros, and I can't ask you for a loan, because there are no prospects for me to pay back a thing like that.

I took a deep breath, and wrote:

How did it go with the manuscript, by the way? Was there a book in the end?

    Regards,
    Lucrezia Latini Orsi

The nights in Mogliano are hot, long, and dark. You can hear the cicadas in the fields, and the air is still until dawn arrives, then a gentle breeze washes across the hills. It was so pleasant lying there on the sofa. The fire burned down in the fireplace, and the air was cool on my feet propped up on the armrest. It was going to be a long night, and the sounds and smells of the place made it impossible to sleep. Too many memories, I thought. I might as well lie here and remember everything as it was then, if such a thing is possible.

I lay on my side and looked into the embers. And I saw us as we were, the summer after Max Lamas had been cursed and came to us to heal. Grandmother, Mother, the waiters. Me, Marco Devoti, and Max Lamas.

As a child, I was neither beautiful nor intelligent, only extraordinarily rich, and I don't think anyone can understand what such a position can do to a person. People who saw me would think: There goes an ugly little child, and not just an ugly little child, but also an incompetent little child, and so I ceased to exist in their eyes. Luckily enough, I was – at least to begin with – wholly uninterested in anything to do with appearance and presentation. I didn't care about my plain features, nor about my transparent skin and the hatched pattern of veins woven underneath like a spider's web. I would turn around in front of the wardrobe mirror, stand in profile, and list my shortcomings one by one, as though they belonged to another creature, as though they'd have no greater impact on my life than a flaking wall in a house I'd never visit. In short, at that time I was one of those lucky girls who never compares herself to anyone else, for whom their own value is as apparent as gold bullion or diamonds.

My deficient appearance aside, in school I enjoyed a sheltered and privileged status. The teachers took great care not to shed light on my limited talent, for the simple reason that my family was the primary financier of the convent school's every operation. Everything, from classes to evening vespers, was afforded, as liberally as conscientiously, by my grandmother Matilde on the tenth of every month. A choirboy would then hurry that short distance between the convent and Palazzo Latini, bill in hand. My mother would ask him to sit down on one of the fluffy sofas in her office, and one of the waiters would arrive with a glass of lemonade on a tray while my grandmother issued the check using a long, elegant hand. Her distinctive script was achieved with a quill, which she slowly dipped in an inkwell made of bronze and moved over to the paper with the same triumphant pleasure in her gaze as an artist spreading oil paint on his canvas. The boy was then handed the check, and before the ink had dried he'd have hastened down the wide marble steps in Palazzo Latini, along the narrow Via del Seminario, and across Piazza della Rotonda. I'd stand at one of the apartment windows that were six feet tall and watch him go, presumably with a crooked smile on my lips.

In the recurrent parent–teacher meetings about me, it was always determined that the best fruits ripen slowly, and that coal and diamonds are in fact one and the same, but the diamond has taken the time to develop its distinctiveness – something my father, who is a mathematician, clung to throughout my childhood as if it were a great truth. In spite of my low grades, he always thought I was a promising mathematician.

"Indeed," he said, nodding to himself, "the best fruits ripen slowly."

My father. My father who sat on the sofa with an absent gaze, writing his formulas on scraps of paper, those that were to hand, and when he'd used up his own scraps he'd continue on whatever was within reach. That might be receipts or the reverse of a watercolor Mother had painted and was drying on one of the tables next to the sofas, or it might be one of the arithmetic books I had left scattered around. As a consequence, my math notebook sometimes contained long, complicated equations, which exceeded the limits of my math teacher's knowledge. I was proud of this, because my math teacher evinced an attitude that noble children suffered from some sort of congenital mental deficiency. Papa's notes in my book were my way of taking revenge, resolutely asserting that at least half of my otherwise perhaps degenerate chromosomes were razor-sharp.

I'm sure that Papa was very happy with us for a time. He walked around in a threadbare corduroy suit and left his blue backpack on the floor in the hall, teeming with books and pens. He cycled to work, cutting his path each morning through the traffic in Rome. No soul born in our city would subject themselves to that, but Papa radiated an irrepressible optimism about the state of things, so irrepressible that even drivers braked as he cycled forth. And he also seemed to harbor a hope that my mother's family could be brought closer to the world, and if not, then the world could be brought closer to us. Mohammed and the mountain . . . Perhaps this was the reason for the gatherings he arranged for his colleagues at the university. They were invited to ours on the last Sunday of the month, at seven o'clock. All were punctual and let in en masse by the porter. Because not everybody could fit at once in the small elevator, they ascended the wide marble staircase as a troupe. They were unusual, academic people who spilled into our hall on these occasions. People Papa had gotten to know in various contexts – doctors, professors, and occasionally students who were somewhat exceptional and granted the favor of mingling with the cream of Roman academia in an extraordinary environment, where the beating wings of times past could be felt as in a Henry James novel. These

were people who were interested in impossible things –
particle mechanics and quarks, or a type of rare dandelion.
In Papa's set, there seemed to be no limit to the breadth or
meaninglessness of the subject one might obsess over. Rarity
was the decisive factor, as well as the adjacent madness and
the confused, occasionally hunted look that made up the
selection criteria for the circle. And it seemed as though the
academics who were the most confused and detached from
the world were at a premium, which followed the logic that
the closer you wished to be to the core of your life's pursuit,
the farther you were from normal, decent understanding
and behavior. Mother would regard them silently as they
stepped into the hall. She'd go to the kitchen and place
chilled white wines on a tray while Papa took his friends
over to one of the sitting areas. Papa might give Mother an
appreciative glance as she went around with the tray. In
that glance, one could read a certain pride, pride over the
fact that someone like him could have a wife like her. My
father's proud expression stood in contrast to the academics'
embarrassment. It was an embarrassment rooted in their
lack of practicality, being so inexorably subpar at moving
through environs such as ours. We were not an academic
authority and so with us, it didn't work to attempt to trump
another with a display of superior learning. One couldn't
advance by dazzling with one's knowledge of Darwin, or
in any other way showing how grounded one was in the
dismal humus of rationality. With us, everything was over-
whelming and mammoth. And here there was nothing of
the bohemian or the attitude of sacrifice and hardship that
people who feel they have a calling can emanate. Whereas,
in their own hovels, they could at most choose in which
chair to sit, at our home you could choose both the room
and the sitting area. Mother enjoyed their embarrassment.

She looked down on Papa's friends for many reasons, but the most important one was that they cared so little about their appearance and couldn't carry themselves. "Those academics," she'd say after they'd left. "Those academics and their traits – a sweet, piercing scent of moldering onion coming from their armpits."

But in the end, he couldn't handle it. Or rather I think he could handle us as a family, but couldn't handle seeing the world persist in regarding us with its cold, penetrating gaze. It's possible that he managed to digest the cruel remarks written about my mother and my grandmother, at least when he saw how little effect it had on them. But he couldn't handle what they wrote about me. When a paparazzo managed to infiltrate the school and gain access to a file that contained my low grades in black-and-white, a stark contrast to the high ones on my final report card – thereby showing how money from the house of Latini distorted the truth – something inside Papa broke. The article was bursting with pictures that had been taken one afternoon when I was sick and alone at home and so, with a swollen face and red eyes, I'd gone out to buy oranges from a fruit shop near Vittorio Emanuele. Somehow the sentiment conveyed by the end of the article was that I was the end of the road for our family, a rotten cherry atop a now-soured cream cake.

"Worse things have been written of us," said my mother, and dropped the newspaper in the wastebasket.

"They attacked my child," mumbled Papa.

And if you hurt a man's only daughter, you hurt him deep in his soul. He could find no way to recover from those articles, and even if he'd never admit it to himself, I think it was precisely the feeling that he couldn't protect me that finally made him rescind his care of me entirely.

The backpack disappeared from the hall. The complicated formulas disappeared from my notebook, and the feeling of fresh air that Papa had always brought with him into the palazzo was replaced with the damp, aged smell of me, Mother, and Grandmother.

Papa's departure from the Palazzo Latini coincided with the start of seventh grade, and my friends blossoming into women. At first, they were unaware of their newfound power over the male of the species, making them even more enchanting. But soon they'd transformed into spoiled, demanding dolls, and the transformation was painfully clear. Having seen this, I stopped yearning for my late-developing body to enter puberty. Which didn't happen either. The only physical change I underwent in those first teenage years was that my face widened. My nose thickened and my hair took on a fibrousness more typical of a woman in her menopause than a girl. My ankles, wrists, and cheeks swelled. It was as though my body thought water retention would best equip it for sexual maturation. My skin – which was expected to be a noble porcelain white – seethed in revolt, and the bridge of my nose and my high cheekbones were plagued by pimples that gave a scratched and inflamed impression. Nobody could do much to hurry nature along: neither my grandmother, my mother, nor the waiters. None of them seemed to understand how to contend with the absence of beauty. That thin hair of mine was pulled back, as with all other women in the family, and put up in a sleek braid that framed my face. And then they regarded me with bewilderment, unable to fathom what they'd done wrong.

For a long time, my eyes were a very pale blue, like a

child's, and only after meeting Marco Devoti did they begin to darken with the typical depth of sexual maturation.

My grandmother never had a rich social life (and I believe the time Max Lamas spent with us was the most social of her entire life). On the other hand, she had a small staff of servants whom she called "the waiters." It consisted of South American men who had been with us for as long as I can remember. My Grandmother had always called them "waiters." Most of her friends called their servants "assistants" or addressed them by name – that was the most common practice, at least when the person in question had lived in the household for several years. But Grandmother, she called them "the waiters" and rarely used their given names. All three of them came from Latin America, and they had all the usual Latin American aches and pains. One had a liver problem, another said he was suffering from a broken heart. The third had no apparent affliction and so was convinced that his was far more serious than the others'. Each of them had his own special relationship to mirrors. The one suffering from a broken heart could gaze at his reflection for many long hours. He did so when he thought he was alone, but sometimes I, Grandmother, or one of the other waiters might chance upon him.

"Are you staring at yourself in the mirror again?" Grandmother once asked.

"No, I'm not staring at myself in the mirror," the waiter replied.

"What are you doing, then?" asked Grandmother.

"I'm looking for something of myself that I think has gone missing," came his reply.

One of the other waiters thought that mirrors were dangerous objects, for they were one of the places where demons were housed. When a person stood in front of a mirror she opened herself to her own reflection, and that's when the demon slunk inside her. From there, it would cultivate the West's worst characteristics inside that person: egoism and self-centeredness. The person reflected would then be heading slowly but surely toward a painful and entirely self-fulfilling demise. Like rust corrodes iron, self-observation rots the human soul, the waiter would say, and one wondered which books he'd read that made him say such a thing.

The third waiter had more of a political angle. He was of the opinion that mirrors were spies. He said that in all societies there was an evaluating authority, and nowhere was it as well developed as in wealthy countries – where people had been taught to observe themselves. Mirrors constituted one such evaluating authority, and there was no need for enforcement, for people subjected themselves to this evaluation of their own free will and even enthusiastically. Several times a day, you'd measure yourself in front of the evaluating authority, suspending yourself dutifully, of your own accord, and you'd do it gladly. And if your reflection did not elate you, as it almost never did, you didn't give up, you set to work on a plan to become exactly what was expected of you.

"Keeping people in check is as easy as hanging mirrors everywhere, because there is nothing stricter," said the waiter, "than the way you gaze at yourself."

The waiters discussed these theories among themselves. And even if they never arrived at a consensus about the true nature of mirrors, they could at least agree that mirrors had the potential for evil, and so for a few days each summer they covered them with sheets. Grandmother laughed dryly at this – presumably she thought all this unnecessary. I, on the other hand, must say I felt a certain unexpected calm spread through the house on those days.

Nonetheless, I never liked Grandmother's three waiters. I disliked them rather severely. Since I was small, I had been the one on whom they could most easily take out their frustrations with Grandmother (my mother showed early signs of being mentally deficient, and approaching her was never in question). I remember how, when I was to bathe, they would scrub me with a brush they said they'd bought in the perfume department of La Rinascente, but which must in fact have been one of those brushes for scrubbing potatoes. This made me hate bathing as a child, and, somehow, I still have a hard time differentiating between the feeling of immersion in hot water and that of a grater against my skin. My skin would end up shining red, and when I told Grandmother, the waiters said I had very sensitive white skin and that was precisely why it was imperative that I be pristine. Rome's exhaust fumes crept into my skin and nestled deep down in my pores, *behind the sebum*, they said to Grandmother, and repeated themselves in Spanish, as if that would clarify anything, *detrás del sebo, doña Matilde, la suciedad se mete detrás del sebo en la piel de la niña.* Grandmother nodded thoughtfully and conceded that the waiters were probably right. Beautiful, white, sensitive but perfect skin was a mark of class and distinction. Such skin destroyed, on the other hand, could devastate any woman's prospects. I simply had to endure, said Grandmother, and by way of consolation she added that she was made to do the same when she was small, and everything had gone well for her.

"Make sure she gets properly clean," she said before leaving, whereupon the waiters looked at me with malicious delight.

*

I remember the first day of school. It was Grandmother who accompanied me, and my skin was shining red, the braid was like a hard whip stretched over my head, and my dress was pulled tight around my waist. Before we left the Palazzo Latini, she sprayed me a few times with her eau de cologne, which now I suspect was something in the style of Madame Rochas or Rive Gauche. So on my first day of school I already smelled like an aged noblewoman, dry and harsh, which the sharp-tongued girls in my class made sure to point out behind my back when they knew I was within earshot. Grandmother and I walked down Via del Seminario and crossed the square. When we passed by the Pantheon, she stopped and touched my shoulder.

"Lucrezia. There's something I must tell you before you begin this very important day in your life."

She looked at me through those thick glasses that she always wore in those days. Her hair was as still and stiff as ever, unmoving in the sultry wind that carried a hint of autumn through Rome. "It's like this," she said as she crouched down, her knees pressed tight together. "You're about to start school, and this means they'll try to teach you many things that they deem important. Some of it will be useful to you, some of it will be of no use to you at all. Some things you'll understand, some you won't, no matter how hard you try. And it's just as well you find this out at once. Honestly, I don't think you . . . "

Here she fell silent and glanced at me. In her eyes was a look of concern.

"What do you mean?" I asked. "You don't think I can learn like the other kids?"

"Yes, of course you'll be able to learn," Grandmother said. "But I don't think, for instance, that you've inherited your father's talent for mathematics. Or your grandfather's sense for German grammar. You must be prepared for the worst, Lucrezia."

"What's the worst?" I asked, my voice trembling.

Grandmother cleared her throat.

"The worst would be if you inherited your mother's talent. It is, in a manner of speaking . . . "

She searched for the word, moving her lips as though it were on the tip of her tongue, but she could only articulate half of it. Then she looked me right in the eye and stated firmly:

"That means no talent at all, unfortunately."

She stood up tall and looked around the square as if she were worried someone might have overheard.

"What I want to say, Lucrezia," she said, smoothing out her skirt where it had creased, "is that you shouldn't expend any of your energy on the sciences. It won't be worth the effort. You should focus on *languages*."

We followed the small street that runs along the Pantheon and to the school. Right in front of the building was Sant'Eustachio, the wine bar. Grandmother took a seat and ordered a glass of Prosecco. As the waiter placed it in front of her, she wrapped her arm around me.

"Remember what I said," she said. "And don't tell your father about our conversation. And for God's sake don't tell your mother."

She sent me on my way with a pat on the back, and I was swept into the excited assemblage of children, mothers, siblings, and backpacks crowding outside the school. I stood alone in the crowd, looking at the large door that would soon open. I had a sucking feeling in my gut, as if there were a deep force pulling my innards down into a whirlpool. Even then I understood what that whirlpool was: it was the fear of finding myself outside of the Palazzo Latini's walls, for I suspected that outside those walls, laws other than ours would reign in the long run. All the other children had their mothers steadying them, and they all looked calm and expectant. When two nuns along with the abbess and our teacher-to-be finally opened the school doors and welcomed us, I turned to the wine bar and looked at Grandmother. Her gaze was trained on me, and she was mouthing through the crowd:

"*Languages*, Lucrezia, *languages!*"

The appeal for languages recurred in one of the two pieces of advice that Grandmother would give to womankind throughout the years. She offered them freely to the press and any woman who could stand to listen, but for the most part it was to Mother and me, and whether or not we could stand to listen seemed not to matter to her at all, for Grandmother would proffer the advice anyway, always with the same urgency. The first piece of advice that Grandmother had was that as a woman, you should love your body, because it is a gift from God.

"It doesn't matter what you look like," she stated. "A deficient appearance is no excuse to give up and devote oneself to obesity and binge-eating. A woman can bring joy to a man, however she is endowed."

"Look at me," she continued. "My body is no longer what it once was. And yet all the men I'm with certify that the pleasure I give them is indescribable."

The second piece of advice that Grandmother had for womankind was that one should leave the sciences alone and focus instead on languages.

"It is language alone," she said, "that can cast us women free of our shackles and permit us to soar over continents."

"That's not true," my mother objected. "Language is destructive, and if you learn too many you'll end up being unable to spell in your own mother tongue. You must be grounded in something, or else you become a legless bird. Someone who can soar over continents, but is unable to land."

"You make your expensive education sound like a great tragedy," was Grandmother's wounded reply.

"People with languages dream of people with languages," my mother said. "Nothing else will ever do. Is that not a tragedy?"

"Well, let your daughter become a woman of the people, then!" Grandmother shouted. "Let her be like her father's mother! Send her to Cassino for a spell, and she'll learn everything she needs to know about life!"

My paternal grandmother. She was the first woman depicted by Max Lamas in *The Polyglot Lovers* during the summer he spent with us. He sat for long hours on one of the living-room sofas in Mogliano and asked about her, diligently taking notes on everything we said. It was when he was still feeling unwell from what he called *the event*, which he had yet to tell us anything about, but which made him grab at anything else he could possibly focus on. Grandmother's voice was precise and controlled when she spoke about my paternal grandmother. Because she didn't want, as she expressed it, to seem "stingy with regard to emotion." But in fact, Grandmother despised Camilla Agostini. She could never fully forgive my mother for allowing the blood her husband represented to mix with ours. My father was fine, but his origins! I believe she thought you had to keep an eye on the genes; they could play tricks, skipping over one generation only to unleash a scourge in the next.

But Grandmother was right about one thing. A woman like Camilla Agostini would never be one to lay claim to continental travel. She was a classic southern woman, one of those who wore dark clothing every day, brown on Fridays, as though she were a widow long before her husband died, which perhaps in a way she was. She went to church every afternoon, sat in the half-light with the other women, and repeated *Santa Maria prega per noi* while inhaling the incense the ambulating priest was spreading in a censer. She was a serious woman who never smiled, for the simple reason that she thought life offered nothing at which to smile. On the odd occasion that there was in fact something to be happy about, she still did not think there was any point in smiling because the absence of a smile was the best protection against envy.

This is what she used to say when Papa was little:

"Enough with the horrible smile, Benedetto. People might think you have something to be happy about."

But she also realized that this way of thinking was typical of her class and origins, and she'd probably sensed, before she met my mother's family, that this wasn't the only way. The life of a woman, she suspected, could hold more than dour insights, downtrodden postures, chapped hands, and the laments of age. There might be something else to grow toward. Something greater than fatigue and a muted daily life with a man slumbering on the sofa. She could sense this aspect of femininity by instinct, but she could not grasp it. She herself had grown in darkness, and she believed this to be her lot.

"Men can die in battle," she said to Papa. "But the far more painful everyday death, that belongs to Woman."

My father's town, Cassino, sits between Rome and Naples and has neither an old town center nor cramped, winding backstreets. There is nothing picturesque, nothing that creates the authentic feeling craved by tourists from Rome, Milan, and northern Europe. Cassino is all perpendicular corners, brick houses, aluminum windows, and ordinary buildings. It is also the town of war cemeteries, and in this respect alone can Cassino be said to be international – here lie Polish and American and German war cemeteries. But international visitors no longer come to the graves. They sit there, as forgotten as they are identical to each other, dilapidated and alone in memory of the lightning-quick devastation of 100,000 human bodies during a few months in the middle of the forties. The train between Rome and Naples does stop, but tourists no longer disembark. They just look out the window, and at most they will think: Why are we stopping here? How unromantic it all looks.

"And how can we be romantic," Grandmother Agostini used to say to my father, "when we're so full of wounds? To expect us to be romantic is like expecting someone with war wounds to be able to dance classical ballet."

And indeed, the town had its wounds. Following the battle during the Second World War, everything was razed yet again by an earthquake in the early fifties. Grandmother Agostini spoke of a roar rising from the earth and a gaping hole suddenly opening. In a few seconds – an eternity for the town and its surroundings – cars and people fell into the abyss. Then the earth closed back up and everything was as silent and satiated as a grave. The destruction was tremendous. Only the war cemeteries were intact, only the grasshoppers from the mountains and the marshes by the sea had not fallen silent, not for one second. Grasshoppers, said Grandmother Agostini, are never quiet.

After the earthquake my father's parents took all of their savings and bought a small apartment in a new building. This is where my father grew up. The living-room window looked out on a wall, the bedroom was cramped, and when the neighbor cooked the stairwell would smell of grease. But from the kitchen you had a view of Monte Cassino, where the convent lay. Papa talked about how Grandmother Agostini spent every afternoon sitting at the kitchen table, looking out at the convent, smoking a cigarette as she drank her coffee. He knew that it was from these moments that Camilla Agostini drew her strength. She knew how to grow without looking down, if you will. Papa often said that his mother had *strength* and *power*, a *real* woman's strength and power, and can't you just hear the barb against my mother embedded in that assertion?

"My mother was the kind of woman who'd never heard of depression, madness, or exhaustion," he asserted with pride. "And all for the simple reason that she never would have had the time for one or the other. She dismissed such things with a snort and a disdainful glance. 'Bourgeois nonsense' she called it, something wholesalers, bohemians, and a certain type of man can allow themselves."

"People like my mother," said my father, "have to think practically. In lire and centesimi and hours and minutes. They can't sit around being pained by their souls."

But as I said, Camilla Agostini suspected there was something outside of her sphere, and that's why she told my father to become an educated man.

"You have to get out of here," she said, "see something else, become someone else. Don't end up a failure like your father."

This wasn't entirely unproblematic, for where were the role models to be found? Camilla made some effort to set a good example. One day she went to Cassino's bookstore with Papa. Papa recounted this episode for me several times. I know it by heart, the way you memorize certain scenes in certain movies that have made a deep impression on you and so you watch them again and again. Sometimes I think this episode with his mother in the bookstore was a turning point in my father's life, an event from which many other events sprung, an impulse to which subsequent movements referred.

I believe it was in September. I imagine the air in Cassino was hot, but no longer burning. And I imagine my father and grandmother had left home around ten, just as the bookstore was opening and the streets were still wet from their morning clean. The pair walked down the town's main street until they arrived at the little store, an orderly space where a husky bookseller reigned from an armchair behind the cash register.

"Can I be of service?" he is said to have asked.

Grandmother cleared her throat and walked timidly to the counter. There she said she wished to have a *great work.*

"A great work?" asked the bookseller.

"Yes. A great work of literature. One of those you're supposed to have read. If you have any such great works here, I should say," she added, looking around the little store.

The bookseller took a long look at her.

"Do you have an idea of what you're after?" he said. "Romanticism? Realism? French classicism?"

"Pardon me?" my grandmother asked.

"You have to have an inkling of *what it is that you want,*" he said, articulating the words slowly and clearly, as though he were speaking with a child or someone developmentally challenged. "Which *literary current* you wish to immerse yourself in."

"I'm telling you," said my grandmother, running her hand over her hair. "I want to have something that one *must read.*"

The bookseller studied his nails. Then he said that if she planned to read the work that all educated people should have read, there was only one really, and that was Proust.

"Well, then I'll have one of them," my grandmother said and took out her billfold. "What does it cost?"

The bookseller grinned, his eyes still on his nails.

"Proust is the *name of an author*," he said. "And the book is not *one* book, but a seven-volume masterpiece. More precisely, *3,600* pages."

He gestured toward a shelf behind him. There were seven luxurious spines all in a row.

"Looks expensive," my grandmother said hesitantly.

"Quality and education have their price," the bookseller replied. "Moving between the classes is expensive. But then it's also an opportunity to – shall we say – become someone new. Like a larva changing to a pupa then a butterfly."

"Did you know that before it turns into a butterfly, the larva has to dissolve into a sauce?" Papa interjected.

"What?" said the bookseller.

"I'll take them," my grandmother said resolutely. "How much do they cost?"

"Do you want them *all*?" asked the bookseller.

"I presume that in order to understand what happens in the third, one must have read the second," was my grandmother's reply.

"Dear Mrs. Agostini," the bookseller said slowly. "Nothing *happens* in these books."

Grandmother stared at the bookseller. However, he did not meet her gaze. Imperiously, he turned his back to her and walked to a narrow, dark aisle behind the cash register. The late summer heat now stifled the room, and the tar-scented steam given off by the asphalt outside wafted in through the open door. From a distance, past the town and toward the mountains, came the music of millions of crickets.

The bookseller pulled out a ladder, ceremoniously climbed up it, and took down the beautiful dark red volumes. One by one he lined them up on the counter in front of my grandmother and Papa, and wrapped them in tissue paper. He handled them slowly and with great care. Papa stood next to my grandmother and watched her clench her ragged billfold.

"Mama, are you really going to buy those books?" he said with unease.

"We've been reading the comics and the sports pages long enough," she replied.

"But I'm not going to read those books," said Papa. "And I don't think that Father will either."

"When you see me blossom, you'll understand," said my grandmother. "Change has to begin somewhere. It must take root properly before it can grow in all directions."

The bookseller was giving her a forced smile.

"How much did you say it was?" my grandmother repeated when all the books lay wrapped in front of her.

The bookseller named the price. Papa had no idea about the sum, but he saw how my grandmother went pale, how her hands and the ragged billfold sank toward the counter.

"It is a very fine limited edition," the bookseller clarified. "One that renders price irrelevant."

In the silence that had overtaken the bookshop, Papa could only hear my grandmother breathing. A whistling came from her chest when she inhaled, and her exhalations ruffled his hair.

"You must excuse me," she said, "but I have to pop into the bank. I'll be right back."

That same evening the biggest fight there had ever been broke out in my father's childhood home. The books had been unwrapped of their tissue paper and were lined up in all their glory on the kitchen table. And almost as red as the books on the table was my grandfather's face as he stood in front of them.

"Are you mad, woman?" he shouted. "Have you completely lost your mind?"

"Do you want your son to become a failure like you?" my grandmother retorted.

"You've never been left wanting since you married me," said my grandfather.

"Thanks to my penny-pinching," my grandmother replied bitterly.

"You're asking for a slap," my grandfather shouted, and raised his hand to my grandmother.

"If you hit me," Grandmother Agostini replied icily, her index finger raised, "then you will never sleep safely in this house again."

Grandfather's hand sank through the air. Then he sank onto a Windsor chair. And there he stayed, rubbing his forehead with one hand.

"With all that we need," he said. "With all that we need, Camilla, you go and buy *books*. We could've bought something we might have enjoyed."

"Maybe that's exactly what I've done," said my grandmother.

"Life is the same wherever you go, don't you understand that? In Rome, in Cassino, in Milan – same nonsense everywhere. There are oppressors and connoisseurs everywhere. What makes you think that our son, with the help of some *books*, will be able to get past them? When we ourselves never have."

When Papa came home from school a few days later, he found my grandmother sitting in the kitchen with the first volume open in front of her. The apartment smelled freshly cleaned and a yellow flower that my grandmother must have bought that day was in a vase on the table. She had combed her hair back along the crown of her head and had fastened it in a knot at the nape of her neck.

"Is it good?" Papa asked, and put his schoolbag on the floor.

He remembered the horror in my grandmother's face when she looked up from the book.

"I think it's too late for me and culture," she said, clearing her throat. "I've never learned book language, and now everything is mixing all together. Your father is right. An old cow will never learn to dance ballet."

After that, the books stood on the bookshelf for the rest of Papa's childhood in that small apartment in Cassino. There they stayed, through the years, as well dusted as they were left alone, with their unbroken spines and unread pages. It was as though they were keeping an eye on the little family. Taking the three of them in as they ate, watched TV, fought, slumbered, and aged.

"When I die you will inherit Proust," my grandmother told Papa when she got old. "You're going to read all seven volumes, and you will see the beauty the bookseller spoke of. I want you to see it for me and your father. Don't stop before you've seen it."

When my grandmother gave up on Proust, the TV constituted her link to the civilized world and her hope for education. She started watching programs about literature, art, and music, programs she had to watch from one of the chairs in the kitchen because her husband wanted to watch different programs on the large television in the living room. Grandmother Agostini jotted down what she grasped in a notebook and told my father, who soon learned never to ask any questions about the disjointed fragments my grandmother used to describe the arts, all the while flipping through the pages in confusion.

"If you meet educated people from Rome, then you must note how they carry themselves," she said in the end. "What they're wearing, what they're eating, and what they're talking about."

And indeed – Papa developed a longing for Rome, not for education and the arts, but for all the pleasure-seeking foreigners he'd heard lived there. He'd heard they moved through the streets and alleys of the capital like white horses through a herd of donkeys. Hungry for love and wearing scandalously little. With his mother's help he registered for university, and together they packed his bags. He found a room to rent at the edge of Rome, and every weekend he'd return to Cassino with a bag full of books and dirty laundry. But Papa wouldn't have too many adventures with strange, foreign women. Only a few days into the first term at university he fell helplessly in love with my mother, Claudia Latini Orsi. She had been registered for the same course by mistake, and the slender, downy nape of her neck became the object of his desire from that very first day of the course and on through the months at university. He himself thought it unlikely. This wasn't what he'd imagined, but now the very sight of a woman's nape made him feel a strong pull throughout his body. Not only that, but it was a nape of guaranteed dark and Italian origin, a nape on which dark hairs lay like iron filings on a magnetic field leading down toward her shoulder blades, and whose owner didn't have the arch look the Scandinavians on Piazza Navona had. No, my mother's gaze was already tired and disinterested, veiled by something Papa couldn't put his finger on, but that he thought was an inner sense of security, a curtain before treasures to be discovered.

After three months, they'd made up their minds: they loved each other and would marry and happily live out their days in Rome. Of course, Grandmother was opposed to the idea, but her husband the marchese granted his approval from Mexico. He thought it was time we got new blood in the mix, and Papa was as good as anyone.

"You may get married," Grandmother Agostini said when he told her about Claudia Latini and the upcoming wedding. "I'll visit when everything is over and done with. Then I'll get to know my daughter-in-law, embrace her as if she were my own. But parties with the nobility in Rome, that's not for your father and me. We'd only make fools of ourselves."

Six years would pass between the wedding and my grandmother's arrival in Rome. I was six years old then, and of course there was no talk of Camilla embracing my mother like a daughter. My mother isn't someone you can embrace like a daughter. Not even Grandmother would attempt such a thing. Camilla Agostini arrived with the train from Cassino, and spent exactly five hours with us. During those five hours, Grandmother and my mother managed to give her a tour of the ten-room apartment in Palazzo Latini in which my parents were living. They also gave a tour of the apartment above, where my grandmother lived. My father's mother was shown all the portraits of our forefathers dating back 400 years. She met Grandmother's waiters and ate their meatballs and tomato sauce. She was shown the Pantheon's cupola from Grandmother's bathroom window and sat under the magnificent trees on Mother and Father's terrace. She could also clearly see that her son worshipped his wife, and that she treated him like a hick, like a know-nothing from the South. In retrospect, I can imagine how brutally unjust the world must have seemed to Papa's mother in that moment. How hard she had fought to get her son to grow beyond the province, the swamp air, and ignorance. All the stairs she'd cleaned. The seven volumes she'd lugged home, which then sat unopened on the shelf. The battles with her husband, all to now see her son as a person of lesser stature, a know-nothing, an attendant to a woman who was the essence of everything that was Other.

Truth be told, as a child I remembered my father's mother only as an ill-dressed old woman hobbling around our rooms, her bag clutched like a shield to her chest. We all sat together in the dining room as the waiters prepared lunch. My mother hadn't gotten ready for the day, but sat unwashed and unbrushed at one end of the table. Across from her, at the other head of the table, sat Grandmother. Between them, my father and I sat on one side, and Grandmother Agostini alone on the other. And no, as Max Lamas later wrote, my mother and my grandmother were not fundamentally mean people. They always listened to what people had to say. But they did so while regarding the person in question as though they represented an insoluble problem, and so also with an utter lack of interest. There are people who can manage to speak when faced with such a look, and there are others who cannot. My father's mother made an attempt. The effort as well as the courage she had to summon must have been colossal. She who had barely been outside Cassino was now sitting in a Roman palazzo, in a room as large as her entire apartment, together with the Marchesa Latini and her daughter. They were two people she'd only read about in weekly magazines, two people she'd always thought seemed made-up and unreal, but with whom she now was to converse. Around her hung portraits of the family's former heads, and from certain large, glossy paintings, jowly, straight-backed women looked down on her, mouths etched with disapproval. Now and then the South American men turned up, and the marchesa and her daughter kept pointing at their glasses to alert them to the fact that it was time for a refill. I remember her catching her breath, and how clearly that breath could be heard in the silence. And then she began to speak. She spoke of the train journey from Cassino to Rome. How full the train had been, how she'd feared that Papa wouldn't be there to pick her up at the station, and how her heart beat in double time when she laid eyes on him, for nearly six years had passed since she'd last seen him. She must have thought that the comment about those six years she'd had to endure away from her son might insult my mother, for then with a tremble in her voice she added:

"He is my only child, after all."

My mother looked at her. It was silent in the dining room, only the sound of the waiters clattering in the kitchen could be heard in the distance. My mother said:

"Why do I get the feeling that you hate me?"

My father's mother opened her mouth and closed it again. She glanced at Papa, who was staring at the table. I could see a vein throbbing in his temple, and for a moment I feared he was preparing to do something significant. I couldn't picture exactly what it might be, but it was as though an explosion were imminent. But before anything could explode that afternoon, Grandmother said calmly:

"Of course she hates you, Claudia. You're married to her son."

Father's mother said nothing more that afternoon. She sat on her chair, blinking over the bloodshot whites of her eyes. Her face was in flames, and dark contours of sweat were spreading under her arms. Eventually the food came, and we ate in silence. I don't have any other memories of that lunch and I've never wanted to ask Papa, but there is a picture that one of the waiters must have taken. In it you see Grandmother Agostini standing next to Mother on the terrace. Mother is glancing off to the side, as if she'd caught sight of something in the air that was more important than her presence in the only picture that would ever be taken of her and her mother-in-law. Grandmother Agostini, on the other hand, is looking straight into the camera. She seems to be biting into ice: her tense jaw stretching her mouth into a thin line, her eyes unsmiling.

Four hours after Camilla's arrival in Rome, we were back at the station, this time to say goodbye. The fast train wasn't going to depart for an hour, and Papa insisted that Grandmother Agostini wait and that we all sit somewhere, someplace cool, and have a drink in anticipation of the departure. But Grandmother Agostini insisted that she would take the usual southbound train. It was one of those trains that seems to stop at every milk stand, but that would save my grandmother from having to spend more time in Rome, the city she already thought of as a wellspring of dishonesty, chaos, and deception.

As she climbed onto the train, she turned to my father and said:

"Never forget who you are. Don't let anyone walk over you."

They were worn-out words, but nonetheless they conveyed a certain drama. A quiet drama, a drama aware of its rung on the social ladder. A drama that would never go to excesses or overflow to make itself known. A drama that would rather flee than put up a poor fight, which, when it comes down to it, is perhaps no drama at all. You could say it was a reserved and, by necessity, suppressed drama. And it left my father paralyzed on the platform.

"I'll never forget who I am," he whispered. "And I'll always be proud of where I come from."

Grandmother Agostini cleared her throat, and she squinted out over the crowds moving between the tracks in the heat. She said:

"The place you come from is nothing to be proud of. The place you come from is a village in a swamp that was bombed to bits. It could be hell. And well, in fact, it is."

She took hold of one of her bag's straps, as if she had to hold on to it to gather the power she needed to say this:

"But you, you have grown like a lotus flower from the shit. And, truth be told, so have I."

With these words, she turned and strode with determination into the train. We lingered outside, and I think my father was trying to catch a glimpse of her through the window, but the sharp sunlight meant that all you could see was the reflection of the outside – the hustle and bustle, the train cars all around, and us. He started pacing the platform. He reminded me of a worried dog. He was mumbling *but I don't see her* and *she's nowhere*, now and then uttering a sound of surprise. I'd never seen him like that, neither after nor before. By my mother's side he always seemed so self-possessed. I assume that's how it is when you join a family that seems to have it all – you cling to the values no one can ever strip you of, which when all is said and done is a matter of pride, and if you don't really know what it is that you're proud of, then there is pride in simply holding your head high, in the gesture itself.

After a while the train rolled out, and it was as though the entire vehicle were Grandmother's back, wholly and implacably leaving Rome. Riding the tracks out past the angular, irregular buildings around the station, with those antennae that every house owner seems to have installed on the roof themselves. The train that contained my grandmother glided past them with its gigantic dignity, and its broken heart. Behind her, she left her only son, and who knew when, and whether, she would ever see him again.

When we walked out onto Piazza dei Cinquecento, my father was crying. He made no effort to hide his tears. He let them fall even though everyone we passed stared at him. In the taxi he dried his eyes, and when we came to our house, the tears were gone. The only trace of sadness was his red-rimmed eyes, which no one would notice for the simple fact that in my mother's family no one looked anyone in the eye without reason.

The cold woke me. It must have rolled in over the land at dawn, and the hills were now cast in a dim light. I pulled the blanket around me, went into the living room, and turned on the computer, but still there was no email from Max Lamas.

Borges writes that mirrors and copulation are abominable, since they both cause the population to multiply. That assertion probably shows a comprehensive goodwill toward nature, because humankind as a creature, at least as seen from above, seems by and large destructive, craven, and detestable. In this it most resembles, at least according to the author Roberto Bolaño, a rat. But contrary to Borges's view, mirrors were, for Marco Devoti and I, the summer he and Max Lamas visited us, more than a way to multiply ourselves – which we thought formidable in and of itself – but also a way to multiply the pleasure of what we eventually undertook in my little bedroom.

Ostensibly, Max Lamas' assignment was to write a piece of reportage for *La Stampa* about my grandmother, portraying her as "the last true marchesa in Italy." In this portrayal, Grandmother would figure as a sort of relic from a time gone by. Even if she was now irrelevant, appearing as she did in her true guise, she still symbolized something real and authentic from Italian history, and the past was something to look back on and rally around at a time like this, characterized, not for the first time in Italy, by deep chaos. That's what the conservative editorial staff at *La Stampa* had thought, Max Lamas said when he called Grandmother for the first time. And it was decided that, in order to really get to know Grandmother, he would spend an entire week with us at our summer house.

It was the end of July that year, and Max Lamas was to fly to Rome, take a bus over the Apennines, and then be picked up by the waiters in Mogliano. His arrival was preceded by detailed preparations carried out by the waiters. Among other things, old family portraits were fetched from the apartment in Rome and hung in the living room in Le Marche. The windows were cleaned and the furniture was moved around over the course of a few days so that the waiters could clean every corner. Once the house had been cleaned, Grandmother's waiters, who were almost never in agreement and whose constant bickering faded into background noise after a few days, traveled down to the market in Mogliano and bought large bouquets of white and orange lilies, which they placed throughout the house. After a day or so, the scent of flowers weighed on every room. Everything was now dust-free, shiny, and heavily perfumed. Grandmother slumbered in her rocking chair, presumably already dreaming of how Max Lamas' pen would portray her in *La Stampa*, and of course picturing something grand. Mother was at the rest home in Mondragón and wasn't expected for a few weeks, if she came down at all that summer. The waiters sat on their sofas. One of them was playing solitaire while the other two discussed something that needed doing at the bottom of the garden and how this might be pointed out to the gardener without insulting him. Then they started to talk about other things – South American things – and suddenly I heard one of them saying *the only calm that can arise under certain circumstances is the calm that follows a shipwreck.* In retrospect I've wondered why – of all the things the waiters said during those days – this sentence stood out from all the rest.

When Max Lamas finally arrived, he had an assistant with him. Grandmother and the waiters stood on the ground floor exchanging confused looks as the pair climbed out of the car. Then Grandmother said:

"No one mentioned an assistant."

When she understood that the assistant would also need to be accommodated, a confusion arose that, combined with the heat, must have made both Grandmother and the waiters momentarily forget how the rooms in the house were arranged. This is how Marco Devoti ended up in the room next to mine.

"You'll have to sleep in the light blue room," Grandmother determined.

We all stood in the hall feeling awkward. Max Lamas with his camera hung by a strap over his shoulder, and a bag with notebooks and pens sticking out which, combined with the blazer, gave him the air of an intellectual from Rome. Marco stood next to him. Tall and still, with a bit of youthful acne, even though he, like I, was surely over twenty. I remember his hands were large and clumsy at his sides.

During the first days with us, Marco Devoti hardly said a word. He walked around with a dark mien and lingered in front of various objects in the house. With his arms crossed over his chest and an expression of restrained distaste, he looked at one family portrait after another. It was hard to understand how Lamas had come to choose him as an assistant when he so clearly despised everything we stood for.

"Oh no, he doesn't despise anyone," Max Lamas assured us. "He just has a hard time expressing himself."

My mother, it has been said, has an excellent nose for wounds, and like a predatory fish she can catch the scent of blood from incredible distances. I don't want to say that I've inherited this ability, but this matter of his speech impediment interested me. I tried talking to him to gain clarity, but he withdrew as soon as I approached him. He, however, occasionally went into the kitchen to talk to the waiters in Spanish. My own Spanish is far from perfect, but if I stopped outside I could hear that Marco Devoti's Spanish, in contrast to Max Lamas' hard continental Spanish, was soft and yielding, as though he had learned it in Mexico or Argentina. And indeed, there was something in the diction – when he said certain words or too many words at once – that seemed to compress entire sentences into a muddle of unintelligible syllables. I laughed to myself. The odd intelligible sentence came out of his mouth. I once heard him say to the waiters *why do you stay, don't you notice how they push you around?* And the waiters answered, talking over each other, *Pero adónde vamos señor, díganos usted adónde vamos, y ella sin nosotros qué hará?* (It was as though they'd gone through this possibility countless times, but every time they'd been forced to dismiss it.) They resumed their conversation, and once again Marco Devoti's words tangled themselves into incredible harangues.

"Grandmother can't manage without them," I informed him before I went to bed that same night.

"You're so fine and noble," he replied, without a trace of the speech impediment. "But you are also a little witch. There's something ugly inside you. It sits at the bottom of you like sediment or slime, because you think you all own the world. You have some sort of entitlement. But things are going to change."

"What have the waiters put in your head?" I asked.

He replied that when my grandmother died, *the end* would come for me and my mother. Everything would come crumbling down, and we would be left without a palazzo, waiters, or property in Le Marche.

"You do know you're living on borrowed money?" he said. "And when Matilde dies, that's the end of the loan. You'll have to sell everything you own and have. The waiters say she's like paint on a piece of rotten wood. And some paint can keep an entire house together, but when the paint finally wears away, everything collapses."

"I don't understand what you mean," I said. "It's as though you aren't quite articulating your words."

Marco Devoti leaned toward me.

"And before your fall becomes a fact," he whispered, "I'd very much like to be with you. Alone. You and me, in your room, in front of your mirror."

"You'll have to try harder than that," I replied.

"Don't make anyone try too long," Marco Devoti answered. "When you're in the shit with the rest of humanity it's not going to be the same as it is now. Do you understand? Come on now."

"You're joking," I said. "Do you really think this is how things are done?"

"Come on," he said.

I got up slowly and took his hand, because the proposal was nonetheless enticing. Perhaps my curiosity was related to the speech impediment. How sure of himself can a man with such a blatant lack be? But Marco was full of self-belief as we walked up the stairs to my room. (I think it's related to mothers. They make their sons feel like kings, however they're endowed.) Marco Devoti locked the door behind us and left me standing in the middle of the room while he took a seat in one of the chairs. But now everything was different, because his self-assurance had vanished. So, this was as far as his self-esteem had taken him, and now it was at its end.

This was also where my own assuredness disappeared, and I felt a knot in my stomach when I saw his shaking hands fumbling to light a cigarette. It was clear that he was not a smoker, because he coughed after he inhaled the smoke, and the cigarette fell to the floor.

"I think I shall rejoin the others," I said.

"Wait," he said and picked up the cigarette. "Wait."

I hesitated.

"Just wait a minute," he repeated.

When he'd finished smoking and stubbed his cigarette out in the ashtray, he stood up and began methodically unbuttoning my blouse. He was so focused that pearls of sweat formed on his brow. His pedantry in unbuttoning, removing, and folding might have seemed normal for a very old man, or someone who had spent his entire life collecting stamps or cataloging butterfly wings. But not someone like Marco Devoti, not a self-professed rebel who tried to stir the waiters to mutiny against Grandmother.

"This feels ridiculous," I said.

Marco Devoti ignored this sentence and began unbuckling his shoes, which he placed neatly against the wall, still avoiding my eyes.

"You're shy," I said.

Still no reply came, but he undid my bra and put everything over the back of the chair.

"You're handling me like a piece of dead meat," I said.

"Right now I'm handling you like a porcelain vase," he replied.

"You're never going to be able to see this through," I said. "You're terrified. It's obvious."

I didn't admit that I too was terrified. Marco sat behind me and unzipped my skirt. And then it was hung neatly on the back of the chair. I was now standing naked before him, and he turned me slowly toward the mirror. I've never liked my own image, so I looked down at the floor. But Marco Devoti got up, put his finger under my chin, and made me face the image. I saw the angular shoulders, the uneasy skin on my body, and the unruly hair. Marco Devoti put his hands on my shoulders and allowed them to glide along my arms, over my hips, and down my thighs. He kneeled behind me. Then he did things you wouldn't imagine someone who'd shaken as he had was capable of. To begin with it was nice – perfectly fine, at least – but when he got going, the encounter escalated. I've tried to write about what happened on more than one occasion, but it's nothing that can be recounted in a calm and collected tone. It demands a sort of irrational state of emergency, or in any case a shut and sealed door. I enjoy offering myself up, because that's part of writing, but I cannot suddenly invite even the most revered reader into my bedroom. (But I can say that he, with his pimples and his freckled back, whispered *puta puta puta, te voy a partir en dos*, and I said I wished I didn't understand and he whispered that of course I did, everyone did, even those who didn't speak Spanish, because it belonged to a filthy ur-language of sexuality.)

Regardless. Minutes later I got up and faced him. Marco Devoti had sunk down in the armchair, his legs crossed. I stared at him and he stared back at me. The room was hot and the air thick with the smell of sex. I opened the window. Marco Devoti fetched paper from the bathroom.

"Don't tell Lamas," he said. "He'll send me away."

He gently dried me off and led me into the shower. He showered me slowly and carefully, as though I were in fact the porcelain vase he had mentioned at the start. He carried over the clothes from the chair and dressed me, item by item. Finally, I stood before him again, dressed just as if the clothes had never been removed. Marco took a seat in the armchair and lit a cigarette, which he smoked without his hands shaking one bit.

"I've always dreamed of having someone of your class in that way," he said, without any speech impediment. "And I must say that it exceeded my every expectation."

We continued to see each other in my room for several days, and always in front of that large mirror. We'd enter a sort of trance lasting as long as several hours, always with our gazes fixed on ourselves. It was rare that we looked each other in the eye. Both of us might have our eyes shut for minutes at a time, as if the other person or the room itself were of no importance. Thinking back, I wonder if those were not the most intense and memorable moments of that summer.

One morning at breakfast Max Lamas gave us a disapproving look, and the same afternoon he announced he no longer needed an assistant. Marco Devoti could go home now. And it was as though Devoti had been waiting for that moment, as though he knew it was coming, because the next day he packed his bag without protest, and one of the waiters pulled up the car. We all watched from the door. As he was about to get into the car, he turned around. He raised his hand at me, and I noticed his pinky was more bent than his other fingers, as though he had a hard time straightening it. When our eyes met I understood something about Marco Devoti. I understood, in spite of my youth and my flagrant inexperience with men, that Marco Devoti was a person who, if you will, cannot make love without love. Standing there, I understood that in the days he'd spent with us I had become a wound in him. The thought was uplifting. At least until I saw the car disappear in a cloud of dust. As the dust settled on the road, I was consumed by a gnawing worry that Marco Devoti was the sort of man a woman could never really be with. One of those men who was perfectly fluent in body language, but who could never stand speaking it with only one other person. One of those who is both a hostage and a gift to femininity. And when I went to bed that night I knew this: Marco Devoti would become a deeper wound in me than I could ever hope to be in him.

By the time Marco left us, almost a month had passed since the article in *La Stampa* was published. But Max Lamas didn't seem to have any plans to return home. On the contrary. For the first time in ages he was feeling very good, he said. And the portrait was expanding. A little at a time, but the forward momentum was constant. The more he saw, the more he wanted to write. He wrote every day, couldn't stop, and when he woke up in the morning the sentences and images were crowding in his frontal lobes. When he said this, Grandmother had a happy air about her. The waiters regarded her skeptically when she smiled like that. But Lamas and Grandmother kept talking. You could hear them going through everything – from the fall of the Roman Empire to mold damage in seventeenth-century Roman buildings and the cadence of Italian in certain libretti written by German composers. Every morning the reassuring clatter of Max Lamas' typewriter could be heard as he transcribed his notes. The sound was rhythmic and precise, as though he were writing without pause, as though everything had been thought through beforehand and did not need to be invented during the writing process. Sometimes the clattering stopped, and all was silent for a few hours after lunch. We'd assume Max Lamas was taking an afternoon nap. Then the water would start running through the pipes, and at five o'clock he'd come downstairs. Freshly showered, perfumed, and wearing a clean white shirt. Grandmother said he looked like the *madrileños* of days past as they stepped out onto the streets at five in the afternoon, rested after their siesta and expectant before the bullfights and the life in general that was about to begin.

"Shall we continue?" he would ask Matilde, as if this were a habit of countless years.

"Of course," Grandmother would say, taking his outstretched arm.

And then they would walk the grounds together. Max Lamas stood tall, as though he were the marchese himself, and beside him Grandmother had more of a stoop. They walked the grounds until dusk, and upon their return Grandmother's hair would be disheveled, as though the wind had finally been permitted to grab hold of it.

And perhaps this newly established routine could have continued had it not been for Grandmother saying one night at dinner:

"My daughter is arriving tomorrow."

A waiter dropped a spoon on the floor and another hurried over to pick it up.

"How lovely," said Max Lamas.

"No," said my grandmother. "Unfortunately, it will not be lovely at all."

"How do you mean?"

"You'll see when you meet her."

Max Lamas laughed and said he'd read everything there was to read about Claudia Latini. He was well prepared. It sounded reassuring as he said it, but of course there are some people for whom no one can be prepared, and whose mental topography is impossible to decipher. You have to stand in front of them, look at them, and sense them, and when you do, it may already be too late to save yourself.

Mother arrived in a white car bearing the Mondragón rest home's logo at one o'clock the next day. We heard the wheels on the gravel as it drove through the gate and onto the driveway, and we got up from the sofas and went to the forecourt. Two caretakers had accompanied my mother, and they were the first ones to get out of the car. The male caretaker opened one of the back doors, and out came Claudia. Her feet were the first we saw of her. My mother had very small feet, which she always adorned in high heels. After her feet came the rest of her, and she got out and stood on the gravel, straightening her white knee-length dress and the sunglasses, which covered most of her face, but didn't hide the spots. Brown spots had begun to spread across her face in recent years, and before he left us my father had said they were advancing in pace with her mental illness. In the beginning, she'd covered them with concealer. Constantly, every five or ten minutes, she'd disappear to the bathroom and use the cover stick. Later she seemed not to care as much; the spots could be as they may, plain as a slap in the face. *Yes, here I am, and everything has gone to hell and I stand by that.* When she smoothed her hair with the sides of the glasses, her dark brown eyes looked even darker against her spotted face. Deeper, and more glittering, but also as if they lay across a border from which it was impossible to find a way back to a normal gaze.

Max Lamas tensely observed my mother. It was silent. No clamor came from the kitchen, no humming from the garden. Even the wind seemed to have stilled, and the bubbling from the pool in the garden had ceased.

"Hello," my mother said, smiling at the cluster of us by the house.

Grandmother breathed a sigh of relief. Was this a good day after all? Did Mother's sober arrival mean that all would go well? Claudia walked past us slowly, into the house, where one of the waiters offered to take her bag and shawl. She held them out, but kept the glasses on. My mother is very short and very slim, almost unnaturally so. Once, one of the waiters said it was incredible that so much ire could fit inside a body as small as Mother's, *increíble – tanta rabia en el cuerpecito de doña Claudia.* Now she was in the middle of the room. Looking at the lilies, the mirrors, the dust motes slow-dancing in the air above the table.

"For God's sake sit down!" she shouted at us. "Don't stand there as if you were guests!"

And, as though she were the house's natural hostess, she gestured to the chairs around us. We sat. The waiters and I on the sofas, Grandmother and Max Lamas on two dining chairs, while the personnel from Mondragón were left standing in the kitchen doorway. Mother stayed in the middle of the room. She slid off her sunglasses and put them in her bag. Her eyes were heavily made up, and the spots shone darkly.

"How do you spend your days, Claudia?" asked Grandmother with a soft voice. "Up there, in Mondragón?"

"I write notes about polyglot people from my past," my mother replied, taking a seat. "And then I look at certain indestructible items a friend of mine has saved in a box.

But I might also dream of a man's hand – a man's hand that, like a plane's powerful engine, will lift me up over the clouds."

Everyone in the room stared at her. The waiters fidgeted on their sofas. Grandmother seemed to be searching through her thoughts for a sentence or an insight about my mother's aggravated state. The only one who looked happy – in fact, he looked as though he'd glimpsed heaven, in Claudia's words – was Max Lamas. But then my mother began to laugh, and it was a drawn-out, unpleasant, mad laugh that caused even the smile on Max Lamas' face to fade. She must have laughed for at least a minute, and that's no short amount of time when a laugh is being laughed in a group of otherwise silent people whose eyes are fixed to the floor. Then she stopped, smoothed her hair, and wiped a tear from the corner of her eye.

"Aha?" she said, looking at each of us one by one.

Max Lamas crossed his legs.

"Aha?" my mother repeated. "And on to my errand. Which of you can find it in your heart to summarize this sordid tale for me?"

For a moment, I thought she'd learned of what had transpired between me and Marco Devoti in my room and that this had occasioned her visit. But her gaze was fixed on Grandmother and Max Lamas.

"Well?" she asked as she wagged one of her crossed legs, so that her shoe was now dangling from her toes, its heel aimed at the room like a gun.

"What do you mean, Claudia?" my grandmother asked with her soft voice. "Of which sordid tale do you speak?"

"Oh, Mother," Claudia said. "Unfortunately, playing the spring chicken doesn't suit you at all. With so many years and experiences behind you, it is quite possibly the only role you cannot play. Don't dissimulate in vain. I'm sure I know what's going on in this house."

Max Lamas stood up, hands clasped behind his back, and said:

"Claudia, there isn't much to say. Except that I'm in love with your mother, and she with me."

A small gasp was heard from where the waiters were sitting. I felt faint myself. Max Lamas and Grandmother? Wasn't he married? And didn't he have plenty of trouble at home, trouble with women, and wasn't that why he'd wanted to come to us, to find peace of mind through hard work and socializing? And Grandmother, at her age? And how had my mother learned of this? The waiters must have called her. Whatever the case, the situation was escalating, and Claudia was the one holding the maestro's baton. And the way she was conducting her surroundings, there was only one possible outcome: total and utter destruction. And now Lamas, so ignorant of our family and its intrinsic mechanics, had begun to engage her in an aside.

"I stand by my feelings for Matilde," he said.

My mother raised her eyebrows, leaned her head against the back of the chair, and looked at the two caretakers.

"Now do you see? Do you understand the gravity of this situation?" she asked. "I had to come. A sixty-year-old opportunist is claiming to be in love with my seventy-five-year-old mother. Ha! And you all wanted me to sit in the park drinking coffee?"

"Fifty-four, if I may," said Lamas. "I'm fifty-four."

"Allow me to elucidate, Claudia," said my grandmother, taking one step forward, "as long as I am alive, I have the right to choose whichever man I want."

"But don't you see?" said my mother. "There's something

behind this. He wants something. He doesn't give a shit about you."

"For all her being unwell and dreaming about polyglots and indestructible items in boxes, your daughter seems very – " Max began.

"Oh!" Grandmother shouted. "Don't make it worse! I'm the one who will suffer if you two don't get along!"

Lamas swallowed, left his chair, and took a step toward Claudia.

"Believe me," he said, pointing in the air, "I understand your concern, really I do. I understand your suspicions, and I understand that you, so to speak, want to protect what's yours. All of yours. But I can assure you that I don't harbor any wish to misappropriate any of what your mother owns. I've even suggested to your mother that we, in the event we choose to formalize our relationship, draw up a contract. So that you and Lucrezia can be put at ease."

"Are you having sex?" asked my mother.

"Excuse me?" Max Lamas asked.

"Are you having sex?" my mother repeated.

Blushing, Grandmother averted her eyes, but Max Lamas recovered quickly.

"Naturally," he said as though this were self-evident. "Of course we have sex. It would be madness not to allow our bodies to express the joy we find in each other."

"Since when has sex been about joy?" my mother snorted.

She began to pace. Then she reached into her pocket and took out a cigarette.

"Dear Claudia," Max said. "Allow me to be completely open and honest. I have always thought that life is like a mirror. Of all the information that a person's eye sends to the brain, the brain selects what it chooses to interpret. If you feel diminished and limited, your worldview becomes diminished and limited. If you think that sex can't be about joy, it's because you haven't experienced it and perhaps aren't able to experience it."

"How tiring he is!" Mother shouted at Grandmother. "Does this drivel constitute your sex life? Old people! Forced to look past the flesh and focus on the degenerate physiognomy of the refined psyche."

She let the ember of her cigarette fall on the thick white carpet.

"Enough of your bullshit, *Don* Max," she said. "That's enough. Now you're going to listen to me, and answer my questions without your greasy pretenses."

One of the waiters got up and went to the kitchen, and across the room the caretakers from Mondragón squirmed.

"I'm an autodidact in male devastation," she continued, "so you can't fool me. I also know a thing or two about the flesh. I know that once the body has begun its decay, there is no return."

"Are you calling me a necrophiliac because I love your mother?" Lamas quipped.

"Flesh is flesh," Claudia said.

"But everything is not flesh," said Max.

"Enough metaphysics. Everyone has understood that you're after my mother's assets. But there is *nothing* here."

Lamas laughed again.

"I choose my women for their personalities. First for their personalities, and then by how they are in bed. Always in that order."

"I can't imagine my mother excelling in one or the other," Claudia replied.

"That's because you don't know her," Max replied. "As a person, your mother is funny, generous, and loyal. And she's a fine lover, but I will keep those details to myself."

"You keep your details to yourself!" Claudia shouted. "But convince me. Convince me that of all the women a man like you could have, of all the intellectual and less intellectual women in Rome, Stockholm, and here in La Marche, my seventy-plus-year-old mother is the best you can get! Convince me of that now. Go on. I'm right here."

But Lamas had sunk down in his chair, deflated.

"You'll only seem like an idiot if you think you can hide it," said my mother. "So confess, then we can move on to the next phase of this conversation."

"I'm not planning on . . . " Max replied. "I'm not planning on . . . "

He cleared his throat and slowly rose from his chair.

"I'll leave it at this: you don't scare me, Claudia."

Claudia, too, got up, and they stood there, facing each other in the middle of the room. Max Lamas' lanky, tall body, and my mother's short figure, braced and elongated because of the high heels. Both had their arms crossed, and they were looking into each other's eyes with an intensity that almost made the rest of us lose our breath.

"Know this, Claudia Latini," said Max, moving closer. "In every woman's life, there comes a point when she blooms one last time. When a woman has gone through all her battles, fought her fights, when she's given birth to her children and done her utmost to be loving, and can look back on a life lived, then she blooms one last time. And she blooms in a way that renders the flesh irrelevant."

"Max Lamas is writing a profile of me," Grandmother interjected. "A book."

"A *book*?" said my mother. "About *you*? What exactly is it going to be about?"

She looked at Max.

"If you know what a book is about before you write it, then you don't need to write the book," Max Lamas replied with a smile. "In that case, a vignette will do."

My mother was silent for a moment. She looked at Max Lamas as she looked at people she was trying to understand deeply. And she did that not as a person looking for the soul's mirror, but more as a practiced fish buyer trying to determine how long a fish has been dead from the clouding in its eyes.

"I want to read what you've written," she said. "Would you be so good as to fetch the manuscript? I'll wait here."

She took a seat in the armchair, her gaze fixed in the middle distance. Max Lamas shook his head.

"I see you're used to getting your way. But when it comes to my manuscript, I call the shots. *En mi hambre mando yo.* In my hunger, I decide."

My mother looked at him blankly, before getting up and walking toward the door.

"I could do with a breath of fresh air," she said.

Max Lamas sank into the sofa next to Grandmother, who retrieved a handkerchief from her pocket and wiped his forehead. They regarded each other and shook their heads. I thought I heard Grandmother whisper *everything will be fine in the end,* or *she'll be fine in the end,* I couldn't hear which. They were interrupted by Mother, who was suddenly back at the threshold.

"I'll admit that I crossed a line," she said. "I apologize."

Confused, Max looked at her and then at Grandmother.

"Will you accept my apology? I misjudged the situation. I've been in that rest home for too long. Too many hours in the company of my friend with the boxes. You see, over the summer we were the only ones left. I hope you can forgive me. I'll take my leave in a few hours, I'll just rest a bit first."

"But you'll stay for dinner?" Grandmother asked.

"Of course, I'll stay for dinner," my mother replied with a warm smile. "Be so kind as to prepare a room and drive the personnel down to one of the hotels in Mogliano."

She took off her shoes and put her feet on the armrest. A moment later she was asleep. And when my mother was sleeping that afternoon, it was as though all of Mogliano breathed a sigh of relief. We left the sofas, and the waiters came and smoothed out the wrinkles that had formed. The doors were opened and a pleasant breeze swept through the house. The pool began bubbling again, and the personnel from Mondragón were driven to the village. Grandmother and Max Lamas went upstairs for a siesta, as did I. The only ones who had no peace when the rest of the house was in repose were the waiters. They began to clean feverishly, and one of them was on his knees despairing over the stain my mother's cigarette had left on the living-room floor.

"Something is about to get crazy," I heard him mumble as I walked by. "Something is about to get very, very crazy."

At four o'clock, we reconvened in the living room, and the waiters arrived with a tray of coffee over crushed ice with whipped cream.

"Don't you cover your spots anymore?" Grandmother asked Mother in a mild tone.

"I do, but I can't find my cover stick," she replied. "It must have fallen out of my bag when I got out of the car."

"I can go look for it," Max offered.

"I don't want to be any trouble," my mother said drowsily. "I'll go."

She stood up and then put her hand to her head, as if suddenly struck by dizziness.

"I'll do it," Max said, getting up. "You sit, I'll go."

He was humming as he walked out the door. But as soon as it shut behind him, my mother got up, crossed the room, and locked it.

"Now, no one here is going to open the door before I say so," she said to us.

And to the waiters:

"Not you either," she said. "If you open up for that clown out there, you'll be on the next train to Rome. Sit down."

The waiters nodded mutely and made their way to one of the sofas.

"You're all going to do as I say now," my mother said. "Lucrezia, go up to Lamas' room and get the manuscript. Meanwhile, I'll be sitting here with Matilde."

I hesitated. Reading the manuscript was intrusive, but on the other hand there would be no danger in it if Lamas had really written what he said he had. It was only a manuscript, in the greatest likelihood stuffed with tiring declarations of love for Matilde, and despite the arid reading, no harm would be done. My mother would be leaving us in the morning, and Lamas would forgive her as soon as he overcame his vanity. I walked upstairs and opened the door to his room. On the desk was the typewriter and right there, next to it, was an orderly stack of paper. I slipped the thing under my arm and walked it down the stairs.

"All right, then," my mother said when I came down. "Let's read."

Now Max Lamas could be heard knocking on the front door.

"Hello!" he called through the door. "I couldn't find the stick. Can you open up?"

"Please, Claudia," Matilde pleaded, wringing her hands. "Don't you understand that I love him?"

My mother smiled at Matilde, and in spite of those spots, it was a healthy smile that could have convinced anyone that what was about to be done was the only right course of action. We sat at the long end of the table. First my mother, then my grandmother, and me further down. Max Lamas was outside, looking in at us through the window while pleading with the waiters to open the door. But the waiters did not move from the sofa, as Mother had instructed, and stared blankly.

It was quarter past four that afternoon when our reading of *The Polyglot Lovers* commenced.

As soon as I began to read, this was clear: authors are the most fundamentally egotistical of creatures, and compared to them the global corps of paparazzi are but a caress on the cheek. When an author sits alone in his chamber, he doesn't write what he should, but what he wants. And though on the surface he may seem like kindness incarnate, the devil himself might be residing in his depths. The surface says nothing about the content. Max Lamas had come to us, lived in our house, eaten our food, and breathed our air, and it was entirely likely that he was also sharing Matilde's bed. Like a sheep or a friendly dog – well, an obedient pet, in any case – he had observed us and established himself in our routines. Then, late each afternoon, he had retired to his room and shut the door behind him.

We were looking from the manuscript to the window. There were long passages we couldn't understand because the text was written in several languages, and not just Spanish, Italian, and French, but other languages with strange letters. Much passed us by that afternoon, but we understood one thing: in spite of the dedication at the start (*To the lovers*), *The Polyglot Lovers* was hardly a declaration of love. The first part of the manuscript was about a curse. Then came the descriptions of Agostini and Grandmother. At first, they were, if not loving, then at least kind. But somewhere in the middle, the tone of the text shifted. The narrator's gaze became coolly investigative, and his descriptions of my grandmother became so callous that my mother hesitated before passing the pages on to Matilde. Now and again barely audible gasps escaped my grandmother's throat as she read, and she put her hand to her chest, as though to fend off an icy wind.

I had thought the Latini women didn't age like others did, Matilde read aloud. *I had thought that age only served to ennoble them, fortifying rather than depleting. Now I see this is not the case. For women age in various ways – some steadily and with regularity, like the precise intervals of a clock's swinging pendulum. There are some who are aged by sorrow – a quick and fitful aging, as though things were always being snatched from them. Some can return; others continue their relentless march to the edge. The light in some goes off, as when a switch is flipped; others retain a flicker of their inner light. Some age like air-cured ham – slowly, still appetizing. A few rot overnight.*

She flipped to the pages at the bottom of the pile in front of her, and read:

How long must I feign interest in Matilde in order to meet her daughter? Today Matilde said: She's coming tomorrow. My throat tightened, and I looked down at my plate in the hope that no one would notice. I have dreamed about Claudia since I read about her in the magazine at the World Trade Center. I have dreamed of her during my entire stay in Mogliano. Is this the end of my journey? First, I dreamed of a fantasy woman. Then of Mildred. Now there is only Claudia.

Grandmother's voice failed her. Mother refused to let her continue reading, got up, and tore the pages from her hands. She gathered the sheets that were spread across the table.

Outside, Max Lamas had put his hands to his face while he looked at us through the window. The waiters were as still as stone pillars and didn't seem to know whether to dare look at us, or whether they could retreat to the kitchen. When Claudia had gathered the papers, she put them in a pile on the floor. Then she pulled up her skirt, pulled down her underwear, and straddled the manuscript. With her eyes fixed on Max Lamas through the window, she squatted there for a while before the sound of water on paper and stone flooring was heard. First it was careful and tentative, like someone being forced to urinate without conviction, but then it gushed over the floor, around her high heels, and toward me at the table. One imagines that a limited amount of liquid can fit in a bladder, especially in people as small as Claudia, but that afternoon my mother demonstrated that this was not the case. We have much more space inside us than we think. Grandmother sat apathetically on her chair and looked at Claudia, then went upstairs. The waiters left their sofa, but Max Lamas was frozen outside the window. Finally, my mother stood up, trampled around in the puddle, and planted one foot on the pile. She tugged her skirt over her thighs and went upstairs. As soon as she left the room, two of the waiters covered the mirrors, while the third fetched a white tub of water and soft soap. He picked up the wet pile of paper and carried it out to the garden, arms outstretched, then he retrieved the tub and carried that out as well. Me, I went up to my room. I didn't understand why the waiters were helping him or why my mother was allowing them to, but from the window I could see Max Lamas and the waiters moving between the tub and the washing line. After about another hour, maybe two, Max Lamas' entire manuscript was hanging from clothespins on the line and drying in the night air.

The days passed without a reply to my email from Lamas. I weeded the garden, raked the gravel on the driveway. I rummaged through old things in the cabinets, found boxes of items that must have belonged to the waiters, which they must have forgotten when they took the boat to South America. A stuffed quetzal from Guatemala, a silver buckle wrapped in paper with a sticker from a market in Belize, and a long hairpin of deep red wood topped with jade stones. I also found clippings about us from magazines, mean things written by ill-willed pens after Grandmother's death. I put them back in the box without reading them. The heat was unbearable. I considered packing my things and traveling to the coast, checking in to a small hotel, and spending some of the money the sale would give me. Not before it cooled off, in a few weeks, would I return to Rome.

But that very night I passed the mailbox down by the road. Out of an old habit, I opened it. There lay a thick rectangular envelope. My name and address were typed, and I was well acquainted with the typeface. I walked back to the house, poured a glass of wine in the kitchen, and went up to my room, sat at my desk, and read.

Stockholm, August

Dear Lucrezia,

I would like to begin this letter with a series of polite phrases.
And I'd like to write a few pages recollecting my time with you.
About how as a person, you think you inhabit a house, but a
house inhabits you as well. Your house has occupied me, I'd like
to say, your house and your garden and all of you have not left
me for a moment since I left you. And the fact that it was I who
crushed Matilde sits like a stone at the bottom of me, refusing to
let itself be broken down. A person dying of sorrow – there is no
consolation, even more so when you yourself are the cause! If this
is any comfort, I have been dealt my punishment. We are but
lovers, I tell myself, and we dream only of understanding. And yet
we have the strength, the power, and even the will to destroy one
another's lives. I'm shuddering at the banality of my words. So, I
will get straight to the point. You're asking me for one hundred
thousand euros and I will give you the money. I'm enjoying a certain, if modest, prosperity. However, I'd like to ask for something
in return.

After what happened in Mogliano, I went home to Stockholm, the
din of ruin in my ears. I hated myself, and I hated my manuscript.
And yet I was unable to part with it even during the journey, and sat
with that wrinkled pile of paper in my lap (and I can assure you it
did not smell like the delicate calves' livers at the beginning of Joyce's

Ulysses — *your mother's venom seeps through every membrane and is apparent in all of her bodily fluids!).*

Once home, I was invited to a pre-Christmas gathering. There, I caught sight of a critic with good judgment, whose path over the previous years had crossed mine in various ways (I'll spare you the details). On impulse, I asked him to read my manuscript. He accepted without hesitation. It was the start of something impossible to foresee. I traveled out to see him with my only copy of the material. The pile, of course, was tarnished, but it was also a slice of life. To force it through a photocopier would have been to kill something undefined . . . It was winter when he received it. I still recall the storms and the cold of those months. He lives by the sea in Stockholm, and Stockholm is a striking city, and in winter it always seems frozen in its own beauty. He was very pleased when I arrived, and his joy warmed even me. He invited me into his home, going so far as to show me the room where the reading would take place. I still remember the look on his face, as though touched by the holy or mystical. He said that this was exactly what he needed to move forward. Something greater than himself, something he could devote himself to. It soothed me, as though I had put my manuscript in the safest place in the world, and everything that would come of this moment would repair the chaos that had characterized my life of late. This is exactly what should be done, I thought, this is the only possibility and the only right option. He showed me into his office, went over to the table, and put down the papers. He did everything with a ceremonious calm, as though this were of the utmost importance for him as well.

"The manuscript looks like it has lived," he said, with a shaky smile.

I wondered how long he'd need to read it. He replied: A few weeks.

Days passed, then weeks. The ease I felt when handing over the manuscript soon disappeared, and was replaced with a worry that became a severe restlessness. I wanted to call him and ask exactly how long the reading would take. But then I'd lose my dignity, and losing your dignity, when it's all you have left, is foolish. I had nothing to live for but the manuscript. My divorce was a fact, and in recent years all I had done was end relationships. When I entered into new ones, I soon ended them, too. I was like a train on the type of Russian railway that's purpose-built to outwit the enemy – whatever I did, the rails would suddenly end and I'd be left standing alone on the tundra. Well. I wanted to know. How many days and how many hours would the reading take? I wanted him to time himself, time how long it took him to read one page, and then make a rough estimate of the total duration. I'm sure you're smiling. But you're smiling because you don't understand. Imagine a mother being separated from her child. Each minute is torment. He could have taken it, and made something of it all his own, or simply allowed it to disappear. Why hadn't I copied it before handing it over? What is the use of that undefinable scent of an original when you stand to lose everything? I fretted, but I was still holding back. I restrained myself, tried to put my energy into getting a grip on my life, and coming up with new things to write. And time continued to pass, without a word from my friend. I convinced myself that he'd found the manuscript so gripping, he was rereading it. I also told myself that maybe he didn't know what to say. I tried to call, but a strange voice that I thought might belong to a cleaner answered and I didn't know what to say, so I hung up. But then I thought all I had to do was be honest, so I called back, but no one was answering anymore. Maybe he's sick? I wondered. But when I inquired with mutual acquaintances, I heard he was healthy, working every day, and had even met a woman, who'd moved in with him.

As soon as the woman was mentioned I knew she was the one who'd answered, and that she also had a hand in the game. My friend must have told her about the manuscript, and maybe he'd let her in on the reading. An unknown pair of eyes, of whose judgment

I knew nothing, had read my intimate story. I wasn't ready for that. I felt like a hatchling, still wet after cracking out of its shell, and I couldn't possibly set out on the first flight: a stranger reading it. I felt naked and enraged – a ridiculous combination, of course. I wanted to go to the critic's house, fling open his door, storm in, and retrieve my manuscript. I couldn't keep these thoughts to myself, so I shared them with my medium, Mildred, who for various reasons knows the critic in question very well. She said she'd conduct inquiries. A few days later she called me up and asked me to forget the whole matter. Forget the whole matter! I shouted into the phone. Forget the whole matter, she repeated. How can I! Just forget it, she said. It's just words and paper. Write another manuscript, do something else with your life. Can I come in for a session? I asked. I'm very busy right now, she replied and hung up.

Everything seemed hopeless and incomprehensible. I told my ex-wife, who's never stopped being supportive. She took my worries in her stride. Don't panic, she said. Slowly, methodically, and steadily, you should get the facts. We're going to get the lay of the land. Then you'll make a plan, and finally, you'll act. Machiavelli's prince couldn't have said it better. She wondered whether the critic still lived in the house by the sea. She advised that I find out his working hours and visit the house when he wasn't home. She'd seen the house in magazines, and knew how it was constructed, the size of its windows, and how easy it was to see what was happening inside. She said that maybe I wouldn't get clarity at once, but if I was patient the situation would open up and reveal hitherto unimaginable possibilities. One must trust that things will turn out as they're supposed to, she said, and I thought, yes, one must learn to have that kind of trust. So, for a few dark afternoons I was supposed to stand there looking into the house, to see what was happening inside. I was to get a sense of the woman. I would see if she was walking around with a stack of papers, reading. I would be able to knock, be honest, and ask for the papers back. But above all I'd have something to do, said my wife. I would become my own little private detective, and it would quell my worries. I said I didn't want to spy. It's not about spying, it's about your manuscript, she said. Your missing manuscript, your child. Honor your work, she said. And this is how my new routine began.

My first visit to the house was on a clear day at the end of January, or possibly at the start of January, that year. I drove out to the suburb by the sea, parked in town, and walked up the little forest road at the end of which my friend lives. The house is encircled by a fence and a gate, but because the garden, so to speak, ends at the sea, you can easily get onto the property by going out onto the ice from the forest. I had to climb over the round rocks at the end of the residence to reach the garden. There were tall conifers with trunks as thick as men. It was four o'clock and a weak, vaguely apocalyptic winter light fell across the archipelago. The house was lit up inside, and from where I stood I could easily see what was happening in each room. I saw the woman. What struck me first was that she was unlike the women my friend usually has, a real downgrade compared with his spectacular ex-wife. For some people, it's all downhill when they break up with their better half, I thought. The woman was petite with mousy hair. Her clothes were baggy, gray and beige. She might have been around forty. She was taking quick, determined steps, as though she were hovering just above the floor, her feet tense. When I first saw her, she was cleaning, moving like a weasel between the rooms. I settled in under a pine tree, leaned against the trunk, and stuck my hands under my armpits to keep warm. My God, I thought. Why is this happening? But such questions have no answers. All you can do under certain circumstances is stay your course, if but to see where it leads. It's a little like asking yourself what the use is of knowing the meaning of peripeteia, or if knowing the meaning of peripeteia will somehow change your life. I'm sorry, Lucrezia. I realize I sound confused. Clearly, I haven't fully recovered yet.

From my hiding place, I saw the woman go into the kitchen and take something out of the refrigerator, only to sit down and watch TV. She was on the sofa for ages, sitting tall, staring at the large screen in the critic's house. I came closer so I could get a better view of the television. I forgot the cold for a second when I saw those moving images. I never watch TV at home. I've always thought that TV series are awful and books are what will endure, but this was an eye-opener. I forgot about the manuscript. Suddenly I felt like I remembered how I used to feel before all of this began, when I was writing different things and my life was heading down a different track. Imagine, all the women I've had, I thought, and now I'm standing here, freezing, alone, and illicitly outside someone else's house. And I thought about what those other women had been like. Hot plants at the bottom of the sea, reaching for me, filled with longing. And now I was standing here and the woman before me was plain, uninteresting, and a TV watcher. Perhaps you're wondering what right I have to complain about her, when I, by spying, was committing the injustice? But it was never my intention to commit an injustice. Perhaps it's a feeble defense, but really it was never my intention. Some might contend that I've done cruel things in my life, but deep down, I'm actually rather nice.

I repeated the same procedure for several days. I traveled out to the house, stood there for several hours from dusk onward, and went home again. It became a habit. And having a habit is calming, even if the habit is meaningless. It gives you a fixed point, and everything else has to arrange itself around the habit. Each morning, I got up, ate breakfast in my small apartment in Kungsholmen, took a walk, ate lunch, rested, and then drove out to the house. I started to enjoy the view as the light dimmed over the water, and the sea's scent hung in the air in spite of the cold. I took pleasure in the sea, it being part of the image of Stockholm in a way that I've otherwise only seen in Venice and Treviso, but the difference is that the sea in

Stockholm has retained its wildness. It's as if the city were brought into nature, not like in Italy where nature is always brought into the city and subordinated to its decadent principles.

But the woman inside didn't watch TV every day. To my surprise she also read the critic's books. She pulled up a chair, reached for the highest shelf of the bookcase, took out a book, and then sat on the sofa with the same concentration as when she watched TV. Apparently, that was how she did things: methodically and one at a time. She rarely looked up from the book when reading, seemingly hypnotized by the text. It was fascinating, because many people, me included, have forgotten how to read with concentration. Maybe it takes a person like that to read in that way, people who naively abandon themselves to the text, whatever the text is like. Sometimes she appeared to be scrunching her forehead, but she never looked up from the book. Standing under the pine tree in the cold, I would have given my right arm to find out which book it was. Clearly it was something from the critic's personal library, and such libraries usually reveal a thing or two, both about the person and about the world order in a wider sense. I unsuccessfully tried to glimpse the title and the color of the book. Then it dawned on me that I could bring binoculars, and the next day I brought my opera glasses with me and saw that she was reading Michel Houellebecq. Michel Houellebecq! I couldn't believe my eyes. Can you imagine someone who never reads anything, because you could see at once that this woman had hardly read anything, reading Michel Houellebecq! It must be like a person who can't swim being thrown into the English Channel or some other body of water that's inhospitable to the human species. There, under the pine, I laughed out loud. As soon as I arrived home I called my ex-wife to tell her, and she too laughed. We laughed out loud together. She said I should break one of those windows, go in, and save that poor woman. I promised to consider it, and we snickered. But I told my ex-wife something else too. I tried to explain to her how I'd never seen a woman do things like the woman in the house did them. Quick and weaselly, and yet with a strange finesse. My wife replied: "It's probably true, Max, that you've never seen a woman do anything at all." "What do you mean?" I asked. "You've never seen anyone. You've only seen yourself, and the women you've had have only been mirrors in which you saw your own reflection." My wife has a knack for grabbing hold of all my nerves at once and giving them a yank. Was this true? In that case, everything was dreadful.

I kept watch outside the house. I knew what time the critic usually came home, and about an hour before that, I'd make sure to be gone. But one day he came home earlier than I'd anticipated, and I had to dive behind a bush at the edge of the property. I watched them going around the house, each one engaged in their tasks. A moment later they were kissing, but that's when I stopped watching and went to my car. Even when spying, you have to respect people's integrity. When a woman takes off her clothes in front of a man, it should be of her own volition; there's nothing more to say about that (even if . . . well, it doesn't matter).

By then, I'd be smiling on my drive home. I felt a soft, hot joy inside me, a joy that can only come from one source. It was as clear as the pulsing in my ears or the blood pounding in my temples when the woman appeared behind the window. For long spells, I forgot the entire manuscript. Maybe my wife was right. It was the first time I'd regarded a woman without trying to see my own desire or the effect of my words.

"It's like reading a blog," she said. "If you read someone's blog long enough, you'll end up liking the person."

I didn't know if I agreed, because I read blogs by people who I know have the right to say what they're saying, but whom nonetheless I find unlikeable.

"You're changing," she added. "It's like something died or is removing itself from you, and underneath is something that can grow. I'm sure that everything will turn out fine, Max."

Her words moved me. You don't know who you marry, but you do know who you divorce, because in moments such as those, all a person's low watermarks are revealed.

"There's no one like you," I said. "You're unique. And part of me will always love you." My wife cleared her throat, said that she would very much like us to be friends, but she'd thank me not to be pathetic.

"What do you suggest I do?" I asked.

"Knock," she said. "Knock and tell it like it is. Say you wrote a manuscript that should be somewhere in the house and you've come to pick it up."

"I don't know," I said. "I don't feel ready."

"Soon it will be spring," my wife said. "Then it will be light, and there won't be any more dark afternoons. Are you going to sneak around the house at night, then?"

"But I have to keep doing this," I said. Watching the plain woman reading her terrible French book, watching her TV shows and documentaries, I couldn't imagine a more meaningful way to spend my time.

"Oh," my wife replied. "Maybe you've fallen for her?"

"But I don't even know her," I said.

"Get hold of the manuscript immediately," she said. "Knock, tell it like it is."

"I'll think about it," I said, and for a few days I sat at home, pondering. But I came to no conclusions, so on the third day I went out to the house to continue my habit. But the culmination of these events had begun on its own, because on the next day, as I was standing in the dark, the critic walked through the gate. Again, I dove behind the bush. The critic entered the house, and they began talking. The woman looked sad, and I'd have given anything to find out what he'd said that had made her so unhappy. A moment later, the door swung open and the critic emerged, went through the gate and toward town. I was standing dead still in the middle of the garden and, by some miracle, he didn't see me. When he'd *disappeared down the hill, I approached the house to get a better look at the woman. The weeks of peeping had made me bold, and I was just a few meters from the window. Suddenly, the woman took three steps toward the window, put her hands around her face, and looked right out, at me. I froze on the spot. Oh hell, I thought. It's all over! I was motionless and hoped for the same luck I'd had a moment before with the critic, but my eyes had already met hers, and by her expression, I could tell she'd seen me and that I'd frightened her. And yet both she and I stood there, frozen stiff. Out of the corner of my eye, I saw snowflakes falling. The pines were still. Slowly, I started for the gate. Almost there, I heard the door being flung open. I turned, and there in the doorway was the woman.*

"Wait!" she shouted.

Our eyes met again. She crossed her arms over her chest to fend off the chill.

"You're the author, aren't you?" she asked.

"The author?" I asked, and for some reason I could only picture the French author from the critic's bookshelf.

"Yes, the author!" she shouted. "The one who wrote the manuscript."

"Yes, that's me," I acknowledged.

"I know what happened to your manuscript!" she shouted. "It burned, and I'm the one who burned it!"

Standing there in the snow, a few meters from Ruben Rondas' house, I stared at her.

"What?" I said and came closer. "Are you saying that the manuscript has been incinerated, and you were the one who did it?"

I was almost at the house.

"I'm so, so sorry," she said in her rasping dialect. "I am so, so sorry. If you want revenge, then take it now. I've been waiting for you and your revenge. Just get it over with so we can be even."

I stood there looking at her, and it was as though everything around us had fallen more silent. As if the pines stood stiller, as if the sea were frozen deep, and everything around us had halted in the midst of the deepest midwinter. Why is the sea silent? I heard myself mumble.

"What did you say?" the woman shouted from the door.

"It's so dark!" I shouted back.

She looked aghast, as if she thought I might be crazy.

"Are you threatening me?" she shouted.

I didn't know what I was supposed to say. Was I threatening her?

"No," I shouted, "I don't think so!"

"Do you want revenge?" she shouted. "Do you want revenge? Then get over here. Get over here and avenge your damn manuscript. Come on! I'm standing right here."

She sounded so afraid. Her voice came out like a tense shriek, and she seemed on the verge of tears.

"But wait," I said, walking toward her. "Don't cry."

"I'm not crying," she said.

"Not yet," I said. "But you're about to."

"What do you care," she said.

I was so close to her, in the doorway. Her jaw was clenched, and her un-made-up face was pale with tension. She's ready, I thought. For what, I didn't know, but she seemed ready for anything.

"Wait, wait," I said. "Why did you burn the manuscript?"

"To get revenge on Ruben for something."

"I see," I said. "I see."

"I've been afraid that you'd come," she said. "And now it's nice that you're finally here, so we can get it over with."

Yes, that's how it is, I thought. That's exactly how it is. Now we're going to get this over and done with. And I searched for the anger inside me, for harsh words. A barely literate person had set my manuscript on fire. I wanted to tell her: "'Where books are burned, in the end, people will also be burned.' Do you realize what writing a book means? It's like burning my child." But, however I searched, I couldn't find the anger inside me. There were no harsh words, *there was no rage. I wasn't even at a loss for words. Instead, I felt a new heat spread through my body, as though she hadn't injured me at all, but rather had given me an unexpected, curious peace.*

"I think I'm supposed to let go of that manuscript," I said. "It's become something else. Let's assume everything is exactly as it should be."

In the distance, I could hear the sea again. I walked to the gate. When I got there, I turned and looked at her. She was still there. I wanted to go back and say something, but I thought twice. I closed the gate behind me and walked down the road to the car.

"Do you have a car?" she shouted.

"Yes, I do!" I shouted back.

"Can you drive me to the station?"

With that ride to Central Station, a different journey began, which perhaps I'll have the chance to tell you about sometime. And now to my question: Could I, in exchange for the money I'm giving you, spend some time at your home to rewrite The Polyglot Lovers? *I think I'd be able to write a different book now. And I could tend to a number of practicalities. I'm not so old that I can't lend a hand if needed. What do you say? Let me know by email. If your answer is yes, I'll book my tickets tomorrow.*

Your devoted,

> Max Lamas

I folded up the letter when I'd finished reading. My bedroom was bathed in the evening light streaming through the window. I put the pages back in the envelope. And I pictured myself returning to Rome to collect the furniture and the mirrors from that tiny apartment, and how they'd finally be freed from that crowded space. I pictured how the rooms of the property would be filled with my family's possessions, how everything would find its place again. I pictured how Max Lamas and his friend with the mousy hair would wander through the rooms and through the fields in the evenings when it cooled.

Or no. The mousy-haired woman would take her evening strolls alone, or with me. Max Lamas would settle in at a table in the garden, and there he'd have paper and a pen in front of him. You'd be able to hear the leaves whispering by the stream, and the crickets from the surrounding fields. He'd pick up his pen, uncap it, and for a few seconds he'd stare into space before putting pen to paper, and beginning to write. My eyes drifted to the mirror, and in that mottled antique surface I met the reflection of myself at the desk.

Marco Devoti, I thought. Where was he living now? Padua? Bologna?

Dear readers,

As well as relying on bookshop sales, And Other Stories relies on subscriptions from people like you for many of our books, whose stories other publishers often consider too risky to take on.

Our subscribers don't just make the books physically happen. They also help us approach booksellers, because we can demonstrate that our books already have readers and fans. And they give us the security to publish in line with our values, which are collaborative, imaginative and 'shamelessly literary'.

All of our subscribers:

- receive a first-edition copy of each of the books they subscribe to
- are thanked by name at the end of our subscriber-supported books
- receive little extras from us by way of thank you, for example: postcards created by our authors

BECOME A SUBSCRIBER, OR GIVE A SUBSCRIPTION TO A FRIEND

Visit andotherstories.org/subscriptions to help make our books happen. You can subscribe to books we're in the process of making. To purchase books we have already published, we urge you to support your local or favourite bookshop and order directly from them – the often unsung heroes of publishing.

OTHER WAYS TO GET INVOLVED

If you'd like to know about upcoming events and reading groups (our foreign-language reading groups help us choose books to publish, for example) you can:

- join our mailing list at: andotherstories.org
- follow us on Twitter: @andothertweets
- join us on Facebook: facebook.com/AndOtherStoriesBooks
- admire our books on Instagram: @andotherpics
- follow our blog: andotherstories.org/ampersand

This book was made possible thanks to the support of:

Aaron McEnery · Aaron
Schneider · Abby
Shackelford · Abigail
Charlesworth · Adam
Bowman · Adam
Lenson · Adriana Lopez ·
Ailsa Peate · Aisling
Reina · Ajay Sharma ·
Alan McMonagle · Alan
Simpson · Alastair
Gillespie · Alastair
Laing · Alex Fleming ·
Alex Hancock · Alex
Liebman · Alex Pearce ·
Alex Ramsey ·
Alexander Bunin ·
Alexandra Citron ·
Alexandra de Verseg-
Roesch · Alexandra
Stewart · Alfred
Birnbaum · Ali Casey ·
Ali Conway · Ali Smith ·
Alice Clarke · Alicia
Bishop · Alison Lock ·
Alison Winston · Alistair
McNeil · Aliya Rashid ·
Alyse Ceirante · Alyssa
Tauber · Amado
Floresca · Amalia
Gladhart · Amanda ·
Amanda Silvester ·
Amelia Ashton · Amelia
Dowe · Amine
Hamadache · Amitav
Hajra · Amy Arnold ·
Amy Benson · Amy
Bojang · Ana Savitzky ·
Anastasia Carver ·
Andrea Reece · Andrew
Kerr-Jarrett · Andrew
Lees · Andrew Marston ·
Andrew McCallum ·
Andrew Rego · Andrew
Wilkinson · Aneesa
Higgins · Angela
Everitt · Angus Walker ·
Anna Glendenning ·
Anna Milsom · Anna
Pigott · Anne Carus ·
Anne Goldsmith · Anne
Ryden · Anne Sticksel ·
Anne-Marie Renshaw ·

Anneliese O'Malley ·
Annie McDermott ·
Anonymous ·
Anonymous ·
Anonymous · Anthony
Quinn · Antonia
Lloyd-Jones · Antonio de
Swift · Antony Pearce ·
Aoife Boyd · Archie
Davies · Arne Van
Petegem · Asako
Serizawa · Asher
Norris · Audrey Mash ·
Avril Marren · Ayça
Türkoğlu · Barbara
Mellor · Barry John
Fletcher · Ben
Schofield · Ben
Thornton · Ben Walter ·
Benjamin Judge ·
Bettina Rogerson ·
Beverly Jackson · Bianca
Jackson · Bianca
Winter · Bill Fletcher ·
Brandon Knibbs ·
Brendan McIntyre ·
Briallen Hopper · Brian
Anderson · Brian Byrne ·
Brian Smith · Bridget
Gill · Bridget
McGeechan · Brigita
Ptackova · Burkhard
Fehsenfeld · Caitlin
Halpern · Caitlin
Liebenberg · Callie
Steven · Cameron
Lindo · Caren Harple ·
Carla Carpenter · Carlos
Gonzalez · Carolina
Pineiro · Caroline
Haufe · Caroline Lodge ·
Caroline Mager ·
Caroline Picard ·
Caroline Smith ·
Caroline West · Cassidy
Hughes · Catharine
Braithwaite · Catherine
Bailey · Catherine
Lambert · Catherine
Rodden · Catherine
Thomas · Cathy
Czauderna · Catie

Kosinski · Catriona
Gibbs · Cecilia Rossi ·
Cecilia Uribe · Cecily
Maude · Chantal Wright ·
Charles Fernyhough ·
Charles Raby · Charles
Wolfe · Charles Dee
Mitchell · Charlotte
Briggs · Charlotte
Holtam · Charlotte
Ryland · Charlotte
Whittle · Chia Foon
Yeow · China Miéville ·
Chris Gostick · Chris
Gribble · Chris Maguire ·
Chris Stevenson · Chris
& Kathleen Repper-Day ·
Christian Kopf ·
Christian Schuhmann ·
Christine Bartels ·
Christine Phillips ·
Christopher Allen ·
Christopher Stout ·
Christopher Whiffin ·
Ciara Ní Riain · Claire
Adams · Claire Ashman ·
Claire Malcolm · Claire
Tristram · Claire
Williams · Clare
Archibald · Clari
Marrow · Clarice Borges ·
Claudia Nannini ·
Claudio Scotti · Cliona
Quigley · Clive
Bellingham · Cody
Copeland · Colin
Denyer · Colin
Matthews · Coral
Johnson · Courtney Lilly ·
Cyrus Massoudi · Dale
Wisely · Dan Parkinson ·
Dan Raphael · Daniel
Arnold · Daniel Coxon ·
Daniel Gallimore ·
Daniel Gillespie · Daniel
Hahn · Daniel Sweeney ·
Daniel Venn · Daniel
Wood · Daniela
Steierberg · Darcy
Hurford · Darina
Brejtrova · Dave Lander ·
Davi Rocha · David

Anderson · David Hebblethwaite · David Higgins · David Irvine · David Johnson-Davies · David Mantero · David McIntyre · David Miller · David Shriver · David Smith · David Steege · David Travis · David F Long · Dawn Bass · Dean Taucher · Debbie Pinfold · Declan Gardner · Declan O'Driscoll · Deirdre Nic Mhathuna · Delaina Haslam · Denis Larose · Diana Cragg · Diana Digges · Dominic Nolan · Dominick Santa Cattarina · Dr. Paul Scott · Duncan Clubb · Duncan Marks · Dylan Tripp · Eamon Flack · Ed Burness · Ed Owles · Ed Tronick · Edward Rathke · Eimear McNamara · Ekaterina Beliakova · Eleanor Dawson · Eleanor Maier · Elena Tincu-Straton · Elie Howe · Elina Zicmane · Elisabeth Cook · Elizabeth Draper · Elizabeth Franz · Elizabeth Leach · Elizabeth Soydas · Ellie Goddard · Elliot Marcus · Elvira Kreston-Brody · Emily Armitage · Emily Taylor · Emily Williams · Emily Yaewon Lee & Gregory Limpens · Emily Webber · Emma Bielecki · Emma Knock · Emma Musty · Emma Page · Emma Parker · Emma Perry · Emma Post · Emma Reynolds · Emma Teale · Emma Timpany · Emma Turesson · Emma Louise Grove · Erin Cameron

Allen · Erin Louttit · Erin Williamson · Ewan Tant · Fatima Kried · Fawzia Kane · Filiz Emre-Cooke · Finbarr Farragher · Fiona Davis · Fiona Liddle · Fiona Mozley · Fiona Quinn · Florence Reynolds · Florian Duijsens · Fran Sanderson · Francis Mathias · Frank van Orsouw · Friederike Knabe · Gabriel Vogt · Gabriela Lucia Garza de Linde · Gabrielle Crockatt · Garan Holcombe · Gary Gorton · Gavin Collins · Gavin Smith · Gawain Espley · Genaro Palomo Jr · Geoff Fisher · Geoff Thrower · Geoffrey Cohen · Geoffrey Urland · George Christie · George Hawthorne · George McCaig · George Stanbury · George Wilkinson · Georgia Panteli · Geraldine Brodie · German Cortez-Hernandez · Gerry Craddock · Gill Adey · Gill Boag-Munroe · Gill Osborne · Gillian Ackroyd · Gillian Grant · Glen Bornais · Gordon Cameron · Graham Blenkinsop · Graham Fulcher · Graham R Foster · Guy Haslam · Gwyn Lewis · Hadil Balzan · Hamish Russell · Hank Pryor · Hannah Dougherty · Hannah Harford-Wright · Hannah Procter · Hannah Jane Lownsbrough · Hans Lazda · Harriet Stiles · Hattie Edmonds · Heather Tipon · Heidi James · Helen Bailey · Helen Brady ·

Helen Collins · Helen Coombes · Helen Waland · Henrike Laehnemann · Henry Patino · Holly Pester · Howard Robinson · Hugh Gilmore · Hyoung-Won Park · Ian Barnett · Ian Buchan · Ian McMillan · Ian Mond · Ian Randall · Ifer Moore · Ilana Doran · Ines Fernandes · Ingrid Olsen · Irene Mansfield · Irina Tzanova · Isabella Garment · Isabella Weibrecht · Isobel Dixon · J Collins · Jacinta Perez Gavilan Torres · Jack Brown · Jack Fisher · Jacqueline Haskell · Jacqueline Lademann · Jacqueline Ting Lin · Jacqueline Vint · Jadie Lee · James Attlee · James Beck · James Crossley · James Cubbon · James Lehmann · James Lesniak · James Plummer · James Portlock · James Scudamore · Jamie Cox · Jamie Walsh · Jane Fairweather · Jane Roberts · Jane Woollard · Janet Gilmore · Janette Ryan · Janne Støen · Jasmine Gideon · Jayne Watson · JC Blake · Jeanne Guyon · Jeannie Stirrup · Jeff Collins · Jenifer Logie · Jennifer Arnold · Jennifer Bernstein · Jen Calleja · Jennifer Fatzinger · Jennifer Humbert · Jennifer M Lee · Jenny Booth · Jenny Huth · Jenny Newton · Jeremy Koenig · Jes Fernie · Jess Howard-Armitage · Jesse Berrett · Jesse Coleman · Jesse Thayre · Jessica Kibler · Jessica Laine · Jessica Martin · Jessica Queree · Jethro Soutar ·

Jillian Jones · Jim Boucherat · Jo Harding · Jo Lateu · Jo Woolf · Joanna Flower · Joanna Luloff · Joanne Marlow · Joao Pedro Bragatti Winckler · JoDee Brandon · Jodie Adams · Jodie Martire · Joelle Young · Johanna Eliasson · Johannes Georg Zipp · John Berube · John Bogg · John Conway · John Coyne · John Down · John Gent · John Hodgson · John Kelly · John Royley · John Shaw · John Steigerwald · John Winkelman · John Wyatt · Jon Riches · Jonathan Blaney · Jonathan Huston · Jonathan Kiehlmann · Jonathan Watkiss · Jorge Cino · Jorid Martinsen · Joseph Cooney · Joseph Hiller · Joseph Schreiber · Joshua Davis · Joy Paul · Jude Shapiro · Julia Peters · Julia Rochester · Julia Sutton-Mattocks · Julia Ellis Burnet · Julie Greenwalt · Juliet Swann · Justine Sless · Kaarina Hollo · Kapka Kassabova · Karen Faarbaek de Andrade Lima · Karen Waloschek · Karen Woodhead · Kasim Husain · Kasper Haakansson · Kasper Hartmann · Kate Attwooll · Kate Gardner · Kate McCaughley · Kate Morgan · Katharina Liehr · Katharine Freeman · Katharine Robbins · Katherine El-Salahi · Katherine Gray · Katherine

Mackinnon · Katherine Skala · Katherine Sotejeff-Wilson · Kathryn Edwards · Kathryn Williams · Katie Brown · Katie Lewin · Katrina Thomas · Keila Vall · Keith Fenton · Keith Walker · Kenneth Blythe · Kenneth Michaels · Kent McKernan · Khairunnisa Ibrahim · Kieron James · Kim Armstrong · Kim Smith · Kirsten Hey · Kirsten Murchison · Kirsty Doole · KL Ee · Kris Ann Trimis · Kristin Djuve · Kristina Rudinskas · Krystine Phelps · Kylé Pienaar · Lana Selby · Laura Batatota · Laura Brown · Laura Lea · Lauren Rea · Laurence Laluyaux · Laurie Sheck & Jim Peck · Laury Leite · Lee Harbour · Leigh Aitken · Leon Frey & Natalie Winwood · Leonie Schwab · Leonie Smith · Lesley Lawn · Lesley Naylor · Lesli Green · Leslie Wines · Liliana Lobato · Lindsay Brammer · Lindsey Stuart · Lindy van Rooyen · Line Langebek Knudsen · Linette Arthurton Bruno · Lisa Dillman · Liz Clifford · Liz Ketch · Liz Wilding · Lola Boorman · Lorna Bleach · Lorna Scott Fox · Lottie Smith · Louise Foster · Louise Smith · Luc Verstraete · Lucia Rotheray · Lucia Whitney · Lucy Brady · Lucy Gorman · Lucy Hariades · Lucy Moffatt · Luke Healey · Luke Williamson · Lula Belle · Lynn Martin · Lynne

Bryan · Lysann Church · M Manfre · Madeleine Kleinwort · Maeve Lambe · Maggie Livesey · Mahan L Ellison & K Ashley Dickson · Malgorzata Rokicka · Margaret Jull Costa · Margo Gorman · Maria Ahnhem Farrar · Maria Hill · Maria Lomunno · Maria Losada · Marie Cloutier · Marie Donnelly · Marike Dokter · Marina Castledine · Mario Sifuentez · Marja S Laaksonen · Marjorie Schulman · Mark Sargent · Mark Sztyber · Mark Waters · Mark Whitelaw · Marlene Adkins · Martha Brenckle · Martha Nicholson · Martin Brown · Martin Munro · Martin Price · Martin Vosyka · Martin Whelton · Mary Byrne · Mary Carozza · Mary Heiss · Mary Morton · Mary Nash · Mary Wang · Mary Ellen Nagle · Marzia Rahman · Mathieu Trudeau · Matt Davies · Matt Greene · Matt O'Connor · Matthew Armstrong · Matthew Banash · Matthew Francis · Matthew Geden · Matthew Gill · Matthew Hiscock · Matthew Lowe · Matthew Thomas · Matthew Warshauer · Matthew Woodman · Matty Ross · Maureen Karman · Maureen Pritchard · Max Cairnduff · Max Garrone · Max Longman · Meaghan Delahunt · Megan Muneeb · Megan Wittling · Melissa

Apfelbaum · Melissa
Beck · Melissa da
Silveira Serpa · Melissa
Quignon-Finch ·
Melynda Nuss ·
Meredith Jones ·
Michael Aguilar ·
Michael Bichko ·
Michael Coutts ·
Michael Gavin · Michael
Kuhn · Michael
McCaughley · Michael
Moran · Michael
Schneiderman · Michael
Ward · Michael James
Eastwood · Michelle
Lotherington · Michelle
Roberts · Mike Bittner ·
Milla Rautio · Milo
Waterfield · Miriam
McBride · Moray Teale ·
Morgan Bruce · Morgan
Lyons · MP Boardman ·
Myles Nolan · N Tsolak ·
Namita Chakrabarty ·
Nan Craig · Nancy
Cooley · Nancy
Jacobson · Nancy
Oakes · Naomi Kruger ·
Nathalie Atkinson ·
Nathan Dorr · Neferti
Tadiar · Neil George ·
Nicholas Brown · Nick
Chapman · Nick Flegel ·
Nick James · Nick
Nelson & Rachel Eley ·
Nick Rombes · Nick
Sidwell · Nick
Twemlow · Nicola Hart ·
Nicola Meyer · Nicola
Mira · Nicola Sandiford ·
Nicole Matteini · Nikos
Lykouras · Nina
Alexandersen · Nina de
la Mer · Nina Moore ·
Nina Parish · Nina
Power · Olga
Zilberbourg · Olivia
Payne · Pamela Ritchie ·
Pat Bevins · Patricia
Appleyard · Patricia
Webbs · Patrick
Farmer · Paul Cray ·
Paul Daw · Paul Jones ·
Paul Munday · Paul

Myatt · Paul Robinson ·
Paul Segal · Paula
Edwards · Paula Ely ·
Pavlos Stavropoulos ·
Penelope Hewett
Brown · Pete Stephens ·
Peter McBain · Peter
McCambridge · Peter
Rowland · Peter Vos ·
Peter Wells · Philip
Carter · Philip Lewis ·
Philip Lom · Philip
Nulty · Philip Scott ·
Philip Warren · Philipp
Jarke · Phillip
Featherstone · Phyllis
Reeve · Pia Ghosh-Roy ·
Piet Van Bockstal ·
Pippa Tolfts · PM
Goodman · Portia
Msimang · PRAH
Foundation · Puck
Askew · Rachael de
Moravia · Rachael
Williams · Rachel
Andrews · Rachel
Carter · Rachel
Darnley-Smith · Rachel
Lasserson · Rachel
Matheson · Rachel Van
Riel · Rachel Wadham ·
Rachel Watkins · Ralph
Cowling · Ramon
Bloomberg · Rebecca
Braun · Rebecca Carter ·
Rebecca Fearnley ·
Rebecca Moss · Rebecca
Peer · Rebecca
Rosenthal · Rebecca
Schwarz · Rhiannon
Armstrong · Richard
Ashcroft · Richard
Bauer · Richard
Clifford · Richard
Mansell · Richard
Priest · Richard Shea ·
Richard Soundy ·
Richard Thomson ·
Rishi Dastidar · Robert
Gillett · Robert
Hamilton · Robert
Hannah · Robert
Hugh-Jones · Robin
Taylor · Roger Newton ·
Roger Ramsden · Rory

Williamson · Rosalind
May · Rosalind Ramsay ·
Rose Crichton · Rose
Webb · Rosemary
Gilligan · Rosie
Pinhorn · Ross Scott &
Jimmy Gilmore · Ross
Trenzinger · Rowan
Sullivan · Roxanne
O'Del Ablett · Roz
Simpson · Rupert
Ziziros · Ruth Chitty ·
Ruth Jordan · Ryan
Grossman · Sabine
Griffiths · Sabine Little ·
Sabrina Uswak · Sally
Baker · Sally Foreman ·
Sally Warner · Sam
Gordon · Sam Reese ·
Sam Stern · Samantha
Walton · Sandra
Hogarth-Scott · Sara
Goldsmith · Sara
Sherwood · Sarah
Arboleda · Sarah
Forster · Sarah Jacobs ·
Sarah Lucas · Sarah
Moss · Sarah Pybus ·
Sarah Smith · Sarah
Watkins · Scott
Chiddister · Sean
Birnie · Sean Kelly ·
Sean Malone · Sean
McGivern · Seonad
Plowman · Shannon
Knapp · Shauna
Gilligan · Sheridan
Marshall · Sherman
Alexie · Shira Lob ·
Sigurjon Sigurdsson ·
Simon Armstrong ·
Simon Harley · Simon
James · Simon Pitney ·
Simon Robertson · Siriol
Hugh-Jones · SK Grout ·
Sonia McLintock ·
Sophia Wickham ·
Sophie Morris · ST
Dabbagh · Stacy
Rodgers · Stefano Mula ·
Stella Francis · Stephan
Eggum · Stephanie
Lacava · Stephanie
Smee · Stephen
Pearsall · Stu Sherman ·

Stuart Wilkinson · Susan Higson · Susan Irvine · Susie Roberson · Suzanne Lee · Suzy Hounslow · Sylvie Zannier-Betts · Tamara Larsen · Tamsin Dewé · Tania Hershman · Tara Roman · Teresa Griffiths · Teresa Werner · Terry Kurgan · Thomas Baker · Thomas Bell · Thomas Chadwick · Thomas Fritz · Thomas Mitchell · Thomas van den Bout · Tiffany Lehr · Tiffany Stewart · Tim Jones · Tim Retzloff · Tim Scott · Tim Theroux · Timothy Nixon · Tina Andrews · Tina Rotherham-Winqvist · Toby Halsey · Toby Ryan · Todd Greenwood · Tom Darby · Tom Franklin · Tom Gray · Tom Mooney · Tom Stafford · Tom Whatmore · Tony Bastow · Tony Messenger · Torna Russell-Hills · Tory Jeffay · Tracey Martin · Tracy Northup · Treasa De Loughry · Trevor Wald · Val Challen · Valerie Sirr · Vanessa Nolan · Veronica Barnsley · Veronica Baruffati · Vicki White · Victor Meadowcroft · Victoria Adams · Victoria Huggins · Victoria Maitland · Vijay Pattisapu · Vikki O'Neill · Volker Welter · Walter Fircowycz · Walter Smedley · Wendy Langridge · William Dennehy · William Mackenzie · Yoora Yi Tenen · Zachary Hope · Zack Frehlick · Zoë Brasier

Current & Upcoming Books

BRET EASTON ELLIS
AND
THE OTHER DOGS

LINA WOLFF
TRANSLATED BY FRANK PERRY